Lights flashing, siren screaming, a patrol car screeched around the corner. Chris looked up at it with relief, but did not fail to catch the panic on Reb's face.

"Shit!" she cried. "Get up, Flynn! Get up!"

"It's okay—I'll tell them what happened," Chris said, trying to reassure her. "She'll probably need to go to the hospital...."

Fiercely, Reb interrupted her. "No! They're just gonna pin somethin' on us and lock us up!" She leaned over her unconscious friend, and with a trembling hand tenderly wiped blood from her face. "Flynn, please, wake up!"

EMERALD CITY BLUES

BLUES

Jean Stewart

Thanks Marie,

Jean Stewart

Also by Jean Stewart

Return to Isis

Isis Rising

Warriors of Isis

EMERALD CITY
BLUES

Jean Stewart

RISING
TIDE
PRESS

Rising Tide Press
5 Kivy Street
Huntington Station, NY 11746
(516) 427-1289

Publisher's Acknowledgments:
The publisher is grateful for all the support and expertise offered by the
members of its editorial board: Bobbi Bauer, Beth Heyn, Hat Edwards,
Pat G. and Candy T. Special thanks to Edna G. for believing in us,
and to the feminist and gay bookstores for being there.

First printing August, 1996
10 9 8 7 6 5 4 3 2 1

Edited by Lee Boojamra and Alice Frier
Book cover art: Denise St. John
Photo credit: Jannine Young, Seattle
Stewart, Jean 1952-
        Emerald City Blues/Jean Stewart
            p.cm
ISBN 1-883061-09-1
Library of Congress Catalog Card Number 95-79034

Acknowledgments

With great thanks to SJH and Robin Houpt for the extensive proofreading work. Also thanks to Beth Mitchum for the gift of her fine editing.

And as ever, deep thanks to Lee Boojamra and Alice Frier of Rising Tide Press.

Dedication

For my Susie, and the real Alf.

And for all the kids out on the street tonight.

"I have come to believe that one of the biggest barriers to gay and lesbian people to achieve civil rights is our inability to see ourselves as one community, united to confront the challenge of discrimination."

—Sherry Harris, Seattle City Councilwoman
Curve Magazine

CHAPTER 1

"Oh, Morgan," Janet whispered. "Don't stop. Please, don't stop."

Dazed and perspiring, Morgan purposefully slowed things down. She moved back, hooked a thick strand of long, dark-red hair behind one ear and studied the naked girl she held loosely in her arms.

Janet Belden was a wonder to her. With her pale blue eyes half-lidded and her long blonde hair sweeping across the old-fashioned quilt, she looked like a seductress in one of those late-night cable movies that Morgan wasn't supposed to watch.

And then, shuddering with delight, the blonde beauty slid a hand behind Morgan's neck, pulling her close. With the tip of her tongue, she opened Morgan's mouth.

Morgan melted.

Aware of nothing but each other, they rolled across the bed, bathed in the late-September sunlight that poured in through Janet's bedroom window. Their backpacks full of school books had been abandoned by the door. Their letter jackets and clothes lay scattered on the floor where they had unceremoniously shed them in their haste to get at one another. Both were salty and sticky from the after-school soccer practice they had left a mere twenty minutes ago, but neither one cared. Janet's

mother and father would not be home from work for another
half hour and this time together, alone in the house, was priceless.

Releasing Morgan's mouth, Janet moaned, "Oh, God,
Morgan...." The undisguised need in her voice made Morgan
quiver in response.

Since the first weeks of soccer camp in early July, Morgan had been enthralled by a new awareness of this teammate.
Although they had been friends all their lives, this summer they
had become incredibly close. Rapidly, they had entered a relationship that mystified Morgan, even as it led her on like a
tantalizing caress. She could only describe it to herself as magic.

Even now, nearly a full month after they had begun
touching each other like this, she still felt a vague disbelief.
Only her fingertips, tingling with friction as they coursed hungrily over Janet's soft skin, convinced her that any of this was
real.

Janet was whimpering as Morgan's hands lingered over
her breasts. "Ohhh," Janet breathed. "You're so good at this...so
much better than Jimmy."

Stunned by the comparison with Janet's boyfriend, Morgan froze, cut to the quick. *She's thinking about him? Now?*

Seeing the turmoil on Morgan's face, Janet whispered,
"You know he doesn't matter." She grasped Morgan's hand and
dragged it between her legs, whispering, "You're the one I want."
Wrapping an arm around Morgan's waist, she entreated, "I'm
sorry. Okay?"

Still uncertain, Morgan nonetheless allowed her hand
to be positioned against Janet's hot, wet center.

"C'mon." Slowly, Janet rocked against her, alternately
nibbling and kissing Morgan's neck.

Does she care for me—like I care for her? Morgan fretted.

And then Janet's lips grazed over that most-sensitive
spot, midway down her neck. A shivering flame of desire flashed
over Morgan. Groaning, her fingers slid through the thick
moisture, searching for and then finding what Janet so badly
wanted her to find. Heated, panting breath shot by her ear,

electrifying her. Suddenly Morgan found herself reveling in the power she had over this girl.

With smooth authority, she played with the arousal, concentrating on the signals Janet was sending her. Gradually, steadily, using all the skill of her hands and mouth, she conducted Janet to the brink.

Let's see you think of Jimmy now, Morgan challenged silently, watching Janet's unfocused eyes and flushed face.

Janet arched. With a sharp inhalation, she clutched Morgan's shoulders, drove her hips against Morgan's fingers, and then was still, her entire body at once taut and trembling. Morgan bent her head to Janet's breast and sucked urgently, all the while plunging her fingers in and out of Janet's soaking vulva.

With a sharp cry, Janet thrashed uncontrollably against her, thrilling Morgan. For an instant, she felt as if she had won a race or scored in a championship soccer game or stepped through the Pearly Gates into Heaven itself.

And then she heard another sound—a long, drawn-out hiss—like air escaping from a bicycle tire.

Glancing over her shoulder, she saw Janet's mother standing in the doorway. Wide-eyed, Mrs. Belden gaped at her daughter.

No, Morgan thought, her hand immobilized inside Janet. *Her Mom came home early....*

Still riding passion with total abandon, Janet had her eyes tightly shut; she was clinging to Morgan and coming with breathless, guttural evidence, over and over.

Enraged, Mrs. Belden gave an incoherent shriek.

Janet's eyes snapped open. Instantly, she lurched up, knocking Morgan aside in her haste to get away from her. Scrambling off the bed, she was already making useless denials. "It's not what it seems, Mother. We were just...we were just..."

Frantic, Janet grabbed up her discarded T-shirt and yanked it over her head. She quickly pulled on her practice shorts, tears of fear and humiliation already brimming in her eyes. "Why are you *here*, Mother?!"

"I had a toothache!" Mrs. Belden screeched. "I left work early and went to the dentist, and then I find you in bed with…" She stopped, and turned a horrified look on Morgan.

In a reflexive attempt to hide her nakedness, Morgan curled into a ball.

"Get out!" Mrs. Belden screamed.

Morgan rolled off the bed and dove for her clothes. Giving a small sob, Janet collected Morgan's red-and-white letter jacket and backpack, then stood aside holding them, her eyes darting wildly about the room.

Within moments, Morgan was fully dressed and crossing the room to take her backpack and jacket from Janet. As she met Janet's distraught eyes, she simply dropped her belongings and grasped Janet's hands.

Janet snatched her hands back.

Mrs. Belden lunged forward, grabbing Morgan's arm. "Don't you *dare* touch her!"

Morgan drew herself up to her full five-foot-nine-inches. "Mrs. Belden, I'm sorry," Morgan began, her voice quavering slightly. "I know this must seem terrible…but…you've got to understand. We love each other."

Mrs. Belden let go of her. She stepped back, whispering, "Oh my Lord. It's more disgusting than I believed possible…." She fumbled for the chain around her neck, found the little gold cross and gripped it desperately.

Swallowing hard, Morgan tried to explain. "We didn't mean for this to happen. But we *do love* each other."

"Morgan!" Janet interrupted. "Stop it! It's not like that!" she insisted forcefully. She sent her mother a look that seemed half genuine apology and half sheer frustration. "We were fooling around—wrestling on the bed," she declared, "and it just happened." With a contemptuous look at Morgan she finished, "It was only this once and it doesn't mean anything, Mother."

"Doesn't mean anything?" Morgan repeated, astounded.

Janet folded her arms across her chest and repeated coldly, "That's right! For me it doesn't mean anything!" She seemed incredulous that Morgan could dispute it. "What's *wrong* with you?"

Open-mouthed, Morgan stared back at her. She was suddenly trembling, as if some part of her intuitively knew what was going to come next.

Mrs. Belden's gaze darted back and forth between them, as if she was not certain whom to believe.

"I mean," Janet argued, "I didn't *say* I loved you—did I?" After a brief pause she answered herself, "Of course not!" Janet glanced quickly at her mother as if this proved something.

In response, Mrs. Belden glared at Morgan. Whatever assurance she had needed, she had just been given.

Morgan felt ill. She suddenly remembered a horror film she had seen years ago. The monster had punched a hole right through the girl's chest, seized her still-beating heart, and torn it out. *This is what it must feel like....*

Morgan stepped closer, close enough to smell the particularly unnerving scent of Janet's skin. Her voice low, quavering again, Morgan asserted, "You can't make me believe you don't care for me."

For an instant, Janet's face softened and Morgan saw her own heated certainty mirrored in Janet's eyes.

Then Mrs. Belden hissed at Morgan, "You stop that right now!"

"It's all right, Mother," Janet said quietly.

Morgan felt ice water pouring through her veins, felt her shoulders turning to granite. There was going to be no escape, no mercy. She could see it in Janet's eyes.

"I'm...not like you," Janet finally said.

Deep within Morgan, a voice was pleading, *Please, don't do this,* but on the surface she was mute, lost in the cold, blue depths of Janet's eyes.

"I love Jimmy. *I'm normal.*"

Reeling as if she had been struck, Morgan turned, wanting only to get out of the room now. She bent, grabbed her team jacket and backpack, then made for the door.

Behind her, Mrs. Belden warned, "You won't get another chance to lead a good girl astray if I have anything to say about it! And I'll call the police if I see you around Janet again! Understand?"

Taken aback by how that sounded, Morgan abruptly turned and faced her. "What do you think was going on here? I never *forced* Janet to..."

Mrs. Belden flew at her, slapping Morgan across the face and silencing the intimation that Janet had actually been willing. Spittle shot out of her mouth as she shouted, "We don't have to put up with the likes of you, Morgan Flynn! The decent, Christian people of this town don't have to put up with *filth!*"

Wiping spit from her face, Morgan looked over Mrs. Belden's shoulder and saw the same mixture of self-righteousness and fear on Janet's face. Dumbfounded, she stumbled into the hallway and down the stairs.

At the front door she hesitated, knowing somehow that she should not leave it like this. But she was too distraught to find the words.

Mrs. Belden, who had followed her down the stairs, was suddenly behind her, shouting, "Go on! Get out of this house! You...dirty *queer!*"

Morgan yanked open the front door, shoved past the screen door, and fled the house at a run.

Shoulders hunched, Morgan walked quickly beneath the cottonwoods that lined the street. Above her, yellow leaves stirred in the slight breeze. Autumn had officially begun a week ago, and after a few chill nights the leaves were already turning color. But Morgan was oblivious to the subtle changes all around her. She was desperately trying to make sense of what had just happened.

She strode past the small, neat suburban houses and well-manicured lawns, traveling the mile from Janet's neighborhood to her own. Then, instead of turning into the street which would take her home, she kept walking until she came to a small park.

She knew she was delaying the inevitable, but she just couldn't go home yet.

Glancing about anxiously, she saw some children playing near the swings, but otherwise the park was deserted. She dropped her letter jacket and backpack beneath a big maple tree. Feeling strangely disoriented, she settled herself in the grassy hollow between two protruding roots and took several deep breaths. It did little to ease her fear.

This is real bad news, an inner voice told her. *You're in deep shit.*

In fiery shades of red, the sun was already setting behind the Cascade Mountains. Almost twenty minutes had passed since Janet's mother had caught them. Morgan's mind was like a hamster on a wheel—endlessly running in circles, and getting nowhere.

Certain that Mrs. Belden intended to inform her parents, Morgan was on the edge of total panic. *She probably already phoned! Shit! What am I going to do?!* Going home was out of the question. She knew beyond a doubt what was waiting for her.

It seemed that in the space of a breath her life had radically changed. Just two days ago she was being courted by the University of Washington for a possible athletic scholarship. As captain of the soccer team and an honor roll student, her chances had looked excellent. And now, none of that mattered anymore.

Her secret was out.

Cradling her head in her hands, she tasted the name Mrs. Belden had called her. "Queer," she whispered to herself. "You're a damn queer."

Now, in place of all that compelling, confusing sexual need, she felt only fear. Fear of what would happen once her father knew. At the mere thought of it, a shudder ran through her.

She jerked her knees to her chest, burying her head in her arms. Taking deep breaths, she tried to calm herself and coax the jumble of events into some sort of order.

Janet plays a mean right wing on the soccer field, but she still looks...feminine. Morgan sighed heavily. *And she also has a boyfriend. That's enough to make her "normal."*

Meanwhile, I'm this big, broad-shouldered, long-legged thing. Okay, so Janet kept saying she liked my looks, liked auburn hair and dark blue eyes—so what?

Then, all at once furious with Janet and crushed by her rejection, Morgan finally couldn't stop the tears.

How am I ever going to deal with this? she groaned. And then, a larger, more immediate problem lurched to the forefront of her mind. *How am I ever going to deal with Dad?*

Apprehensively, she glanced at her watch. *I've already missed dinner. I oughtta go right now. Putting this off is only gonna make him worse.*

It was nearly 8:30 p.m. when Morgan slowed her resolute pace at the foot of the driveway. By the time she was midway across the lawn, she had come to a standstill, gazing anxiously at the house. Warm, yellow light shone from all the windows, falling in long strips on the dark lawn. For some reason, it reminded Morgan of a lighthouse warning ships away from the rocks.

Uneasily, she hitched her backpack higher on her shoulder. *C'mon. There's nowhere else to go,* she told herself, stepping into one of the shafts of window light.

From the corner of her eye, she noticed a shadow rise up from the small cement porch by the front door. Moving quickly, the shape came hurtling toward her. Startled, she instinctively began backpedaling, but he was already upon her. She recognized the faint smell of him—stale pipe smoke and Old Spice aftershave—as he grabbed the collar of her jacket. Before she had time to even get a protective arm up, the first blow blasted into her jaw.

Suddenly, the darkness of the front lawn exploded into fireworks for Morgan. Bright, streaking lights were shooting through her head, spinning like pinwheels before her eyes. She found herself on her hands and knees, disoriented, wondering at the enormous pain on the left side of her face. Seconds later, something hard crashed into her stomach, launching her up and sideways. She landed on the grass with a thud, rolled over onto her face and lay there in rigid agony, trying to capture a breath.

Oh, God! He's already kicking me! The kicks usually came later, after the fusillade of slaps had steadily escalated into punches. She was in real trouble if the kicks were being delivered so soon. Her mind flashed a terrifying insight. *He might kill me this time.*

Somehow, she was up, scrambling to get away from him. He seized her by the collar again as she made it to her feet and his fist drove her backwards and down twice more before she stayed down for good, finally curling into a ball to take the series of brutally hard kicks.

When he finally stopped he panted, "Star of all the sports teams! Honor student! You had everyone thinking I was so hard on you. But I knew..." He let loose a stream of curses, then stood over her, accusing, "I knew all about you, *long before you did!*"

Her backpack was gone. She was stupefied, shivering so uncontrollably hard with delayed panic that her teeth were chattering. She'd wet herself at some point during the beating and now her long, baggy soccer shorts were soaked and clinging to her legs. She was ashamed and terrorized and she ached all over, but none of it hurt as much as the things he was saying to her.

"You're a disgrace to this family! You're no daughter of mine," he sneered. "What were you doing with that girl? Huh?" His voice was pure hate. "You want to do that sick, disgusting shit?" he demanded. "Well, you're not going to stay here and do it! You're not going to ruin *my* good name in this town!"

Oh God, help me, Morgan thought. Through the fog of pain and fear, a strong sense of foreboding overtook her. *He's really gonna make it count this time....*

"Get up," he growled.

She tried, honestly tried, but she was so dizzy that she couldn't rise from her kneeling position on one knee.

"I said get up," he hissed by her ear.

He grabbed a handful of her long hair and pulled her toward the front porch. She heard it, felt it, tearing out by the roots. In excruciating pain, she lurched along on her hands and feet, half-crawling, trying to stay even with him. Somehow, she got up the cement steps and he opened the door. With a hard shove, he sent her through it before him, then stepped inside and slammed the door closed.

She blundered toward the stairs, hearing a sharp intake of breath as she passed someone standing by the archway that led to the living room. Stifling a sob, she lost momentum and sank to her knees.

Her mother's voice entreated, "Why do you have to make him do this to you? You get him so mad—it's not his fault...."

And then the blathering rush of nonsense was left behind as her father grabbed her hair again and hoisted her up, dragging her with him as he ascended the stairs.

Over his shoulder, he threw an order at her mother. "Run a bath and clean her up. She's not spending another night in this house."

At the top of the steps, he pinned her against the wall with one straight arm, allowing her mother to slide past them.

Nervously, Morgan glanced at the steep descent of stairs that yawned mere inches from her feet. Her mother scooted down the hall and into the bathroom, out of sight.

And with a gleam of conquest in his eye, he glanced at the stairs and warned, "Careful."

Sickened, she trembled and averted her eyes, betraying her horror as he subtly pushed her, moving the upper part of her body so that she was off balance and leaning over the top step.

Why does he have to do this?! she asked in a silent, internal scream.

"You're always so clumsy, aren't you?" he whispered. "So clumsy on the stairs..."

Suddenly, something deep inside of her broke loose. She was fighting him, fighting with all of her might. He was bigger than her, heavier than her, but he was no longer angrier than her. Elbowing, pushing, she surprised him and almost fought her way clear, before she realized how precarious her position was. They were wrestling wildly only a foot away from the top step of the staircase. Twisting, she tried to lunge the other way, tried to dive for the safety of the hall—and almost made it.

Then her father caught her shoulder and shoved her— hard—driving her right over the edge of the stairs. For a moment she was airborne, then, with a helpless shriek, she managed to tuck in her upper body as she hurtled down. First she felt the bite of pain in her shoulder, then she was rolling over and over, until she banged the back of her head and abruptly lost consciousness.

Pain washed over her as she opened her eyes and heard her father growl, "Get up, you little slut."

Though barely conscious, she concentrated on getting her feet under her. It was all she could do to stay upright, and then she was being dragged up the stairs again.

"Please, no more," she pleaded, completely broken. "Don't throw me down the stairs again, please."

"I didn't throw you, you clumsy idiot!" he raged. "You fell! You did it to yourself!"

Gripping her by the hair, he roughly guided her down the hallway to the bathroom, then shoved her inside. Morgan fell heavily against the towel rack and slid to rest on the cold tile floor.

Her mother waited by the tub, twisting a washcloth in her hands.

"Get your clothes off, you slut," he hissed from the doorway, then slammed the door and left them.

In a daze, Morgan began fumbling with her clothes, desperate to comply. She glanced up at her mother and her mother averted hard, unforgiving eyes. "Don't look for sympathy from me."

A short time later, her mother had her in the bathtub, washing her with a cursory briskness. As Morgan cringed away from the sponge passing over the bruises on her back, a tempest was gathering inside her. Now that the terror was subsiding, pure fury was taking over. She couldn't look at her mother for fear she would start uncontrollably screaming at her.

Silently, she raged, *Sympathy? How about mercy? He beats me to the ground and you turn away. How can you let him do this to me? What's wrong with you?*

She heard her father talking heatedly with someone on the upstairs phone. She heard the words "Doctor Baxter" and the phrase "I want your help on this." Doctor Baxter must have been stubbornly resisting, because her father was shouting, "She's sick and I want her put away! She's doing this to defy me!"

Seeing that Morgan was listening, her mother explained brusquely, "It's for your own good. I hear they can cure...people like you." Morgan looked up at her, staggered by the knowledge that her mother, too, believed she was sick.

"You call yourself a doctor?!" her father was shouting. "You're a danger to society! And you won't stop me, you know. I'm sure one of your colleagues will understand a father's concern for his daughter!" The sharp slam that followed told her that he had smashed the receiver into the cradle. Cursing, he stomped past the closed bathroom door and thundered down the stairs.

With a calculating glance at the door, her mother said, "We're through here, Morgan. Let's get you to your room." She reached over, supporting Morgan by the elbow.

Using the side of the tub, Morgan pushed herself up. Pain displaced her anger and a low moan escaped her as she stood.

Her mother's eyes were cold, devoid of pity as she perfunctorily toweled Morgan dry. "Your father's a good man," she stated fiercely, as if she was trying to assure herself, as well as Morgan, of the fact. "He just...has a temper...." Her voice grew bitter, and her eyes hardened. "And you defy him, Morgan. You've always been such a difficult child."

She's blaming me! Morgan thought bitterly. *Is that how she makes peace with herself for siding with him and ignoring these crazy attacks? She tells herself that it's my own fault?* Looking away, torn between despair and outrage, Morgan thought, *Somewhere along the way, you chose him over me, Mom.*

Lips set in a tense line, her mother helped her into a robe and led her across the hall to her room. At the door, she stopped, watching Morgan use the wall for support as she crossed the distance to her bed. "Get into your pajamas and try to go to sleep," her mother instructed, glancing down the hallway. "I don't think you'll be going anywhere tonight."

Again, they heard her father on the downstairs phone, barking demands. Although anger still rang like steel in his voice, Morgan could tell he was trying to sound reasonable. Morgan swallowed hard, knowing that sooner or later he would successfully make his case and convince someone with medical authority of the need to get her "placed somewhere."

Meeting Morgan's distressed eyes, her mother said, "I'll try to get him to reconsider, but...I think you've gone too far this time, Morgan." Suddenly embarrassed, she whispered, "I can't believe you did that! You and that girl. It's...*filthy!*" Her face was red, her eyes cold, as she turned and left the room.

For a moment, Morgan stood there, staring at the space where her mother had been. Her gut was churning with hot resentment. *Damn! I fell in love! All I did was fall in love!*

With great effort, Morgan made her way back to the open door and pushed it closed. She hesitated there for a second, tempted to lock it. Then she remembered the time when she was fourteen and she had dared to run upstairs to escape.

In her mind's eye, she saw it again. Her father kicking the door open, cornering her, then hitting her over and over.

She was out of school for the next two days.

She told her friends that she had crashed her bike, and it seemed everyone chose to believe her. Then again, the adults in a small town like Wenatchee had a long pioneer custom of minding their own business. But she'd catch her classmates staring at her out the corners of their eyes. Though they never challenged her stories of one accident after another, they never really believed them, either.

By the time she was fifteen, Morgan had begun to realize that her father's brutality toward her had little to do with her own behavior—good or bad. She began to see him for what he was, besides being her dad. He was a man facing the computer age with a high school education. At the insurance firm where he worked, time after time he was passed over for promotion. Frustrated and embittered, he often came home from work in a rage.

To survive, she began focusing all her energy on a dream: she would earn a college scholarship, and escape his house—in triumph.

In the shelter of her room Morgan read and studied with a fervor few of her classmates understood. She went for long, solitary runs, or holed up alone in the garage, skipping rope or lifting the free weights she had bought at a garage sale. Patiently, she prepared and she waited...and silently endured the beatings when they came.

That autumn of her seventeenth year, Morgan was methodically applying to dozens of colleges, aware that her chances of acceptance and even a scholarship were very, very good.

And now I've lost any chance of college. Morgan shuddered, one hand on the closed bedroom door. She automatically began biting her lip as she worried, and then winced as she made contact with tender, swollen flesh. *I can't let him do this! So he goes ballistic—why can't I fight back?*

Trembling, she retraced her steps to the bed, praying that he had vented his fury enough for one night. *What am I going to do?* she thought, wincing as she lowered herself to the mattress. *I can't take any more of this.*

Slowly, the bedroom door began to open and Morgan froze. Her heart pounded in her ears.

Her younger brother's head poked around the side and he looked at her, then away, obviously appalled by what he'd seen.

"Shit," John muttered, shutting the door behind him. "He's calling every psychiatrist in the phone book, trying to get someone to certify that you're 'troubled and rebellious.'" John's thin, fourteen-year-old frame was stiff with fury, and he blinked back tears. "So far he's striking out, but he's swearing he's gonna have you locked up by the weekend."

Morgan shook her head, then instantly regretted doing that. The room went into a slow, sickening spin, making her even more nauseous.

"What are you gonna do, Morgan?" her brother pleaded. "I've seen shows on TV about what they do to queer kids in those places. Drugs and messin' with your head and tryin' to turn you into someone you're not—it ain't right."

Realizing that he was both frightened and outraged by her father's brutality, she felt a tremendous relief. "You mean," she said, then stopped and put a hand to her sore jaw, trying to master the pain that shot through her face, "you know about me? And...it's okay? I'm still your sister?"

With an anguished grimace, John dashed tears away. "Of course you're still my sister! You're the only one worth shit in this whole family!"

"John, it'll be okay," Morgan lied, hoping to soothe him.

"It won't," John replied desperately. "He hates you...."

"Don't worry. I'm leaving," Morgan said, more to calm him than anything else. However, once she had said it, it really did seem to be the only solution. "I'm leaving tonight," she repeated decisively.

They traded a long, hopeless look, then John nodded.

"Run," he choked, "before Dad gets some sort of wagon sent around and they shoot you full of shit and carry you outta here."

Clenching her teeth together, Morgan stood. "C'mere," she whispered, motioning him closer with her hand. *I don't want to go,* she thought, wanting to dissolve into self-pitying sobs. Instead, she prompted, "Get my big navy blue pack. It should be under my bed, near the wall."

John obligingly searched beneath the bed, then rose and handed the backpack to Morgan. She ruffled his hair, a gesture of affection she had used all her life with him. Bending his head, looking overwhelmed with emotion, John hugged her quickly then made for the door.

He paused there, not looking at her, then blurted, "Don't phone or write. It won't...be safe." Opening the door, he slipped out.

Morgan stared at the backpack in her hands. She felt paralyzed by the enormity of what she was about to do. Then, gradually, she became aware of her father talking in another part of the house. His voice was muffled; she could not clearly hear the words, but the rage was still audible. As if in counterpoint, her mother's softer, higher voice was trying to reason with him. And then, gathering both volume and fury, her father began shouting, until her mother could not be heard at all and her father went into a loud, belligerent tirade.

"She's a Goddamned dyke!" he screamed. "And I'm not going to have it! If the people I sell insurance to get wind of this—I'm finished!"

He said more, but Morgan didn't bother to try and listen.

She moved slowly, quietly about her room, dressing herself for the journey she was about to undertake. With great care she selected and packed the few extra clothes she would take with her, along with several cherished books. She lifted the small steel money box from her dresser, thankful that she had saved so much of her summer earnings for college.

As she settled the money box into her backpack, she blinked back a rush of tears. *No college now. No chance for a scholarship when you're a runaway....*

Before she could get caught up in the anguish of what she was doing, she fastened the pack and began pulling on her letter jacket. As she moved to slide her arm into the second white leather sleeve, she had to grit her teeth to keep from crying out in pain. The muscles all along her back and ribs were throbbing and sore. Carefully, she lifted and then shouldered her backpack, wincing as the weight fully settled on her shoulders.

She considered writing a note before leaving, then decided that there was at once both too much and absolutely nothing to say.

Aching all over, she limped to the door and stood there listening. When she was sure that her parents were still in the kitchen, at the back of the house, she opened the bedroom door and crept down the hall. Her bruised legs were shaking as she skirted the floorboard that always creaked. Concentrating on stealth, she descended the stairs and crossed the hall to the front door. She placed her hand on the knob, turned and tugged, all in one motion. Then she froze, wondering if her father had heard the slight noise of the front door opening.

Down the hall, in the kitchen, she could hear him banging his pipe in a glass ashtray as he cleaned it out for one last smoke.

"Can you believe it? Washington state law says a kid over age thirteen can't be involuntarily committed," he griped bitterly. He sounded as if he were finally tiring; his tone was lower and the relentless thud of his pacing feet had ended. "Well, that last doctor told me a thing or two about how to handle this."

Morgan shivered and closed her eyes. *Jesus, help me.*

"There's a place he told me about, Rivendale of Utah," he declared. "They'll break her of this shit or just plain break her! I don't much care which."

Soon he would be muttering and heading for bed, dismissing any thought of her until the next morning, when he would awaken rested and fresh...and dangerous again.

Her doubts dropped away from her. *I have to leave,* Morgan thought. *What could be worse than living like this?* With a suddenly fierce resolve, she stepped over the threshold, and then, with great care, pulled the door closed.

Once outside, she tiptoed off the small cement porch and quickly crossed the dark lawn. Without a backward glance, she escaped into the chill, black night.

CHAPTER 2

That same Thursday evening, on the other side of the Cascade Mountains, another seventeen-year-old was alone on the streets.

Small, thin as a reed and clad all in black, Reb was leaning against a telephone pole at the corner of Olive Way and Broadway. Though she appeared bored and half-asleep, she was shrewdly observing every detail of her surroundings, alert to all the comings and goings. She was aware of the soft late-afternoon sun hovering just above the Seattle skyline. From the corner of her eye she was watching the women converging on Bailey/Coy Books, farther down Broadway. Dorothy Allison was there tonight, signing her books, and Reb felt tempted to go down and try to see her through the window.

Naah. You got business to attend to, she reminded herself. She focused on the construction worker who was approaching. He had a six-pack of beer tucked under one arm, and as he passed her, he crooned, "Hey, baby. Five bucks to suck me off."

Reb averted her face, but not before she spied the red-and-white box tucked into the rolled-up sleeve of his white T-shirt. The man continued by her, laughing, swaggering, full of himself. A moment later, Reb slipped into step right behind him and deftly plucked the Marlboros from his T-shirt.

"Hey!" he shouted, staring at his shirtsleeve, stunned to find that it was empty. "What the...?" Angrily, he turned to see who had stolen his cigarettes.

By that time, she had skillfully blended into the crowd and was just another scurrying pedestrian.

Roughly twenty minutes later, Reb was walking down Eleventh Avenue, enjoying her second cigarette. As she passed the cars parked perpendicular to the crumbling remains of a curb, she slouched a little, a posture which allowed her to peer quickly inside each vehicle she passed. Finally, she saw what she was looking for: a backpack partially covered by a plaid flannel shirt, both of the prizes carelessly tossed onto the back seat of a blue Chevelle. With a quick glance around, she confirmed the fact that no one else was in sight. Casually, she finished the cigarette, dropped it and snuffed the butt under her boot.

As usual, the cigarettes had helped cut her ravenous hunger, but that wouldn't last long. Reb crouched down, then moved into the space between the Chevelle and a Pontiac. The big warehouse behind her was casting a convenient shadow, and she knew she would be hard to see as long as she stayed low. Slowly, she withdrew the wire hanger from its hiding place under her oversized black sweater.

Suddenly, Reb stopped, arrested by her own reflection in the Chevelle's passenger window—a heart-shaped face with large, fawn-like brown eyes, framed by straight black hair. She was rather proud of the stylish bowl-cut; she had done it herself, and it had come out mostly even, ending just above her ears.

She smirked at herself and mocked softly, "You look about twelve," before she got down to work.

Deftly, she inserted the straightened hanger into the rubber seam that ran between the metal car door and the glass window. At seventeen, she was still small and thin, yet she was strong enough to steadily push the wire down, deep into the door. Wiggling it about patiently, she finally snagged the hidden bar that controlled the lock mechanism. Within a couple of minutes she had the lock jimmied and the door open. She pushed the passenger seat forward and eagerly unzipped the backpack, only to find it empty. After picking up the flannel shirt, she discovered it reeked of male body odor, and promptly tossed it aside. In two more minutes she had thoroughly searched the car and emptied the glove box, and all she had to show for her work was a package of spearmint gum.

Disgusted, Reb pocketed the gum, shut the door and moved to the next car.

At that moment, a large white pickup turned the corner onto Eleventh Avenue and came rumbling over the rough pavement. Reb dropped down, shoved her wire hanger beneath the Pontiac beside her, then crawled under the car after it. Lying perfectly still, she listened intently as the truck moved steadily closer.

The Ford pickup slowed as it approached her hiding place. "Olson, Morrissey & Wheeler Enterprises, Home Renovations & Sales" was painted on the driver's door. Reb had only seconds to read it before being distracted by the striking features of the woman behind the wheel. Thirty feet past her, the truck turned and glided into a parking place across the street. That was when Reb spotted the pink triangle sticker on the truck's rear bumper.

So...you're queer.

The man and woman who got out were slow about leaving the vehicle. They stood in the late-September sunshine, trading remarks as the man drank from a dark-brown bottle. They were so close Reb recognized the label: Emerald City Ale.

Micro-brewery. Which means they're probably yups.

"When you invited me to dinner," the man was saying, "I thought you were actually *making* it. Silly me."

"Don't start, Nelly," the woman replied dryly, causing the man to laugh. "I wanted company, not nagging."

I'm available... Reb thought, wondering why a gorgeous woman like this was at a loss for companionship.

Reb slithered closer to the Pontiac's bumper, daring to risk being seen in order to keep the woman in view. Tall and lean, her curly, blonde hair cut close to her head, the woman looked like a construction worker. She wore big, buckskin-colored boots, a gray sweatshirt and faded blue jeans, all of which were spattered with colorful splashes of paint. Her face had a sturdy, androgynous quality with bright, light-colored eyes. It was the eyes that drew Reb's gaze—like the glimpse of a lake through forest trees; that unexpected flash of something luminous that makes a person look again, straining to see more.

"So, Chris," the man was saying. "Have you thought any more about that piece Gary wants to do on us for the *Seattle Gay News?* It'll be free publicity, you know. Great for the business. He's even got a headline: 'Contractors Turn Capitol Hill Into Castro.'"

"Castro," Chris scoffed, though she grinned as if pleased. "Probably just means that you've been getting carried away with the gingerbread trim on the last few houses."

Tom lifted and resettled his Mariner's baseball cap, for a moment revealing a pink, bald head. "Victorian houses require gingerbread," he proclaimed saucily, his hand on his hip. "It's de rigueur."

As he spoke, Chris was removing a leather tool belt from the truck cab and then climbing into the back of the truck. "Well, in the 'de rigueur' department, don't forget, we're going to be needing a couple of house painters." She knelt and fiddled a few minutes with something Reb couldn't see. "With Allen and Jeff going back to classes at the university next week, it's gonna be just you and me on the job site. Allison wants us to finish by December."

As she lifted the lid of a large wooden box built into the space just behind the cab of the truck, her blonde curls caught the slanting sunshine. Chris stowed the tool belt inside, and closed the box. She swung her legs over the side of the truck gracefully and landed in the street beside her friend.

Smiling appreciatively, Reb thought, *Wow. A fine butch lady who wears a tool belt and makes her livin' fixin' up houses.*

"I notice you're spending a lot of time with Miss Allison," Tom commented archly.

"It's strictly business," Chris answered, appearing distinctly uncomfortable. "The real-estate end of buying, and then reselling stuff gets pretty involved sometimes."

"Uh-huh," Tom said, his disbelief clear.

They began to move away from the truck. Reb took a deep breath, trying to ignore the tremendous ache in her stomach.

"Girl, when are you going to start dating again?" Tom asked, draping his arm around Chris's shoulders.

"I'll get around to it eventually," Chris answered, a determined grin tugging up one side of her mouth.

Yet Reb, well-schooled in reading facial expressions, saw grief in her eyes.

As they began to move up the street, Tom's last remark floated back to Reb. "Sure you will. And Auntie Tom can't wait to play matchmaker."

Tom gave her a solid hug, then let her go. They continued to talk, but they were too far down the narrow road now for Reb to hear them.

Gripping her wire hanger, Reb quietly started sliding out from under the Pontiac. She stayed on all fours, scurrying to the end of the Chevelle, then leaned against the fender. She watched Tom and Chris reach the corner. As she expected, they made the left turn on Pike Street, heading around to the front of the old, red brick building. The entrance to the Wildrose restaurant was within fifteen feet of the corner, and Reb had no doubt that the Rose was where they were going.

Carefully, she surveyed the length of Eleventh Avenue. She was once more alone.

They'll be eatin' for at least a half hour, Reb thought. *Plenty of time....*

When she stood, a wave of dizziness hit her, and she had to lean a hand on the trunk of the Chevy till her head cleared. Then, moving as casually as she could, she crossed the street to the white pickup.

She tried the driver's side door first. It was locked. With a grimace, she moved around the truck and tried the passenger's door. Also locked. Going up on her tiptoes, she stretched her short, skinny frame and began threading her hanger between the glass and the window seal. Patiently, she jiggled the wire around in the unseen recesses of the door unit, taking extra care to catch the internal metal bar. She was at a disadvantage this time because the height of the truck ruined her leverage. Still, a few minutes later she had the door open and began picking the glove-box lock with a thin, professionally designed blade she carried in her pocket for exactly this purpose. She made short work of the cheap mechanism; the glove-compartment door fell open with a thud.

Immediately, she spotted the Styrofoam coffee cup wedged beneath a paint-speckled Mariners ball cap. *Ten to one that's parkin' meter change!*

She drew the cup out and found it was not only half-full of quarters, it also held three twenty-dollar bills. Hurriedly, she stuffed both coins and bills deep inside the pocket of her black jeans. Moving with expert efficiency, she pushed the empty cup back into the glove box. Not bothering to re-lock it, she simply closed the compartment and then locked and closed the passenger's door.

She took three steps away from the truck, thrilled with her find, then spun about, remembering the wooden box built against the back of the cab. *Wonder what she has in there?*

Grunting, she used a foot on the back tire to climb over the side wall and into the back of the truck. Crouched low to avoid being seen, she focused on the large wooden box built into the space behind the cab. A thick Yale lock secured the lid.

After a few moments, trying to repeat her success with the glove box, she grew exasperated and abandoned her efforts. "Shit," Reb muttered to herself.

Engrossed, she studied the thickness of the wooden lid, itself. *Hmm. Only about an inch.* She reached into her jeans and brought out a pocket-sized screwdriver, then began to whittle the wood away from the lock clasp. Roughly five minutes later, she pried the screws from the lock clasp and, grinning, pulled the lid open.

Inside, she found several different power tools and extension cords, along with Chris's tool belt containing a top-of-the-line Craftsman collection. But Reb ignored all of that and grabbed the pair of brand new construction boots sitting in the corner. She dropped the boots at her feet, then, with a soft squeal, grasped the long flashlight that had been wedged behind them. But the best was yet to come. As she was lifting out a canvas tarp and a coil of orange safety rope, she discovered the battered black leather motorcycle jacket underneath.

I'm rich! she crowed to herself.

Glancing up and down the street, she pulled her plastic trashbag out from beneath her sweater. She stuffed boots, flashlight, canvas tarp, rope, and leather jacket into the bag. Deviating from her usual hit-and-run style, she took extra time securing the lid and fiddling with the broken lock clasp, trying to make it look undamaged. For some reason, she didn't want anyone else seeing the busted lock and taking further advantage of this woman.

I'll warn her about it, Reb decided, feeling magnanimous, *tell her to get it fixed.*

She fished in her back pocket, found her stub of a pencil and the small notepad she used for jotting down lyrics. Thoughtfully, she composed her note, then folded it and kissed it.

After lowering the bulging trashbag into the street, she vaulted over the side. Knowing she had already spent too much time here, she dashed to the front of the truck. Quickly, she lifted the wiper blade and stuck her note underneath, then returned to her bag. She grabbed it, and immediately headed in the opposite direction from the one Chris and Tom had taken earlier. After a fast walk for half a block, she broke into a full-out sprint.

At the end of the street, she stopped at the edge of the intersection and looked back at the white Ford pickup. Suddenly, unexpected remorse pierced her. *Talk about dissin' somebody! Here I am admirin' that fine-lookin' woman, then I go and jack her stuff!*

But then it occurred to her that now she had money to eat, and the supplies she needed for an outdoor shelter. Giving a helpless sigh, she swung the trashbag of loot over her shoulder and turned away. *Got to keep body and soul together somehow,* she thought. *And anyway, I'll probably never see her again.*

Driven by her gnawing hunger, she bent her head and began hurrying along East Union Street. The Capitol Hill Shop Rite was only about six blocks away.

Night had fallen by the time Chris slid into the truck, feeling better for the meal and Tom's company. Beside her, Tom was yawning, remarking that he thought the Wildrose served the best Reuben in Seattle. Agreeing amiably, Chris started the engine. She turned on the headlights, and suddenly noticed the small, square shape under the wiper blade.

A note. For a few long heartbeats, she stared at it, thinking it was from Joyce. Then, right behind that thought, savage memory slashed her, sinking its teeth into her heart.

Was it really five years ago? she wondered, the pain still disconcertingly fresh. She sat there, vividly remembering the folded notes Joyce used to leave on her truck, under the wiper blade, just like this.

Turning to Tom, feeling disoriented, Chris asked, "Do you see that?"

He nodded impassively, then seemed to wait for her to retrieve the note.

Chris brought her gaze back to the paper. Tom had obviously forgotten all about Joyce's penchant for leaving notes. Provocative messages like, "See you in bed," or "Get your fine ass home," tucked under the wiper blade whenever she saw Chris's truck parked in front of a job site. Sweetly tender phrases like, "How are you, Beautiful?" Chris sighed, admitting to herself that it was the sort of thing that only a lover would cherish and remember.

Oh, God, Joyce, she sighed inwardly. *I miss you.*

Opening the door, she held onto the steering wheel and half-stood, reaching for the paper. She tugged it free of the wiper, then plunked back into her seat. Inwardly shaken, she unfolded the note beneath the overhead cab light.

Yo Lady,
Be sure to check your box in the back. I only took what I really needed, and I'm very sorry I had to mess with your truck.
A Friend

Chris growled, "Shit!" She shut off the truck engine, then, suddenly outraged, pounded the steering wheel with the heel of her hand. "I think I've been robbed!"

"What?" Tom asked.

She thrust the note at him. He moved the paper beneath the overhead light, reading the neat printing, while Chris jumped out of the cab and climbed into the back of the truck.

Unable to see much in the dark, she smoothed her hands over the box and found the lock by touch. She gave the cool little square of sturdy steel a testing tug. Screws popped out of their wooden holes and jingled as they fell into the black depths of the truck bed. The steel clasp slid completely off the box.

"Aw jeez!" Chris griped, throwing the lock down angrily. "It's broken, all right!" With her other hand, she slammed open the lid.

Tom came out of the truck, saying, "This is almost a thank-you card."

Leaning into the box, Chris was taking a quick, tactile inventory of the contents. "Where's the damn flashlight?" she complained. "They must've stolen the thing, for cryin' out loud!" Then after a few minutes of fumbling over what remained in the wooden bin, she announced, "They didn't take the tools! I can't believe it! Not even the power stuff...."

"'They?'" Tom countered. "It's one name here. 'A Friend.'"

Oblivious, Chris lit a match, then rattled on, "...but my new boots are gone and so is your motorcycle jacket...."

"That ratty thing?" Tom commented, squinting against the dark as he tried to peer into the box. "I only kept it in the truck for those chilly mornings when the fog just won't quit. I mean, I'm sorry about your boots, but thank goodness he passed up the tools, which are really worth something." Tom scratched behind his ear. "Don't you think that's strange?"

"And the paint tarp isn't here, and, like I said, the flashlight." Frowning, Chris shook her hand up and down, putting out the match. She straightened and let the lid bang closed. "Why would thieves steal that junk and leave the stuff they could sell?"

"Don't know," Tom said. "But if they were desperate enough to break into the toolbox, you're lucky you didn't have anything tempting in the cab."

"My meter money!"

Quickly, Tom moved back into the truck and checked the glove compartment. He pulled out the small white coffee cup, then sighed and turned it upside down. "How much was in here?"

"*Shit!*" Thoroughly angry now, Chris hopped from the truck bed down to the street. "They wiped me out!"

Tom handed Chris the empty cup. "It was just small change, right?"

"I had sixty bucks in there!" Chris retorted. "Money I won in the football pool! While we were unloading the truck this afternoon, Allen handed it to me and I popped it in here!" Furious, she crushed the coffee cup. "For cripe's sake!"

Tom stuck his head back inside and commented encouragingly, "But they left your high-priced radio and tape deck unit alone. Not a scratch on it, or the ignition box."

She peeked over his shoulder, frowning. "Well, that's certainly weird."

Tom backed out of the cab and bumped into her. "All in all, it *is* rather small-potatoes thievery, isn't it?"

She nodded. "Why did they pass up valuable tools and an expensive sound system?"

"I don't think it's more than one person," Tom answered. "And according to what I've heard from our cop friend, Thea, this has all the earmarks of being done by a street kid."

"Well, I better not get a hold of that 'kid,' that's all I have to say," Chris muttered, tossing the crumpled coffee cup into the back of her truck. "I'll take that sixty dollars out of him in hard labor—the absolute worst job I can think of—like scraping all the paint off the exterior of a three-story house!"

"Such as our current project," Tom remarked, regarding her with a boyish grin that belied his forty-three years. "Looking forward to next week's slated activity that much, are we?" He pretended to lift a phone receiver to his ear, dialing a number. "Hello? Governor Lowry? Listen, we have this great plan to stop youth crime. However, we need a few thousand metal paint scrapers and all the kids you can send us from juvenile hall...."

He went on with his monologue, but Chris had stopped listening. *I thought it was a note from Joyce,* she thought, feeling raw and betrayed. *And it was some little punk...breaking into my truck, robbing me, and then leaving a note to jeer about it...* No longer able to endure Tom's teasing as well, Chris heard herself lashing out at him. "If a kid needs money, he can *work* for it, God damn it! Just like I did!"

His pale blue eyes were concerned as they searched her own. "Okay, you're right. It's not funny." He reached out and placed a gentle hand on her shoulder. "I'm sorry, Chris."

"Stupid kids!" Chris snapped, giving her anger full voice. "What the hell are they doing running around this late on a school night! They oughtta be home...doing their school-work or washing up after dinner or...*something*. Anything besides breaking into my damn truck and stealing my property!"

"They're homeless, Chris," Tom said softly. "You've seen them—those scruffy-looking kids up on Broadway. Runaways, throwaways, whatever you want to call them."

Giving him a withering look, Chris marched around the truck and swung into the driver's seat. "I don't want to hear another liberal lecture about the need for more social programs! We need tougher judges and sentences for hard time!"

As Tom settled himself beside her, she slammed the door closed and started the truck engine again. She felt herself putting a distance between them, shrinking into that familiar cavern of pain and emptiness she carried inside her.

"I take it you're not going to phone the police," he ventured.

In answer, she backed the truck out fast, screeching the tires as she braked. "Why? What good would it do?" Seething, she thrust the stick into first gear. "All the cops will do is make a report, tell me not to leave my valuables in the truck, and then go drive around some more in their cruiser."

Tom stayed quiet, only lifting his baseball cap and re-settling it. He was obviously trying to give her space.

Angrily, Chris demanded, "What's happening to this country, anyway?"

A few minutes later, Chris turned the truck onto Six-teenth Avenue, and then into her drive. She steered the vehicle down the gravel lane and into the small garage at the edge of the backyard.

She had dropped Tom off at his place a few blocks away, and received a strong, longer-than-usual hug from him as they parted. They had been friends since high school and business partners for fifteen years, so she was not surprised to realize he had read her mood. Once the anger had passed, grief, ever waiting in the wings, had swept over her.

Well, Joyce always did tell me my face was an open book, she mused.

Grimly, she turned off the truck engine and simply sat there, gripping the steering wheel. Five years had passed in a haze of anguish—the longest five years of her life. As often happened when she sat still for any length of time, memories overtook her.

Leaning against the rail, rocking with the motion of the ferry boat, I slowly twist open the urn. The wind catches the gravelly contents as I toss what is left of Joyce into the air, into the churning, deep-blue waters of the Sound. A feeling of numbness and hollowness wraps itself around me; the nearby tourists stare. "It's what she wanted," I say quietly.

Chris covered her eyes with a hand. *But it's not what I wanted. God, no, it's not what I thought I'd ever be doing.*

Now, each evening, after the twelve-hour days and the working weekends, she still came home to an empty, silent house.

Stoically restoring order to her thoughts, Chris leaned back in her seat.

She had to admit that over the past few months, the misery had begun to recede. Joyce's absence was no longer the first thing she thought of each morning. Whole days went by sometimes without a thought about her. As time went on, Chris was both surprised and irritated to find that she was recovering.

It made her feel guilty, as if her slow healing was, in reality, a betrayal.

I'm getting over it. Baffled, Chris sighed. *Aren't I?*

Alf's barking at the back door brought her back to reality. He was seven years old now, and clearly annoyed that she'd left him at home today, something she rarely did. Usually she parked him in the Ford cab on the rare occasions when she went out to eat, so in his mind, tonight's abandonment was an outrage. However, it had been fairly warm that afternoon, and she hadn't wanted him to suffer in a stuffy truck when he could lounge on a sofa at home.

As Chris left the garage, she flipped the inner light on and left the door open. Walking quickly, she followed the brick walkway and climbed the deck stairs two at a time. Key in hand, she crossed the broad stretch of wooden planking, and seconds later, opened the back door.

With hysterical glee, the brown-and-white springer spaniel threw himself at her, nearly knocking her over. His small nub of a tail wagged excitedly as he ran across the deck and down the steps. Laughing softly, Chris followed after him, watching him race out of the light cast from the garage. She could hear him whuffling busily as he charged about, and even in the dark knew what he was doing. Back by the line of oaks and alders at the end of her acre of property, Alf's dutiful, if compulsive, search for squirrels had already begun.

She went back to the garage and thoroughly examined the truck beneath the bright electric lighting. Amazed to find no scratches on the body paint of either door, or damage to the lock mechanisms, she grew thankful that at least her thief had had some skill.

Yawning, she reached into the truck cab and removed her paint-stained Mariner's cap from the glove box. *Thank the Goddess, he didn't take this.* On cold, rainy days, she always felt warmer within minutes of putting that hat on her head. Tom said it made her look like a man, like "a skinny Spokane redneck," to be exact, but Chris loved the hat. With a small, stubborn grin, she yanked it over her hair, pulling it low on her brow, and left it on.

She shut off the garage lights and tugged down the overhead door. Whistling, she looked around for Alf, but Alf didn't come. She squinted into the shadowy depths of the backyard and saw no telltale patches of white scooting around.

Then a car drove into the driveway she shared with the house next door.

The new neighbor. Chris remembered feeling a strange mixture of curiosity and annoyance when the moving van had arrived.

Allison had not said much about this latest sale, mentioning only that a woman had bought the property. The house next door had been empty for some time, almost three months, since Joel and Frank had put it on the market in an effort to finance Frank's AZT treatment. The house had been an Olson & Morrissey project, four years before Joyce's death. Chris found she almost resented anyone else owning and living in the splendid two-story Victorian that had once belonged to good friends.

The photo-sensor lights of both houses flicked on, flooding yellow light over the matching wraparound front porches and the shared driveway. Midway down the drive, Chris watched the new Saab lurch to a stop. The car horn beeped—a sudden, loud sound that cut through the quiet Seattle night. As Chris watched, a woman quickly emerged from the driver's side.

She stomped her high-heeled foot and yelled, "Dammit to hell—get out of there, you!"

Astounded, Chris stood in the dark, unseen, as Alf came slinking across the driveway from the neighbor's front yard. Even from this distance, she could see that he was carrying something in his mouth. To her amazement, the slender figure in heels and a tailored business suit gave chase, as Alf loped into Chris's yard.

When Chris rounded the bushes by her front porch she found both dog and neighbor involved in a showdown by the steps. The neighbor was cursing and Alf was actually growling. Seeing Chris, Alf ran up the painted wooden stairs to the front door, where he began whining and trotting around in nervous circles.

The woman turned, demanding, "Is this your dog?!"

For an instant, Chris just stared at her, taking in her pale, Celtic skin and flashing blue-green eyes. Then she noticed the curvaceous figure and the sleek, light-brown hair which was gathered and pinned in a twist at the back of her head. She was an arresting and unexpected vision, and she was angrily glaring back at Chris as if the bold appraisal had made her angrier still.

Before Chris could open her mouth, the woman asserted, "This dog is a menace. Just *look* at what he's done!"

Chris followed the wave of the woman's hand and saw what Alf was guiltily guarding. Well over two dozen muddy tulip bulbs were strewn over the welcome mat, bits of wet dirt still clinging to them. And Alf's front paws, normally white socks with a few brown springer freckles, were dingy with mud.

"Aw jeez, Alf," Chris sighed, mortified.

Alf gave Chris a sorrowful look, full of contrition. The small stub of tail was wagging hopefully.

"He tore up the entire flower bed!" the woman shouted. "All across the front of my house! I worked so hard all week...hauling in wheelbarrows of dirt and fertilizer. With a tight breath she finished, "And now it's all ruined!"

Lamely, Chris began, "He has this thing about digging...."

The woman interrupted, insisting, "I slaved over that garden! And I intended to accomplish more than provide buried treasure for your rampaging beast!"

"I'm sorry," Chris began again. "I'm Chris Olson..."

Once more, she was promptly cut off. "Can't one thing in my life go right, for God's sake? Don't I even get a *chance* to start over?" Waving a hand at her yard, she addressed Alf directly. "Can't I even hope for a little something in the spring?!"

Then, as if realizing that she had said too much, the woman snapped her mouth closed. She gave Alf a mean stare, and then marched past Chris.

Not ready for her to leave yet, Chris found herself hurrying after the neighbor as she headed back to the Saab. "I'll replant your flowers for you," she offered.

The woman reached into the car and brought out an expensive-looking leather briefcase. "Don't bother!" she said, slamming the car door. As she continued around the vehicle, toward her house, the new neighbor threw over her shoulder, "Just keep your dog in your own yard, Mister!"

Brought up short, Chris stopped and watched the woman go. "*Mister?*" she repeated. "What kind of crack is that?"

The woman ignored her and briskly tripped up the front steps. High heels clicked across the wooden porch. With an imperious fury, she unlocked the door, sailed over the threshold, then slammed the door behind her.

Miffed, Chris turned and strode across the yard to her own porch. "Don't even tell me your damned name, why don'tcha?"

She stomped up the stairs of her front porch, glowering at Alf, then yanked off her ball cap. "Of all the stupid stunts," she complained, pulling her gray sweatshirt over her head. Once it was off, she spread it on the porch and used her arm to sweep tulip bulbs onto it.

Alf promptly picked up one, and tried to trot around her, but Chris snagged his collar, ordering him to drop it.

With a glum look, Alf complied.

"This is ridiculous. You stay out of that lady's yard," she ordered. Trying to simplify the message, Chris employed a stern voice, "No! Bad dog! Stay home!"

Alf huffed a snort, then sat down with his back turned toward her.

Feeling chilly in just her T-shirt, Chris picked up her discarded Mariner's hat and jammed it over her hair. She grabbed up the few remaining tulip bulbs, then used her sweatshirt like a sack and carried the load across the yard to her neighbor's flower bed.

Working quickly, Chris replanted the bulbs one by one. When she was finished, she wiped her muddy hands off on her jeans, and signaled Alf.

"Better to mend fences sooner than later," she told him. "So she's a knockout? So what? Like we care, right?"

Alf trotted along beside her, his tail wagging happily.

CHAPTER 3

The next day, Friday evening, found Morgan walking along a busy street in Seattle. She peered at the folded map in her hand, then examined the street sign on the corner.

She was approaching the intersection of Olive Way and Broadway. Clad in baggy, faded jeans and an open, blue-green plaid flannel over her T-shirt, she was more than a little relieved to realize that she was blending right in with every other kid in the crowd. Then the wind swept her loose, auburn hair back from her face, and she caught the curious glance she drew from a man who was passing by her.

Keep your head down, she chided herself. *You've got a mean black eye and you don't need any questions about how you got it.*

Worriedly biting her lip, she shoved the map in the back pocket of her jeans. Her backpack was feeling heavier by the minute. Even as she gripped the shoulder straps of the pack and tried to shift the weight, she knew it would do little good. What she needed was to find someplace to curl up and sleep.

It was nearing six o'clock, and the afternoon warmth was quickly fading. Almost twenty hours had passed since she had sneaked out of her parents' house. A bleak twenty hours, marked by tightly controlled anxiety and an increasing feeling of bewilderment.

She had spent the previous night sitting in an alley near the Wenatchee Greyhound terminal. Her back propped against a rough brick wall, Morgan had resolved that no matter what happened, she would never go home again. Strangely, there had never been any question in her mind about where she was going.

She had grown up hearing about Seattle, the city over the mountains. Surrounded by water and nestled atop seven hills, it was fondly called "The Emerald City," because the surrounding country was so green. Her father had often sneered that the place was "full of half-breeds and queers," and seemed to think that was disgusting. Morgan had never understood why mixed races or gay relationships in a city hundreds of miles away would concern him so much. It followed logically, then, that what would cause her father to despise the place would make her love it.

And so, earlier that morning, just before 7:30 a.m., she had walked into the Wenatchee Greyhound terminal. Resisting the compulsion to check over her shoulder every five minutes for the police, she had paid twenty-five dollars for a ticket to freedom and then climbed aboard the shining, silver bus. During the morning ride, as the bus threaded its way up through the Cascade Mountains, she had dared to close her eyes. But three hours of sleep had done little to repair the damage of last night's beating.

Now, late in the afternoon, the large navy-blue bruises that covered her legs and back had taken on a fiery ache and she was tired beyond belief. Despite the black eye, she had spent the day walking, canvassing this section of the city and applying for jobs. Between the coffeehouses, fast food restaurants, and numerous small businesses, Capitol Hill had immediately seemed like a good place to look for work. However, no one had seemed to even want to talk to her, let alone hire her. Worse, she hadn't lined up a place to spend the night. She had looked up the YWCA address in the phone book and knew the general direction, but it was located on the other side of the city. And she had been delaying that trek, hoping to land a job before she began to spend money on room and board.

*I feel so alone...*she realized. For a moment she wondered if Janet even knew she was gone, then made herself put the thought from her mind. *Janet doesn't want me. She wanted sex—not me. Get over it.*

Exhausted, she wandered into Dick's Hamburgers, a Fifties-style fast food joint, for the second time that day. As she stood beside lines of milling, impatient customers, Morgan observed that the "Help Wanted—All Shifts" sign was still hanging by the entrance. She pushed her way through the people moving steadily to and from the counter, and then stood by the cash register not in use, trying to catch the manager's eye.

He looked right at her, then frowned and looked away.

Undaunted, Morgan called out, "Excuse me, sir."

When he stood before her, still frowning, she said, "I put in a job application this morning. You told me to come back tonight and maybe I could start..."

He contemptuously cut in, "I phoned the number you wrote down, kid, and the woman who answered never heard of you."

Hunching her shoulders, Morgan lowered her eyes. "I can explain...," she began.

"So, then," the manager continued, paying no attention to her, "I asked the woman who ran the desk if the Y could be considered your place of residence, and guess what?" His voice was rising. People in the counter lines were turning to watch. "According to the hotel desk, you don't *live* there."

In a direct appeal, Morgan looked at him and asserted, "I really need this job."

"No fixed address, no job," he sneered, "you're a runaway! I'm operating a business here, not a charity. Want some advice, kid?" When Morgan turned and began to wearily walk away, he shouted after her, "Go home—where you belong!"

As she reached the door and pushed it open, she felt someone close behind her. Instinctively, she turned and found herself face to face with the same man who had passed her on the street a few minutes earlier. Powerfully built, in his late twenties, he was well-dressed in a business suit and a striking, rakishly loosened tie.

"You looking for work?" he asked.

Morgan just stared at him. Though the man smiled disarmingly, some inner alarm began ringing.

"I got a job for you," he said, then slipped his hand into the crook of her arm and tugged her sideways. "Come on."

Moving quickly, he dragged her past the glass windows that encased the front of the restaurant.

Recovering from her initial shock, Morgan dug her heels in, trying to jerk her arm free. "Hey—quit it!"

He laughed and continued around the side of the building, taking her forcibly with him. There was suddenly no one else in sight, and the huge glass windows that made up the front of Dick's were gone. This side wall was solid brick, and the building itself was effectively preventing anyone in the front section of the parking lot from seeing them.

His coal-black eyes were riveted on her, slithering over her, and there was suddenly ice water shooting through Morgan's veins.

Trouble! This is trouble! Morgan's mind wailed.

"Come on. Don't you wanta make a quick twenty bucks?" he asked, tightening his grip, increasing his pace. "If you're good, you can stay overnight. Maybe earn yourself a little extra...."

Stumbling beside him, Morgan protested, "No! Let go...." Before she could say anything else, he slapped her. Hard.

She lost her footing and he pulled her against him, whispering in her ear, "You already got a black eye, sugar. You want another one?"

This was familiar—horrid and terrifying—and yet so impossibly familiar that at first Morgan couldn't understand her own response to it. Almost on cue, that strange detachment came over her. An invisible, thick, cottony wall seemed to rise up within her, insulating her from the terror.

"Get used to the idea, baby," he whispered, then gently ran his tongue around the edge of her ear. "You're gonna work for me, and you're gonna like it."

A surge of bile rose in her throat. *He isn't Dad!* she reminded herself. *Think! You can't shut down! Think!*

"Don't scream, sugar," he warned her. "I'll make you awful sorry if you scream." With one last quick look around, he hustled her toward a cream-colored, older-model Cadillac parked at the corner of the building.

Frantically, she clawed at the strong fingers locked around her arm. As they neared the driver's side, just as he reached to open the door, she managed to locate and isolate his pinky finger. Remorselessly, she snapped it straight back, all the way back to his wrist. She heard—felt—the bone break.

Screaming, he released her. His face was a mixture of fury and astonishment, and he clutched his hand to his chest, gasping.

Morgan took off at a dead run. She hurtled through space, her arms and legs rising and falling like pistons, the heavy backpack thudding against her spine. Behind her, she heard hard-soled shoes slapping on pavement, and knew he was already in pursuit.

She was gulping air as she dashed into the busy rush hour traffic streaming along Broadway. Watchful of the approaching cars, timing her dodging path between the vehicles, she weaved and stutter-stepped her way through four lanes of automobiles. Dimly, she heard the car horns blasting as she was narrowly missed by a black Jeep and then a bright blue Miata. Once across, she sprinted down the sidewalk for the perpendicular street fifty yards ahead. As Morgan cut the corner, turning left, she looked over her shoulder and saw the man relentlessly moving along the double yellow line in the middle of the road. He wasn't desperate enough to challenge the solid waves of traffic moving along the street at thirty miles an hour. Temporarily at least, he would be unable to follow her.

Terrified that he might cross at any minute, she charged down Denny, and raced several blocks before turning right on Eleventh Avenue. Gasping with relief, she sighted the small city park there. She stopped and bent over, her legs trembling as she carefully checked the street behind her. When she was certain that she wasn't being followed, she jogged across the grass, into the park. Behind a bush, she fell to her knees. Her stomach heaved, but there was nothing much in it to vomit. Gasping and shaking, she wrapped her arms about herself, blinded by tears.

Why? she wondered frantically. Why *the hell did he do that? Like I was...his for the taking?*

For several minutes, she rocked back and forth, trying to compose herself. *God, that was close,* she kept thinking, as she wiped her eyes with shaking hands. Deep within her, she suspected that this was how those female corpses turned up in the forests along the Green River.

After half an hour of hunching there, afraid and nauseous, she gradually became aware that the crisp autumn night was growing downright cold. Listless now that the adrenaline rush was over, she dug her red-and-white letter jacket out of her pack and slipped it on over her flannel shirt. Although she was grateful for its warmth, she was vaguely fearful of wearing the jacket. The huge letters on the back, "Wenatchee High," seemed to identify her to the world as a runaway. She was just starting to understand what an easy target being a runaway made her.

Gratefully, Morgan pushed open the door and crossed the lobby. She saw the bold sign reading "YWCA Hotel

Accommodations, 2nd Floor" and the arrow pointing up the stairs. She couldn't help the groan that escaped her. It had been at least a three-mile walk from Broadway to this side of the city, and after everything else she had been through today, the thought of climbing two flights of stairs seemed impossible. Somehow, though, she managed to keep putting one sneakered foot in front of the other, and climbed the steps one by one.

She reached the second floor and crossed the ancient linoleum to the hotel desk. A clock on the wall told her that it was almost eight. Noticing the service bell, she tapped twice and then looked around. As she waited, she pressed her fingers against her temple, trying to relieve the fierce headache she was developing.

A plump woman with frizzled, gray hair came through an open door behind the desk. Her name tag read "Molly," and as she smiled at Morgan, Morgan saw the pricing sign behind her.

Surprised, Morgan croaked, "Thirty-five dollars a night?"

It seemed like a lot of money. She hadn't been clear on just what the room would cost, but this still seemed exorbitant. Even with all her savings, at thirty-five dollars a night, she'd be broke inside of a month.

Surveying Morgan with concern, Molly replied, "I'm afraid we're full."

"Full?" Morgan echoed, unable to process what was being said to her. She rubbed her burning eyes with her hand, then asked, "You mean I can't stay here?"

In a gentle voice, Molly said, "That's right. We're at capacity right through next month." She waited until Morgan looked at her again before saying, "I'd need to see some I.D. first, anyway. No offense, but you look mighty young and we don't rent to anyone under seventeen."

Dismayed, Morgan pulled her eyes away from the woman's penetrating scrutiny. She had left her driver's license and anything else with her name on it back in Wenatchee. As far as she was concerned, Morgan Flynn was dead.

She gathered her courage and answered, "I'm seventeen. But I...don't have anything to prove it."

Slowly, Molly leaned across the desk, and in a soothing voice, like a person might use with a child lost in a shopping mall, she coaxed, "If you're in trouble, maybe I can help."

Morgan's stomach rolled over. Her heart began thumping and she could barely meet the woman's gaze. "No, uh...I'm just passing through and I, uhm...need a place to sleep, and it was getting late, so I..." Realizing that she was rambling, Morgan stopped and simply stood there, at a loss.

"Look," Molly was saying, "let me see if I can get you placed in a shelter for the night."

Is she trying to trick me? Morgan thought, her throat constricting. *Is she going to pretend she's helping me, and then turn me over to the cops?*

"I can call the Shelter, over on 46th Avenue South," Molly explained, reaching for the phone. "It's an emergency facility exclusively for young people." Her pale blue eyes worried, she elaborated, "I'll be honest, it's usually hard to get into, but maybe they'll have an opening."

"No, that's okay. I've changed my mind," Morgan murmured, backing away. "Um...thanks anyway."

"Please," Molly entreated, "don't go. You look like you could use a friend."

Uncertain, Morgan hesitated.

She had quickly realized that this part of the city was scary. Whereas Broadway had been made up of small shops and universities, and was bustling with young people, Fifth Avenue was a markedly different place. The area around the YWCA was dominated by tall office buildings, theaters, posh hotels, and cavernous parking garages. As she had walked along Fifth Avenue on her way here, she had passed one business suit after another. The speculative male eyes had lingered on her, until after only a few blocks she had entered a new realm of fear. Never had she felt so naive and defenseless. Worse still was traveling the last block, when several drunken homeless men had shuffled out of the shadows. Trailing behind her, they had mumbled entreaties for cigarettes and spare change. When she ignored them and hurried on, they had shouted lewd threats after her. The queasy feeling in her stomach had worsened with each block.

After a moment's hesitation, Morgan knew she'd do anything to avoid going out on the street again.

"Stay here with me for a little while," Molly invited softly. "I'll find you a safe place to sleep."

Wearily, Morgan blinked, wanting so much to trust her.

Taking Morgan's indecision for agreement, Molly pulled a folder from beneath the desk and busied herself with the phone.

Incapable of staying upright another minute, Morgan went over to the ugly, orange vinyl sofa placed near the lobby wall. She shrugged off her backpack, dropped it to the scarred linoleum, then gratefully sat down. Relieved that someone was willing to help her, she sighed and leaned back against the cushion. Molly was into her third call, her courteous inquiries a soft comfort in the background, when the exhaustion Morgan had fought for hours rose like a wave and swept over her.

Some time later, she heard another voice asking, "So what does this one call herself, Molly?"

Briefly, Morgan tried to open her eyes, but they were just too heavy. She was down deep somewhere, held in the grip of an overwhelming fatigue.

"Don't know. We haven't gotten that far yet," someone replied. "I've spent the last half hour trying to get her shelter somewhere, but this time of year it gets tough."

With a start, Morgan realized they were talking about her. She forced her eyes open, blurting, "What?"

Before her stood an African-American woman in a blue police uniform. A badge flashed on her chest. A holstered revolver was snug on her hip.

"Oh, shit," Morgan breathed.

"Hi there," the police officer remarked, her eyes flitting over Morgan's face. They were direct, calculating eyes, with none of Molly's warm compassion.

Morgan sat up fast, darting a nervous glance at the stairs. *Go, go, go, go...*her inner voice screamed.

"Now, don't panic, girlfriend," the officer counseled. "I'm just stoppin' by. This place isn't even on my beat and..."

Distressed, Morgan swung her gaze to Molly, who was hurrying around the side of the long hotel desk.

"Oh, hey. Don't look at me like that. I didn't betray you, kid," Molly insisted, sounding flustered. "This is Officer Jance, a friend of mine. She just stops in to chat over a cup of my bad coffee...."

Morgan wasn't listening. She was watching the police-woman turn toward Molly. She saw her opportunity and seized it. With one hand she grabbed her backpack, then tucked her shoulder down and shot forward.

Her tackle caught Officer Jance in the midsection. With a loud "Uhhn!" the policewoman went down and Morgan kept going, past her, to the stairs. She took the steps in a series of open-legged leaps. At the ground floor, she shoved open the glass doors and took off down Fifth Avenue, carrying the bulky backpack under her arm like it was an oversized football.

Without consulting the map, she raced down the streets, zigzagging from one to the next. She heard the whoop of the police siren as she tore through an alley three blocks away, and with a rush of panic realized that she was getting impossibly lost. It seemed as if several squad cars had begun to crisscross the area, their red and blue lights flashing, painting the menac-ing, dark streets in surreal shades. She finally stopped to slip the backpack straps over her shoulders, and then a police car was suddenly coming up the alley behind her. Gasping and frightened, Morgan moved close to the old brick wall and slid behind a dumpster.

They're gonna catch me, she thought, fighting panic. *They're going to call Dad and I'll end up drugged out of my mind and locked up for the rest of my life!*

Indistinctly, she heard querulous voices—men's voices—and peeked around the side of the metal dumpster to determine the source. Nearby, beneath a dim overhead light, she saw some men sitting on a warehouse dock, sharing a bottle. They were arguing over whose turn it was to take a drink, and abruptly the quarrel got louder. The squad car swept a searchlight over them, catching two of the men grabbing a third. They were shouting curses and grappling for the bottle when the squad car stopped. As Morgan ducked back behind the dumpster, she heard the glass smash.

Another peek revealed that the officers had jumped out of the car. They began chasing the men, who had jumped off the dock and were running away from Morgan, to the opposite end of the alley.

In the resulting excitement, Morgan crept unseen through the darkness, and exited the alley onto the next street. While the adrenaline was still buzzing through her system, she began running up the hill stretching before her, not needing the map to know which direction to go.

From the day's travels, she had learned two things. One, that Seattle was a series of monstrous hills, all of which rolled up from Puget Sound. And two, the more highly urban side of the city was on the western side of Interstate 5, the major highway which divided the city into east and west.

Without hesitation, she headed east, back to Capitol Hill.

As Morgan trudged uphill, she heard a church bell tolling the hour and automatically began counting. Massaging her neck, trying to think of something beside her headache, she got to eleven and then knew why she felt so sick. Hungry and tired, she knew her body was in complete rebellion.

I've got to get a room somewhere, she resolved. *I'll spend whatever it takes. I just have to get a safe place to lie down.*

She wasn't sure why she didn't change direction when she saw three figures standing close together on the sidewalk about fifty yards ahead. By now, she was so used to trudging uphill that she felt as if she were in a trance. She was simply leaning forward and placing one black Converse sneaker in front of the other. When the hill leveled out, she was breathing hard and squinting against the halogen street lights.

At last, she found herself on the corner of Olive Way and Broadway, a busy intersection even this late at night. Not five feet away from her, two young teenage boys were shoving around a girl, trying to intimidate her into letting go of what looked like a trashbag.

"Stupid little dyke," one boy snarled.

"I'm warning you, Leper!" the girl yelled at the taller one. "You too, Moon," she shot at the boy with a shaved head. "It's *my* stuff! Go get your own haul!"

Fearlessly, the much shorter girl continued to fend them off, kicking out at the boys while she clutched the plastic bag with both hands. But the boys were laughing, deliberately taking their time and wearing the girl down. She was breathing hard, tiring.

For a moment, Morgan watched in disbelief, then glanced around, angrily wondering, *Why doesn't somebody help her?* Cars were whizzing past the dispute, not even slowing down. Pedestrians, all of them seeming extraordinarily young—some years younger than herself—were averting their eyes and hurriedly passing by the scene, all of them looking frightened. *What's the matter with everyone?*

Morgan returned her attention just in time to see the taller boy haul back his fist and punch the girl, knocking her to the ground.

All at once, Morgan's vision was awash in red. Blood hammered through her head, her hands clenched into tight balls and an inferno of shaking rage demolished some brittle inner barrier. The blast ripped through her, sweeping her along. In an impetuous rush, she peeled off the heavy backpack, dropping it to the sidewalk. In a fury, she grabbed the boy's shoulder and spun him around.

To her surprise, she found herself looking into a face that couldn't be more than fourteen years old; close enough to see the patches of inflamed acne along both cheeks, and a cruel, chilling sneer on his lips.

"What's your fuckin' problem?" Leper barked. "You want some, too?" He raised his arm, ready to backhand her.

Without conscious thought, she chambered up her right arm. Of its own will, her fist shot forward, straight from the shoulder, and she nailed him.

Leper went down.

Within seconds, Moon let go of the trashbag he had wrested from the girl dressed in black. He glanced at his friend, sprawled on the concrete sidewalk, then menacingly advanced on Morgan. She stood her ground, yelling things at him, things she couldn't quite seem to make sense of, even as she heard and felt them booming from her own throat. He looked at her strangely. Then, almost as if he were fighting more out of some bullying habit than out of real anger, Moon gave a nasty laugh and quickly closed the space between them.

She dodged his first punch, blocked his second, then got him square on the nose with a right cross. Shocked, wincing with pain, Moon clamped his hands over his nose. As Morgan moved toward him, shouting, still not really clear what she was saying, the boy cowered back. He looked as if he had no idea what to do. When he finally moved his hands away from his face and saw the stream of red gushing down onto his sweatshirt, he burst into tears.

Without a backward glance, Moon began scurrying down Broadway, blubbering, "She hurt me! The bitch *hurt* me!"

Nearby, astounded, Leper still remained sprawled on the sidewalk, rubbing his jaw. As she wheeled on him, the boy spit blood, then scrambled to his feet, muttering, "C'mon, bitch!"

The girl with the trashbag was yelling, "Go, girl, go!"

This time Morgan barely managed to weave out of the way, and Leper's punch glanced off her shoulder. But while he was close to her, Morgan was able to land a left uppercut. Leper's jaw snapped shut with an audible crack of teeth. His eyes rolled up into his head and then he slumped to the pavement.

Wild with anger, Morgan stood over him, shouting, "Come on! Try and hit me! I'm through taking your shit! I'm through—you hear me?!"

She came to herself with a jolt. At last, she comprehended what she was saying. *Sheee-it!*

Breathing raggedly, realizing that she was out of control, she backed up and stumbled into the girl with the trashbag.

Then, suddenly, she was aware of motion behind them. As she turned, she saw that the boy with the shaved head and bloody nose had returned. Slowly, she registered that Moon had been busily rooting through her backpack while she was fighting Leper. Hardly daring to believe her own eyes, she watched Moon lift her small metal cash box from the backpack. With astonishing quickness, he tucked the box under his arm and began to run.

My money! she thought, dumbfounded, then hollered, "No!"

Infuriated, Morgan gave chase, but after only a dozen steps a swirl of black dots abruptly rose before her eyes. Winded, dizzy beyond belief, she staggered to a stop, then bent over and gripped her thighs.

That was when she heard the scream of a police siren. It seemed far off, but she instinctively knew it was heading her way. Gasping with fear, Morgan straightened.

Large, round brown eyes peered up at her. "You're not crazy or anything, are you?" the girl asked.

Dazed, drained and unnerved, Morgan admitted, "I fell in love with Janet." Swallowing hard, she reasoned, "That's crazy enough, isn't it?"

The girl's eyes swept over her, measuring, evaluating. "I don't know. Was she cute?"

Grimly, Morgan whispered, "Beautiful."

The wail of the siren was getting louder, quickly coming closer.

The girl's face became resolute. Briskly, she collected the clothing the boy had tossed out of Morgan's backpack, hurriedly stuffed the assortment back into the pack, then re-zipped it.

"He stole all my money," Morgan wailed, her voice strained with disbelief.

"So you're broke?" the girl asked, helping Morgan slip the pack over her shoulders.

"Yeah," Morgan was barely able to whisper. Her throat was painfully tight and she thought for a moment she was going to break down and bawl like a baby.

Next to her, the short, dark-haired girl slung the bulky trashbag over her shoulder and reached for Morgan's right hand. With a firm tug she set off, walking quickly away from the scene.

Morgan tried to keep pace with her. She could feel herself shaking all over, but some cool, detached part of her mind was telling her that none of this was real. First a crazy fist-fight and then the theft of every cent of her hundreds of dollars—it just seemed impossible.

"Hey—listen—my name's Reb," the girl stated with a swift smile and a reassuring squeeze of the hand. "And I'm sorry about your money, but I'm sure glad you were on my side."

The siren was getting progressively louder.

Her breath catching with fear, Morgan glanced behind her, verifying that there was a boy back there lying on the sidewalk. "Is he okay?"

Keeping a tight hold on Morgan's right hand, Reb pulled Morgan forward. "He'll live. Don't sweat it."

"W-why were they picking on you?" Morgan asked. She glanced at the trashbag Reb carried. They *wanted something in that bag badly enough to attack her.*

"Aw, it's gang shit," Reb relayed, grimacing. "They're Ghouls. It's just a small-time local gang, but they got big plans of expansion. And it's the same deal: you're either in or you're out."

"And you're not in the gang?" Morgan clarified, squinting against her dull headache.

Reb hefted the trashbag meaningfully. "No way!" she said vehemently. "I'm a lone wolf! I jack my own haul."

Not sure what she meant by that, Morgan stared at the bag.

"Now keep moving," Reb urged, "and we'll blend right in with the rest of the wandering Trolls by the time the cops get here."

"Trolls?" Morgan repeated, wiping the cold sweat from her face with her free hand. Now that the adrenaline rush was receding, she was feeling nauseous and thick-headed. She badly wanted to sit down and rest.

"Keep movin'," Reb coaxed as she felt Morgan slow. "You on somethin'?"

"What?"

"Are you usin'?" the girl demanded.

Frowning, unable to make any sense of this conversation, Morgan repeated, *"What?"*

"You're weavin'," Reb chastised. "What are you? Drunk, stoned, tranked?"

Blinking, Morgan disclosed, "I haven't slept or eaten much for a couple of days. I think I'm kinda crashing." Then, seeing how suspiciously Reb regarded her, Morgan confessed, "I...um, had some...trouble at home yesterday. I left."

Behind them, a police car entered the intersection. Abruptly, the whooping siren shut off, but red and blue lights continued to sweep frenziedly over the shop windows and buildings that lined Broadway.

In propelling Morgan along, Reb had managed to put a full block between them and the boy on the corner. Morgan was relieved to see the boy struggling to his feet as the officers approached him.

Purposefully, Reb guided Morgan into a crowd of fifteen or so youngsters, all of whom were traveling away from the squad car. At the heart of the small mob, Reb slowed. They waited with the others for the traffic light at Thomas Street to change. Glancing casually back at the police, Reb reached into her jeans pocket and pulled out a box of Marlboros.

"Smoke?" she asked Morgan, offering the pack.

"No," Morgan mumbled.

Reb put a cigarette in her mouth, then shoved the Marlboro pack back into her jeans. Morgan watched her, noting how practiced she seemed as she pulled a lighter from her jeans pocket, flicked a flame and lit up. Something about the way she did it made her seem very hard core. When she exhaled, she narrowed her eyes against the smoke. Numbly, Morgan realized that Reb was taking the opportunity to study her, as well.

"You been havin' a rough time," Reb commented.

Morgan swallowed. *Shit. Is it that obvious?*

Reb parked the cigarette at the corner of her mouth, like Humphrey Bogart. With a small smile, she took Morgan's hand again.

The light changed, and they crossed Broadway with the rest of the young people around them. Noticing that several boys were glancing at their clasped hands, Morgan tried to free herself from Reb's grip.

Reb told her, "Hey, chill. I'm just returnin' the favor." Seeing Morgan's bewildered look, she elaborated, "My turn to get *you* out of a mess. Okay?"

Bemused, Morgan made no reply. The fog that was hazing the edges of her mind crept in a little more. Her head hurt, her stomach was flipping and twisting. She was afraid that if she didn't lie down soon, she would pass out.

As if she read Morgan's increasing weakness, Reb asked, "Got a squat?"

She blew smoke in Morgan's face as she spoke, and Morgan couldn't help coughing.

"A what?" Morgan choked.

"A crib—a place to crash besides under a bridge—like a Troll's gotta do when the cash is low."

Under a bridge...I could have just crawled under a bridge....

Patiently, Reb was waiting on her answer. Morgan shook her head, no.

"You're welcome to hang at mine."

Morgan looked down at her, examining the bowl-cut, straight dark hair, the thin build emphasized by black jeans and the oversized pullover. She had a youthful, intriguing face, but the brown eyes were flashing with devilment.

Can I trust her?

Again, as if Morgan's expression gave her away, Reb smirked a little, then assured her, "I'm lookin' for a partner, here. I won't jack what's left of your stuff."

"What?" Morgan asked, then blushed, annoyed at how often she was saying that. She knew she was sounding very inexperienced.

With a precise flick of her fingers, Reb tossed the cigarette away, and Morgan gratefully gulped clean, smokeless air. Making direct, sincere eye contact, the small girl shifted the trashbag that draped over her shoulder like Santa Claus's sack.

"I won't steal from you," she stated. "Like I said, I'm a lone operator and I've been havin' some problems with the Ghouls. Problems you just put a stop to like I never could."

Mute, unable to think of an answer, Morgan let herself be led down the block. The line of small shops they had been passing ended with an all-night laundry on the corner. Several men lounged in the doorway there, passing a brown bag that only barely disguised a pint bottle of hard liquor. One of the men began hissing sexual overtures at them.

Reb swung around and said briskly, "Your mouth's too big and your dick's too small."

The other men roared with laughter, drowning out the insulted man's angry reply.

As they left the men behind, Reb cast a wary gaze back at them. "Here's your first lesson, Rookie. Don't whore and don't beg. No matter what. Eat trash, but don't *be* trash. Just because you're temporarily on the street don't mean you gotta lose all pride."

Morgan glanced over her shoulder, hoping that the man with the big mouth wasn't following them.

"And don't do drugs," Reb added. "That's the highway to hell."

Reb continued to tow her along by the hand. They were leaving the commercial district behind. Large brick apartment buildings and old, leafy oak trees began to dominate the street.

"You got a tag?" Reb asked softly, watching her, then amended, helpfully, "A name?"

Don't tell anyone your name....

After a brief silence, Reb reached over and touched a finger to the small embroidered letters on the left side of the letter jacket Morgan wore. Squinting down at "M. Flynn, Captain," written in white thread for all the world to see, Morgan groaned.

Reb grinned. "What's the M stand for?"

Feeling incredibly stupid, Morgan scowled. *Why didn't I take that off?* Reb was openly laughing at her. *She probably thinks I'm a total stooge!*

"Let's see," Reb mused. "Are you—Mary? Margaret? Or should I just call you Rookie?"

"Quit it," Morgan muttered, stone-faced. *Man! She's obnoxious.*

Seeming to read her mood, Reb let the matter drop. Then, farther down the block, she asked, "Okay if I call you Flynn?"

"Yeah," Morgan mumbled, wearying, allowing herself to relent a bit. Despite her need to stay remote and guarded, she liked the feel of Reb's warm hand pulling her along. "Where are we going?"

Giving Morgan's hand another squeeze, Reb soothed, "You just concentrate on stayin' on your feet. I'll get us there."

Some time later, Morgan wasn't sure how much later, Reb was cautioning her to stay in the shadows of the huge old brick building they were passing. Then, Reb had her by the arm, guiding her into a narrow alley. After the lights of the street lamps, the darkness of the alley seemed oppressive and frightening, and instinctively, Morgan hung back.

"It's okay," Reb whispered. "We're almost home."

Unconvinced, Morgan planted her feet, tore her arm free. *Why am I just letting her take over? What if this is a setup?* Gasping for breath, trying to clear her head, Morgan tried to retreat and ended up leaning helplessly against the brick wall.

"Look," Reb was whispering by her shoulder, "I know what you're thinking. This ain't no sellout. Unlike most people—my folks among 'em—I got ethics. And..." Reb broke off and made a quick scan of the alley. "I *need* you. This is a business deal. I got what you need: grub and a squat to crash in. And you got what I need: muscle. Okay?" There was a small hand inserting itself into hers, shaking it. Reb finished with, "Deal?"

What else can I do? Morgan wondered, rubbing her eyes. *I've lost all my money. I can barely walk. My head hurts so bad...* Admitting to herself that she was far too tired to even conceive of another way, she didn't resist as Reb pulled her away from the wall and deeper into the alley.

At last they came to a steel door, and after another quick look around, Reb dropped the plastic trashbag and pulled something out of her pocket. The small girl stood close to the door, calmly turning what looked like a long, thin blade back and forth in the lock. Finally, there was a quiet click and Reb pushed open the door. She hoisted the trashbag in quickly and pulled Morgan inside with her.

In the darkness, Morgan stood swaying, listening to Reb close and lock the door behind them. The rest was a blur of blackness as Reb took her farther into the building and then up endless flights of stairs. Using her hand to keep her balance, Morgan felt the wall change from broken plaster and exposed boards to a smooth, cool brick surface. They climbed higher and higher; Morgan was panting, tripping on the iron and concrete steps as her thigh muscles turned to lead and refused to lift her feet.

Then Reb stopped and Morgan heard her digging through the trashbag for something. A minute later, she clicked a flashlight on, and they used the beam of light to cross a cluttered floor.

"Sorry," Reb said quietly. "Couldn't use this too soon. No sense riskin' the chance that someone on the street might see the light through one of the second-floor windows."

While Reb was lithe and quick, ducking under what looked like a fallen beam and then slipping around a row of dusty wooden packing crates, Morgan proceeded slowly. Suddenly, she fell over something she couldn't quite see, something alive that ran away from her. Morgan ended up down on her hands and knees; with a sigh, she sank to the floor.

Time seemed oddly suspended. There were soft forms, furry beings, rubbing along her arms and legs, but though they frightened her, Morgan was too tired to try to move away from them. A door was open somewhere before her, and a soft, golden light was falling, cast from the threshold to where she lay. The small beings were meowing, skittering toward the door and a girl who was calling her.

"C'mon," Reb encouraged. "Mealtime at Mi Casa Loca. You have to help me, Flynn, 'cause I can't get you in there by myself."

It took everything Morgan had left to get to her feet. Half carrying, half dragging her, Reb brought Morgan through the door, into a room that seemed filled with candlelight. There were magazine cutouts on the walls, bookcases filled with books, a battered acoustic guitar leaning against a small wooden table. Though Morgan longed to crawl into the low bed in the corner of the room, Reb deposited her in a banged-up wooden rocking chair. As Morgan sat down and dropped her head into her hands, Reb was issuing directions in a soft but firm voice.

"Take your jacket off. Then all your clothes."

Wide-eyed, Morgan clutched her open letter jacket closer about her chest. *Is she after sex?* Morgan thought. *Is that how I'm supposed to pay for this?*

Chuckling, Reb commented, "You oughtta see your face."

She moved off, and Morgan watched her pull a steel tub out of a pile of odd junk near the far wall.

"I'll be right back," Reb stated, then disappeared into the dark hall with the flashlight.

When she came back a few minutes later, she was uncoiling a length of garden hose. She reached the tub and then knelt down, carefully arranging the length of hose so that it would stay in the bottom of the tub without her aid. Satisfied, she finally twisted the nozzle attached to the hose end, and water began to gush into the steel tub.

She rose then, and approached Morgan. "All my new strays get the same treatment." She reached out and stroked the small gray cat sitting near Morgan. "First a bath, then a meal. And then, only if they want it, some pettin'." She looked into Morgan's eyes, and the hand stroking the little cat moved to Morgan's cheek, barely touching the purplish-grey bruise below her eye.

Instinctively, Morgan shied away.

"Only if you want it, Flynn," Reb repeated quietly, her brown eyes full of commiseration. "And I promise I will never hurt you."

They regarded each other in silence for a moment. And then, powerless against the fatigue dragging her down, Morgan shuddered.

Without a word, Reb pushed the backpack straps from Morgan's shoulders. Then the red-and-white letter jacket was pulled off, and Reb examined the back, reading "Wenatchee High" aloud. As Morgan struggled to peel off her plaid flannel shirt, Reb studied the big W on the front of the jacket, fingering the small embroidered emblems depicting soccer and basketball.

"Some kind of major jock, huh?" Reb asked, her tone teasing.

Morgan nodded.

"Well, what's the big deal, then?" Reb demanded. "Haven't you undressed in front of girls for years now?"

Making a great effort, Morgan pushed herself out of the chair and crossed the room. Get *it over with fast,* she told herself, yanking her green T-shirt over her head.

She stopped by the tub, untying her black Converse sneakers and tugging them off. She opened, unzipped, and dropped her jeans. Then she made quick work of the socks, the bra, the panties. She was shaking again as she stepped into the steel tub.

Expecting the water to be cold, she was pleasantly surprised to find it was hot. She sat down, hunching over with the relief the water immediately imparted to her sore legs. Reb was soon beside her, pulling the hose out. For the next several minutes, Reb held the hose above Morgan, letting the hot water splash over her back, soaking her long hair. Morgan quickly lost awareness of her embarrassment in the luxurious feel of the heated water streaming over her. There was a bar of soap placed in her hand and as Morgan washed herself, the overhead water slowed and then stopped.

With brisk efficiency, a handful of fragrant shampoo was worked into her hair. Relaxing into the small hands creating suds across her scalp, Morgan soon dropped the bar of soap in the little tub and though she halfheartedly searched for it she couldn't find it again. Sighing, she felt Reb's hands traveling all over neck and shoulders, slippery with shampoo, massaging her muscles and skipping the more discolored patches of flesh. Then, the hose was overhead again, squirting the pain and dirt away.

The water stopped, and Reb was helping her to stand, saying, "Almost done, Flynn." There was a large white towel draped around her shoulders as Morgan stepped out of the tub. "Dry yourself off," Reb instructed. Fumbling wearily, Morgan rubbed the towel over her arms and legs, then dried her hair.

Reb moved across the room and began rooting through the trashbag she had been carrying when they met. She pulled out two packages, smirking slightly as she brought them over to Morgan.

"Put these on for now," Reb said, removing a gray sweatshirt and a pair of gray sweatpants from their plastic wrapping.

She placed the stiffly folded new clothing on the wooden table before Morgan. As Morgan put the towel aside and picked up the sweatpants, she frowned with suspicion.

Blithely, Reb announced, "They fell off the back of a truck."

Morgan stood there nude, hesitating. Then, realizing that Reb was inspecting her quite blatantly, she hustled into the soft clothes. "University of Washington" was emblazoned across the front of the sweatshirt in large gold and purple letters. Morgan felt a stabbing irony. She had planned on going to the university as recently as seventy-two hours ago. It seemed a cruel joke that this was how she had ended up in these particular sweats. A rush of tears blinded her, and she fought back the almost overpowering urge to cry. Somehow she knew that if she started she would never stop.

Reb handed her a comb, then steered Morgan back to the rocking chair. As Morgan sat down and began trying to tug the comb through her tangled mane, Reb set about pouring dry kibble into two large bowls. Cats came running from every direction, serenading Reb. She talked to them softly, calling each of the twelve or more animals by name as she took the bowls out into the hall.

Then, as Morgan worked with the comb, Reb cleared away the hose and tub. Curious, Morgan stopped and watched Reb drag the nearly full tub off into the hall. In the darkness, Morgan could hear her dump the water somewhere.

When Reb came back and Morgan asked about it, the girl shrugged and muttered, "Only thing the elevator shaft is good for...."

Feeling more and more dazed, Morgan had made little progress with her hair. After Reb had changed into sweat clothes, too, she came and helped her.

For a while, Morgan clenched her teeth as Reb snagged knot after knot, then abruptly, she ordered, "Just cut it."

"Really?" Reb asked, her voice full of disbelief. "It looks great on you—so shiny and thick."

"I have to...change the way I look," Morgan stated earnestly. "Someone might be trying to find me."

"Who?" Reb asked. It was the same gentle, soothing tone she had used with the cats. "The same someone who gave you all those bruises?"

Morgan couldn't answer her. Uneasily, she gripped the comb in her hands. *What must she think of me? She saw all the black-and-blues when I took that bath. Everything.*

The comb was removed from her hand. Reb got up and began searching through some cardboard boxes. Morgan huddled there, blinking with weariness until Reb came back with a pair of scissors.

There followed half an hour of careful snipping while Reb turned Morgan's head this way, then that way. To Morgan, it seemed to go on forever. Long lengths of wet, dark-auburn hair fell across Morgan's sweatpants and bare feet, creating a deepening pile. Eventually, Reb was hardly cutting at all, just arranging the style into a short bowl-cut similar to her own. Morgan's head felt remarkably unencumbered as Reb took her chin in her hand and turned Morgan's face to the side.

"Hey," Reb breathed, sounding amazed. "You're even *more* of a babe."

Morgan blushed. "Yeah, right."

If there was one thing her father had managed to drum into her, it was that she was *not* pretty. Perplexed, Morgan studied the girl before her.

She had a face like Wynona Ryder: large, expressive brown eyes and a perfect complexion. *If anyone's pretty, it's you.*

"Ready for some grub?" Reb asked, her eyes continuing to take in the new haircut with evident satisfaction.

"Please, no offense," Morgan pleaded, not certain she could keep her heavy lids up for one more minute. "You've been great, Reb. But I'd really like to just lie down, if that's okay."

"Sure," Reb returned.

She took Morgan's hand and helped her out of the chair. When Morgan tried to sink to the hard wooden floorboards, Reb laughed, pulled her up and pushed her toward the corner. Before Morgan's bleary eyes, the bed seemed to rise on a platform of wood, supported by cinder blocks. It was broad—a queen-sized mattress—covered with real sheets and several warm blankets, and Morgan trembled with anticipation.

"I can't take your bed," she protested weakly.

"We're sharing," Reb stated matter-of-factly. Then, seeing Morgan's instant tension, Reb reminded her, "Hey. We're business partners, Flynn. No funny stuff."

Unable to help herself, Morgan obeyed Reb's gentle push and rolled gratefully between the sheets and blankets Reb had pulled back for her. As Reb tucked her in and turned away, Morgan caught her hand.

"I'm not who you think I am, Reb," Morgan confessed, her eyes closing, even as she willed them to stay open. "What you saw me do tonight...I've never done anything like that before."

Reb sat down on the bed, and Morgan opened her eyes one more time, fighting to stay conscious long enough to get a reply. Her face inscrutable, Reb just watched her.

"I'm not tough," Morgan mumbled. "I won't be much good as 'muscle.' You probably won't want me...."

"I won't, huh?" Reb replied softly. She grinned a little, then soothed, "Don't sweat it, Flynn."

Morgan's mind became a swirl of thoughts that just couldn't find expression in words. With a long sigh, she closed her eyes.

A deathlike sleep claimed her.

CHAPTER 4

That same Friday evening, on the other side of Capitol Hill, Chris Olson stared into her clothes closet and frowned. Quickly, she checked the red numerals on the clock radio beside the bed.

Nearly six. Gotta hurry. Tom said he'd come by for me at six-thirty.

Behind her, curled up in a tight ball on the bed, Alf groaned his displeasure. He knew from past experience that whenever she stared into the clothes closet like this, he was definitely not going to be invited along on the outing.

What the hell am I going to wear? Chris wondered.

Allison Wheeler was giving a house party, and Chris had agreed to go only because it was primarily a business function. Some of their Capitol Hill friends and a few of their more recent customers were expected for cocktails and a buffet. These affairs were Allison's astute yet genteel way of concluding a big-money transaction. She claimed she loved introducing new residents to the old standbys, but Chris knew such social gatherings were ultimately profitable. Frequently, satisfied customers tended to recommend Olson, Morrissey & Wheeler to their friends who were house-hunting. And that was good for business.

Chris couldn't believe it was already ten years since she, Tom and Allison had formed a mutually beneficial business team: Olson, Morrissey & Wheeler Enterprises. They routinely evaluated any houses that went up for sale in the Capitol Hill area, specifically in the blocks surrounding Volunteer Park. Chris and Tom managed all the property selections and renovations work, while Allison handled the real-estate dealings. They pooled their funds, bought low, remodeled creatively, and then resold the property—sometimes earning double their initial investment. What was even more pleasing was the fact that their clientele was largely lesbian and gay.

Maybe my new neighbor will be there tonight, Chris thought, briefly intrigued with this possibility. But she quickly grew annoyed with herself and banished the thought. *I don't even want to go to this stupid thing!*

No question about it, these days she faced any social affair reluctantly. Inevitably, she seemed to end up sitting alone, feeling vaguely uncomfortable and melancholy.

A quiet sigh escaped her as she selected a light pink silk jacket from the closet and hung it on the back of the closet door. Then she reached for her pleated black pants and white shirt. With a frown, she realized she was once again assembling her standard "dress-up" outfit: pink silk jacket, black pants, white, pleated tuxedo shirt. Tom would no doubt break into laughter when he saw her.

After hesitating a moment, she reached into the bottom of the closet and drew out her black Doc Martens with the rainbow shoelaces. Tom would roll his eyes when he saw them on her feet. "You're ruining the effect," he would hiss. "You should have worn heels, preferably stilettos."

Chris grimaced at the mere thought. After a day in steel-toed construction boots, climbing around on a steeply pitched roof, her feet hurt. Laying new shingles took more out of her these days than it once had. She was forty-two, and she felt it.

I'm dressing for comfort, she resolved. *I don't care.* Tossing her robe on the bed, she went to the bureau for underwear.

Besides, who am I trying to impress? I don't want Allison to be any more aware of me than she already is.

She wasn't sure just why she was resisting Allison. The woman was damned attractive, in a blonde-bombshell-ish, curvaceous way. Assertive, polished, professionally successful—all the dynamics that were supposed to matter in the equal-to-men Nineties. Still, there was something about Allison that just plain spooked her.

The woman's a collector, Chris decided. *Clothing, shoes, retail properties, women....*

It was a disquieting realization. She knew that she was ripe for a seduction, so wired with unrelieved sexual tension that the right touch from Allison at the right time would probably be her undoing. And like a master chess player, Allison had been carefully moving her around the board as Chris tried to avoid check and mate.

So, I'll dress as I like, she silently affirmed. *Maybe put Allison off with my total lack of style.*

She rummaged through a drawer for underwear. *Tom can wear the high heels, if he likes them so much!* She laughed, imaging her well-muscled, balding friend mincing into Allison's party, utterly delighted with his footwear.

Alf wiggled his nub of a tail.

"Oh, you think it's funny, too, huh?" she asked him, chuckling.

In answer, he rolled over on his back, making a shameless demand for a belly-rub. Chris stopped everything and joined him on the bed for some cuddling. A few minutes later she sighed, "Couldn't manage without you, buddy-boy," and reluctantly resumed her preparations for going out.

Once dressed, she checked herself in the mirror. For an instant, in the soft lamplight, her face clearly reflected her Norwegian ancestry.

I'm starting to look like my father, she thought, remembering the cold blue eyes that had so often bored into her own.

"You are a woman and a woman should marry," he had frostily informed her when she had told him she wanted to take college preparatory classes in high school. "Besides," he had finished contemptuously, "you are not smart enough. You will make yourself a laughingstock."

After all these years, the death of that dream still hurt.

She shook her head, and urged herself to get moving before she was late. Tom would be picking her up in five minutes.

Jennifer sipped her glass of Chardonnay and scanned the room.

Six men were clustered around the grand piano in the corner, lustily singing Cole Porter's "What Is This Thing Called Love?" To Jennifer, fresh from the staid environs of Philadelphia, the scene seemed so screamingly gay-guy that she almost giggled.

Behave, she told herself, striving to keep a straight face. She plucked a piece of lint from her tweed pants, glad now that she had decided to wear the matching blazer, with a brown cashmere pullover beneath it. Seattle had a damp that penetrated to the bone, and she was not used to it. She felt as if she had spent the last weeks constantly freezing.

However, when the sun shone, the city seemed to gleam with magic. Newly constructed skyscrapers etched vertical slashes of glass into the deep, pristine blue of the sky. The shimmering waters of the Sound provided a glorious backdrop, and beyond the water rose the granite-gray crests of the Olympic Mountains.

Jennifer thought she had never seen such a beautiful city. Except for the fact that she still didn't know a soul, and was feeling increasingly lonely, she was quite satisfied with her decision to move to the West Coast.

She looked around the room again and thought of the papers she had to grade. Teaching Literature 101 always guaranteed lots of paperwork, but right now, even the writing of freshman college students suddenly seemed preferable to this dull party. She had hoped to at least meet somebody interesting here. Someone she could talk to for a while.

Oh, come off it, she told herself. *You've sworn off love, remember?*

She shifted her eyes to the only other woman in the room. Round-faced, plump and energetically pounding accompaniment on the keyboard, this one had been introduced earlier as Molly Webster. Molly reportedly worked as a women's counselor at the downtown YWCA. She was obviously a big favorite with the boys.

Through the broad archway, Jennifer could see Molly's partner, Dorothea Jance, meandering around the buffet table. Even out of uniform, it was obvious that the broad-shouldered black woman was a police officer. Jennifer would have figured it out even without the introduction and brief exchange of pertinent personal data that had taken place upon her arrival, fifteen minutes earlier. There was an aura of no-nonsense and competent authority about Thea, as they called her.

With a sigh, Jennifer swirled the last bit of Chardonnay in her glass, then went in search of her hostess. She had fulfilled her sense of obligation and put in an appearance, and it was now time to go. After all, she had only bought the house to secure a tax write-off. The money she'd recently inherited from her grandmother had dropped into her life like manna from heaven, releasing her from a life of scrimping by on a college professor's salary. Certainly buying a house didn't mean she was embarking on a quest for the Happily-Ever-After, as Molly and Thea seemed to be doing. Yet she had to admit she was disappointed not to have met anyone interesting so far this evening.

Gliding across the room and down the hall, she found Allison Wheeler, her realtor, talking on a cellular phone in the kitchen.

Jennifer stopped at the threshold and waited for Allison to notice her. But Allison merely went from being partially turned, to being completely turned away from her. As Jennifer lingered, she heard some of Allison's conversation.

"Yes, Chris will be here," Allison was saying. "You know I can't get anywhere with her, so why worry?" A soft, slightly seductive chuckle, then, "Well, of course I won't give up. Five years of celibacy—can you imagine what she'd be like once you got her going?!"

With a glance at the clock above the refrigerator, Allison smoothed the short skirt of her rust-colored wool-knit business suit, then adjusted the jacket. "Saturday night was wonderful," Allison assured her phone partner. "You know I'm interested. *Very* interested, but I'll be tied up here all night, I'm afraid." Allison's free hand moved on to fluff her blonde-streaked, shoulder-length hair, and it dawned on Jennifer that she was readying for someone's entrance.

Probably this "Chris."

Abruptly, Jennifer moved back down the hall, wondering where Allison had put her raincoat. She had spent the last weeks adjusting to a new city, a new job, and a whole new way of life. She was just too tired to deal with dyke drama, too.

She polished off the last of her wine in one quick drink.

How is it some women can be sleeping with one lover while focusing most of their energy on getting the next "person of interest" into their bed?

The woman behind her in the kitchen was clearly gearing up, preparing to win her next trophy. *It's too much like Gail,* Jennifer thought.

Jennifer stopped in the hall and briefly closed her eyes, remembering last year's excruciating ordeal. At first, Gail had subtly flattered her, then pursued her, and ultimately seduced her. And as Jennifer's heart opened and embraced the woman, Gail had lost interest and dropped her like the proverbial ton of bricks. Gail, who had seemed so fascinating and gregarious, had been a player. There had been other women—always denied, of course—as if keeping Jennifer in the dark had been the most satisfactory part of the game. In the space of ten months, Jennifer had been given every reason on earth to evade future love affairs like the plague. Bitter and wounded, she had left Philadelphia and moved three thousand miles west. And yet, apparently, here was another version of Gail, this time in the form of a bottle-blonde realtor.

Where's my coat? she thought, exasperated. *Just find it and go—don't start plodding through the emotional swamp!*

As Jennifer emerged from the hallway, the front door swung open to admit a balding man wearing suspenders and dapper gray flannel trousers. Behind him came a tall, lean blonde in a pink silk suit jacket. They seemed to be sharing a joke about something, for the man was laughing.

Striding inside, the man in the gray flannels turned toward the woman, demanding, "That crazy dog dug up her tulips and stashed them on your front porch?"

Stunned, Jennifer focused on the woman and forgot to breathe. *Not a man at all....*

"When Frank and Joel lived next door he used to dig up their gladioli bulbs every spring. And now this beautiful woman moves in and he's already got us off on the wrong foot...."

"You mean paw," the man returned.

She called me "beautiful," Jennifer couldn't help noting. Even so, she fixed the lean blonde with a searing stare.

"It's not funny, Tom!" the woman insisted, though her mouth did quirk up to one side, causing her square jaw to temporarily lose the gaunt shadow below her cheekbone.

Too thin, Jennifer commented inwardly. *Thin as if she has to be careful, now, not to lose any more weight.* She caught herself wondering about that, and then knew that this was the notorious Chris. *Celibate for five years. Why?*

As if feeling the intense stare, Chris suddenly turned and met Jennifer's eyes. Blinking in disbelief, Chris visibly gulped, then gouged an elbow into her companion's side, muttering, "Tom!"

Tom followed Chris's startled gaze and spotted Jennifer. With a charming smile, he promptly dragged Chris over for introductions.

"*You* must be Chris's new neighbor!" he declared.

Chris, meanwhile, firmly disengaged Tom's hand from her elbow, almost scowling at him.

"I'm Jennifer Hart," Jennifer said as she politely gave Tom the briefest of glances. She leveled a stern look at Chris. *Tell funny stories about me, will you?*

She was rewarded with the sight of Chris going scarlet.

As Chris began studying her shoes, Tom was saying, "You're the professor from Philadelphia, right? You taught literature at Penn?"

Jennifer nodded. "That's right." Her eyes barely left Chris. *How on earth did I miss the fact that she's a woman?* "I've just taken a position at the University of Washington."

In return, Tom nearly chirped, "Tom Morrissey and Chris Olson, Home Renovations and Sales."

"Did you two work on my house?" Jennifer asked, finally facing Tom.

He had a merry, apple-cheeked face, and his eyes crinkled at the edges. "We did," he said triumphantly. "It was one of our earlier projects."

"Excuse me," Chris blurted, not quite interrupting, but close to it. "I'm really thirsty." She stepped around Tom and moved toward the buffet table. "Anybody else need anything?" she asked, attempting to be polite as she back-pedaled away from them.

Coolly, Jennifer held up her empty wine glass.

After a second's hesitation, Chris dutifully returned for it. If possible, the woman was blushing a deeper shade of red than before, and at close range, Jennifer noticed that she had vividly blue, blue eyes.

Stop staring, Jennifer thought. "Chardonnay," she said.

For some strange reason, she made sure their fingers brushed as the long-stemmed crystal changed hands.

Chris lost her grip on the glass. It fell to the polished wood floor and shattered.

"Aw jeez..." Chris groaned, crouching at Jennifer's feet. Glancing up, genuinely solicitous, she asked, "You're not hurt, are you?"

Affected by the evident concern, Jennifer murmured, "I'm fine, thanks."

Impulsively, Chris reached for the only remaining recognizable part of the glass. Her finger had no sooner made contact with the stem, than she promptly sliced the skin on a razor-sharp edge.

Noticing how she yanked her hand away, Tom and Jennifer bent beside her, both of them reaching for the hand she cradled.

Allison bustled up to the edge of the group, commenting dryly, "I believe you're supposed to use the fireplace for the glass-smashing routine."

Quietly, Tom told her, "Chris just cut herself." With an ease that displayed how used he was to taking care of her, Tom drew Chris to her feet, firmly telling her to go with Allison and get bandaged.

Since blood was running along the side of her hand and dropping on the floor, Chris simply sighed and acquiesced. "Sorry," she called back to Jennifer, looking chagrined.

Jennifer was disconcerted by the alarm she felt, watching Allison leading Chris down the hall, toward the kitchen. Without preamble, she asked Tom, "Think you can you handle the cleanup on your own?"

He gave her a perceptive look, then grinned like the Devil himself. "Go, girl!" he enthused.

As she smiled back, he laid a hand on her arm and leaned closer. "But let me warn you," he confided. "She's got bigger walls than Troy."

Reflecting on that bit of news, Jennifer paused. *Oh, great! Reserved and cautious professor meets reserved and cautious construction worker. Platonic friendship, here we come.* She was astonished by how disappointed she felt.

Grinning, Tom lifted an eyebrow and whispered, "I saw how you handed her the wine glass. Keep teasing her like that." With a glance toward the kitchen, he elaborated, "But do it subtly, while you're pretending you're not at all interested in her."

Half in wonder, Jennifer nodded.

"Allison's been doing every vampy thing except roping the poor woman and hog-tying her to the bedposts," Tom confided, rolling his eyes. "Believe me, that only makes Chris run for the hills." Again he gave Jennifer an approving smile. "She's already very aware of you, I can tell. So *befriend* her. And then drive her crazy with want."

Feeling like she had just entered some predestined, Faustian pact, Jennifer let him escort her down the hall.

"Oh, Allison," Tom called sweetly. He grabbed Jennifer's hand and pulled her behind him.

They found Allison positioned tightly behind Chris, who was wedged up against the sink. Chris was getting her injured hand washed by the arms reaching around her. Though Allison stepped back quickly when they came in, Jennifer could have sworn she'd almost had her lips on Chris's neck.

"What is it?" Allison demanded, the annoyance in her voice unmistakable.

"Where do you keep your broom and little dustpan?" Tom asked innocently. "So I can clean up the glass."

"Right here," Allison answered curtly, marching over to the closet by the rear staircase. She opened the door and brought out both items, thrusting them impatiently at Tom.

By the sink, Chris swayed and gripped the counter with her good hand.

"Uh-oh! She's fainting," Tom called to Jennifer.

Coming quickly alongside her, Jennifer grasped Chris by the upper arms and steadied her. Chris's face was alarmingly pale now, and the blue eyes were staring fixedly at the faint traces of blood washing down the drain of the shiny steel sink.

Briskly, Jennifer tore a handful of paper towels from the dispenser over the sink, and then wound them tightly around the small cut on Chris's finger. "Take a deep breath," she instructed calmly.

Chris drew a shaky gasp.

It's barely a flesh wound, Jennifer thought. *Why is it affecting her like this?*

"You're okay," Jennifer soothed quietly. She turned off the faucet, then guided Chris over to one of the four chairs around the small kitchen table.

Chris's knees buckled, and she sat down with a thump. Limp and unprotesting, she allowed Jennifer to gently apply pressure to the paper towels wrapped around her finger.

Allison appeared at Chris's side, smoothing the damp, blonde hair back from Chris's ashen face. "It'll be all right, honey."

"Do you have a first aid kit?" Jennifer prompted.

"It's only a little cut, for heaven's sake," Allison began, looking genuinely peeved by Jennifer's presence. "Tom and I have been through this before with her. It's not a big deal."

Irritated, Jennifer insisted, "She nearly passed out."

"Chris always gets woozy when she sees blood," Tom revealed quietly, and Jennifer could tell by the glance he cast at Chris that he was betraying a confidence in trying to explain this. "It's an understandable reaction. I mean...considering... the accident and seeing Joyce..."

"Tom!" Chris growled warningly, and Tom broke off.

They froze. Something huge and unspoken hung in the air, making all three business associates silent and ill at ease.

"I'll go upstairs and get a Band-Aid," Allison announced, throwing a lethal glare at Jennifer. "I'll just be a minute."

As Allison's high heels clicked up the steps, Tom carried the broom and dustpan past Chris and Jennifer. "A Nellie's work is never done," he commented to no one in particular.

Jennifer smiled.

And then, all at once, she and Chris were alone in the kitchen, sitting very close together. Awkwardly, they looked at one another and then away. Chris eased her wounded finger from Jennifer's hand and used her own hand to apply pressure.

"I'm sorry you were hurt, Chris," Jennifer offered tentatively. "I wish I had just gone for the wine myself, now."

"Hey, call me Grace," Chris jested quietly, then frowned at the bloodstained paper towels decorating her finger.

With her other hand, Chris wiped the sheen of perspiration from her brow. Without pause, she plunged that same hand up and into her crown of gold-blonde short curls, and ruffled the lot of them in what was apparently a nervous habit. But though Chris had destroyed the carefully groomed look, her hair ended up looking better than it had before. It was tousled now, slightly wild, probably the way it looked when she rolled out of bed. Suddenly, Jennifer wondered what that fair hair would feel like in her hands.

I could get in trouble real fast with this one, she realized, and moved her own chair back a little to gain some distance.

"Sorry about..." Chris gestured lamely toward the sink, "all that." She swallowed. "It's the blood. I...don't handle it well."

Though she was curious, Jennifer murmured, "No need to explain."

"No, I..." Chris began, then cleared her throat, "I want you to...hear it from me."

This was unexpected, to say the least. Jennifer had thought that a person with walls would be anything but forthcoming.

"It happened five years ago," Chris confessed, "New Year's Eve." She leaned back in the chair, took a deep breath and closed her eyes.

Jennifer watched her preparations, wondering if the woman could finish what she had started.

Chris exhaled slowly. "We were on our way home from a party." Her voice became different, almost hollow-sounding. "It was late. I was driving...stone-cold sober. I saw these head-lights.... They told me later that a drunk crossed the double yellow lines and hit us head-on. All I really remember, though, is holding Joyce afterwards. She...bled to death in my lap."

Jennifer watched her open those blue, blue eyes and stare at her injured hand. "Just when I think I'm over it..."

Gravely, Jennifer offered, "Some things a person never gets over."

Color began returning to Chris's face. She searched Jennifer's eyes, as if she heard the sound of personal experience behind that platitude. She asserted, "But I want to get over it. I need to go on. I didn't die that night—Joyce did. But, it's like I can't get beyond it. I try, but I can't." Looking confused, Chris dropped her eyes.

For a moment, Jennifer simply watched her. The sorrow on Chris's face was deep and weary, but there was something in the set of her jaw, in the line of her mouth, that told Jennifer the woman had also developed an immeasurable strength from this experience.

You're just finding out that you're glad you're alive, Jennifer thought. *And you don't know what to do about it.*

In a whisper, Chris said, "I still miss her. But I can't cry anymore. Is that...faithless?"

"No," Jennifer said softly, "grief is a strange beast." She probed her own recollection. "It arrives uninvited and takes over your life. And just when you think it will never leave, and you've kind of gotten used to that relentless, ever-evolving, gnawing pain..." Jennifer faltered. The old wound in her heart opened and memory assailed her. *Oh, God.* She suddenly felt so exposed.

Chris lifted her eyebrows.

Concentrating on maintaining her poise, Jennifer finished, "Just when you think the grief will never leave, you find yourself enjoying the simplest things. Even savoring them, with an awareness and an appreciation you were not capable of before."

Chris was listening, watching. "You lost someone," she ventured softly.

"Years ago," Jennifer admitted. "And it was hell. But time goes by, and here I am...." She frowned and moistened her lips. "Whatever that means. Sorry if I'm not imparting any pearls of wisdom here."

The barest glimmer of a smile moved over Chris's face. Jennifer felt an odd delight race through her, pleased to have provoked even that spare response.

"You're doing fine." She patted Chris's knee reassuringly. "You'll be all right."

Just then, Allison clattered down the stairs. Holding up the Band-Aid, she took charge of Chris.

Minutes later, all three women walked into the dining room to join the guests gathered around the buffet table.

Dorothea Jance was telling a story to several friends gathered around her. "...so I stop by to say hi to Molly, like I usually do after work. And as I cross the lobby, I see this kid sitting on that uncomfortable wreck of a couch they have in the lobby. Her head's back and she's sound asleep—a real good-looking white girl with this wicked shiner."

Allison gently pulled Chris toward the buffet, disclosing, "I picked up an Umberto's lasagna, just for you."

Left by herself in the center of the room, Jennifer noticed Tom waving to her. She moved to where he stood with Thea and Molly and several men.

After making sure everyone knew each other, Tom explained to Jennifer, "Thea was assaulted last night while on duty."

"Shit, Tom—it wasn't an assault," Thea clarified, laughing. "Just knocked down by a panicky street kid. You make it sound like 'NYPD Blue' or something."

Molly elaborated, "This girl had wandered into the YWCA Hotel, where I work. Eight at night, and there she was...."

At the buffet table, Jennifer noted that Allison's hand was cupping Chris's elbow as she steered Chris from one serving dish to another. For a moment, it disturbed her that Chris was so passive about being managed by Allison, but then she reminded herself that it was none of her business. Finding Tom's eyes on her, Jennifer bent her head and tuned back into the police story.

Thea took up the thread of the tale. "The kid woke up, saw me, and her eyes got real big, real fast." Casting Jennifer a troubled gaze, she said, "Fear like that on a bruised face... Makes you wonder what the hell went on at home, you know?"

Jennifer nodded. She had been teaching for ten years now. She knew about that kind of wondering, all right.

"You should have seen the look that kid gave me," Molly said. "I know she thought I called the cops on her."

Thea ended the story. "The girl tackled me low, like a linebacker, putting me on my ass before I even had a clue." Marveling, Thea clasped her hands behind her back. "By the time I got up, she was gone. Fast—some kind of track star, I'll bet. I called in a couple of squad cars. We chased around for a while, trying to spot her."

With a gaze at the others, she explained, "After that reaction, I thought it was important to get her to talk, maybe ease her fears some, get her some food. When a kid is scared of cops, it means she won't come to us for help when she really needs it."

Holding a fine china plate with colorful, if meager, amounts of food arranged upon it, Chris moved to the periphery of the group. Allison was right behind her, wearing a peevish expression.

"We lost her, though," Thea related, looking very disappointed. "God knows where she is tonight."

"She must be guilty of something to run like that," Allison commented.

"Aw, c'mon, Allison. She's a runaway," Tom protested, looking annoyed by Allison's assumption. "As in 'on the run.' From cops, from counselors, from anyone who might try to force her to go back home again."

"She's also probably a thief," Allison retorted cynically. "That's how they survive, you know. Hooking and stealing. So don't feel too sorry for her."

"That's a rather sweeping generalization," Tom sighed.

Allison turned on him with an edge in her voice. "You said yourself that you thought it was a street kid who broke into Chris's truck last night." Raising her eyebrows meaningfully, Allison addressed the group, "Sixty dollars stolen from the glove compartment."

"Anything else?" Thea asked Chris.

"Some stuff was taken from the truck-bed box," Chris confessed, her eyes sheepish. "Plastic tarping, rope, my flashlight." She paused, thinking. "And Tom's old black leather motorcycle jacket. Just junk, really. He left the tools, which I couldn't believe."

"What makes you so sure it was a he?" Allison inserted, casting Tom an arch glance.

"It *does* sound like squatter's gear," Thea remarked thoughtfully, then chided, "Chris, you know better than to leave money in the glove compartment."

"Yeah, you're right," Chris returned quietly. "I won't do it again. And tomorrow I've got an appointment with the Ford dealership. I'm getting the wooden box torn out and one of those all-weather steel boxes installed in its place."

Satisfied, Thea nodded.

"What the heck is 'squatter's gear?'" a boyish-looking man asked. Jennifer recalled that Tom had introduced him as David.

Tom answered, "People who are homeless call the places where they settle 'squats.' A big waterproof tarp like the one that was in Chris's truck would be a real prize. Tie the rope between two trees and throw the tarp over the rope and it may not be the Hilton, but it's a dry night in the woods."

"Oh, I see," David replied, as understanding dawned on him.

Molly interjected, "It's common practice when the shelters are all full—like now—and people have nowhere to go."

Wide-eyed, Chris asked, "You mean, you couldn't find a place for that girl last night?"

With a grim expression, Molly confessed, "That's exactly what I mean."

"Then even if she hadn't run off like that," Chris concluded, her words slow with disbelief, "she would've spent the night on the street anyway?"

"I turn away thirty to forty like her a month, Chris," Molly sadly explained.

Thea placed an arm around Molly's shoulders, giving her a supportive embrace. "You knock yourself out, Mol. You do your best for them."

"But it's not enough," Molly declared. "There are so many kids out there—sleeping in doorways, living under bridges, hiding in condemned buildings. They're frightened and hungry and completely on their own. It isn't right."

"They ought to just stay home," Allison observed briskly. "Nothing could be as bad as what they must go through out on the streets."

"Oh yeah?" asked Thea.

"Well, let's face it," Allison pursued, "they're ill-prepared to take care of themselves. None of them ever get *real* jobs, so they can live like decent people."

"Shabby clothes, unwashed, no permanent address, no references," Thea enumerated, then added with a sharp edge to her voice, "I'd like to see who would hire any of us in similar circumstances."

Allison faced her. "Oh, please, Thea. Give it a rest. Their skills probably consist of picking pockets, breaking into cars, and performing blow jobs in dark alleys. It wasn't a homeless waif that broke into Chris's truck—it was an experienced hood."

Alarmed, Chris swung her troubled gaze to Allison.

"Let me guess," David murmured to Tom. "She's a Republican."

Allison heard the comment and retorted coolly, "We're not living in The Great Society any more, fellas."

"Well, recent studies..." Molly began.

"Studies be damned," Allison declared flatly. "These kids are drug abusers and dropouts. In a word—losers."

"That's not true," Jennifer stated in a low voice that nevertheless carried enough snap to turn heads.

It was the first time she had spoken, and all eyes fell on her at once, surprised. For a moment, Jennifer considered holding her tongue, but Allison's smug, I-got-mine attitude was just too much to bear.

"Most often, they're on the run because they've been abused. Physically, sexually, spiritually—some of them *horribly* abused." Jennifer's voice rose as she spoke. "A lesser number of them leave home or are *thrown out* by their parents during a period of fairly normal teenage rebellion. And then there are the ones that have been ignored or neglected for years. They finally just wander off, looking for love and a sense of belonging. They usually find some twisted version of it in among the gang-bangers."

Thea added, "By the time the parents reevaluate the family situation and decide to find the kid and work things out, it's way too late." She sighed heavily. "The police and social services are understaffed to begin with, and there's just too many kids for us to deal with all the missing-persons reports that are filed. Within three days of leaving home, a pimp is after them, and you know the rest of that story. I'll bet that half those kids we pass on Broadway are already dying of AIDS."

Astounded, everyone began talking among themselves.

Jennifer watched Chris lower her head, looking anguished by that last piece of information.

Molly raised her voice to be heard. "And according to the commonly held ratio of one in ten, probably at least ten percent of the kids on the street tonight are gay and lesbian youth."

Silence followed that revelation.

"I've heard estimates as high as twenty-five to thirty percent," Jennifer amended.

Tom remarked, "No wonder they hide. They're such easy targets. America's last socially condoned one, to be precise." He shoved his hands in his pants pockets. "It used to be 'kick the Kike,' or 'lynch the Nigger.' Now it's 'off the Fag.' Or the Dyke...you fill in the dehumanizing slur of choice."

David shook his head. "All those kids! Man!"

Then Tom asked softly, "Meanwhile, what are we in the gay community doing about taking care of our own?"

The guests surveyed each other thoughtfully.

"Oh, for Christ's sake," Allison muttered.

CHAPTER 5

"I'll kill her!!" her father was roaring.

Horrified, Morgan rolled over and saw him coming through the doorway of her bedroom, raising his fist for the first vicious strike.

Whimpering, she tried to free herself from a morass of covers. Someone's arms closed around her, pulling her down. She screamed, fighting to free herself.

"Flynn!" the high-pitched voice was shouting. "Stop it —you're hurting me!"

Morgan stared into a pair of worried brown eyes. This was not her father. This was a girl. "Reb," she gasped, finally recognizing her.

Still in a panic, she tore her gaze away and checked the room. It was obviously *not* her bedroom. In the dim light, she could see several cats of varying sizes and colors. Perched on pieces of Reb's makeshift furniture, they observed her with startled expressions.

"You had a nightmare," Reb soothed, firmly holding on to her.

Morgan surveyed the closed door, trying to slow her breathing. "It seemed so *real.*" She sank back into the sheets, relieved, and then realized Reb's arm was pinned underneath her. "Oh. Sorry," she mumbled, rising up to allow Reb room to move away from her.

Disoriented from the sudden waking, Morgan didn't notice that Reb had shifted closer until she was lying down again and Reb was leaning over her. Wordlessly, Reb lingered, less than a foot away. Her eyes were intent, her mouth partially open. She looked as surprised to find herself poised there as Morgan was.

Morgan heard her own breathing speed up. On the heels of terror, another sensation was suddenly beginning to register. Unexpectedly, desire slammed in. Her heart was racing, her skin was prickling with the need to be touched and warmed. Now that she was less befuddled, she felt the clammy cold that permeated the room, and the inviting heat that emanated from the thin body stretched so close to her.

Reb must have read the need she felt, for she slid a little closer. "I really want to kiss you," she ventured, her voice a hoarse whisper.

Staring back at her, Morgan could not answer. She found herself focusing on the sweet shape of Reb's lips.

Slowly, Reb leaned down. It was a light yet enticing kiss, and Morgan lifted her head, chasing it as Reb withdrew. That seemed to please Reb, for she gave a gratified sigh as she moved back in for more. This time, as their lips met, she fully lowered her wiry, sweatsuit-clothed body onto Morgan's and sent her hands into Morgan's hair.

Feeling Reb's fingers sifting through the short, thick strands, Morgan remembered, *My hair! Most of it's gone!* And then, abruptly, she lost that thought. *This is different than with Janet... She feels different—like she's made of gristle and bone... She smells and tastes like cigarettes, but God, she can kiss....*

Hungrily, Reb deepened the kiss, and Morgan found herself being led into a dazed and eager response.

And then, Morgan's empty stomach made a long, loud rumble. Reb ended the kiss, snickering into Morgan's neck. The short bursts of breath on sensitive skin electrified Morgan. She couldn't help trembling.

"Hmmm," Reb murmured, leaning back on an elbow to study her. "When did you eat last, Flynn?"

Morgan frowned, trying to remember. "Noon yesterday."

Reb stroked Morgan's hair back from her face. "It's past three o'clock in the afternoon," she informed her. "Over twenty-four hours on empty." A small, warm hand slipped beneath Morgan's sweatshirt, smoothing over her stomach, and Morgan gasped slightly. "You have to eat regular while we have the means to do it," Reb continued, looking serious. "We can't risk your gettin' sick."

Morgan regarded her, thinking, *Because I'm the "muscle" of this...this...whatever this is that I've gotten myself into. What exactly does she need muscle for, anyway?*

"Cuz if you get sick enough," Reb went on, "you have to go down to one of the free clinics. Some of the bigger shelters have them. And the docs there will give you free meds, but they might decide you're too sick to be out on the streets. And the next thing you know you're bein' handed over to some tight-assed bureaucrat."

And they'll either ship me back to my parents or park me in juvenile hall. Comprehending at last, Morgan nodded gravely. *I'll never go near one of those free clinics. I can't risk it.*

"You gotta stay strong, Flynn," Reb murmured, bending lower. "I got great plans for you." Softly, she kissed Morgan again, slipping the tip of her tongue in for a sizzling punctuation of the point. "I like the way you look, the way you move," she whispered, moving her warm hand up under the sweatshirt, caressing Morgan's breast. "The way you get hot."

Closing her eyes, Morgan felt helpless against the desire Reb was stirring. She was dumbfounded by Reb's boldness, by her own breathless reaction to it. With Janet, she had progressed slowly from friend to lover, driven as much by emotional as by physical delight. And yet, Reb was somehow jumping past all that, gaining direct access to the most vulnerable part of her.

She loved Janet, even now, even when she carried the indelible memory of Janet's disgust for her. Just as damaging as her father's beating, Janet's ruthless rejection had ripped her apart. Yet somehow, some part of her still belonged to Janet Belden. She couldn't understand it.

But this—what I'm doing with Reb—this has nothing to do with love, Morgan thought. *I'm on fire! And just two days ago I swore to myself that I'd never do anything like this again!*

So what am I doing? she wondered, feeling agitated and perplexed. She was breathing fast now, caught in a whirl of carnal pleasure she had thought she could only feel with Janet. Abruptly, she ordered, "Stop."

Reb's hand moved lower, skimming across Morgan's flat stomach. "You sure?" Reb crooned in her ear. As if to emphasize the temptation, Reb slipped her fingers beneath the cotton waistband, caressing as her hand traveled still lower.

Morgan caught hold of Reb's wrist. "I said stop," she repeated quietly. As if on cue, her stomach gave another resounding gurgle.

"Damn," Reb muttered, sitting up and sliding out from under the covers. With a mischievous grin, Reb crawled over Morgan and left the bed. "Sorry. Couldn't help myself," she said, laughing.

She pulled on a pair of wool socks before padding across the cold wooden floorboards and kneeling by a small plastic cooler.

Morgan cast off the covers and followed her, suddenly wondering what Reb did about a toilet. "What day is it?" she asked.

"Saturday mornin'. Sorry, I don't have a TV, so no cartoons." Opening the cooler, Reb pulled out a box of granola bars and two bananas, then placed them on the scarred wooden table. "But there *is* breakfast," she announced.

With a glance at Morgan's bare feet, she instructed, "Put those socks on," nodding at a new pair resting on the rocking chair, still in the plastic wrapping. "The can is down the hall."

As Morgan hesitated, socks in hand, Reb prodded, "C'mon. Hurry up—I have to go."

Morgan picked up the package of socks. "Why is everything new?" she asked, needing to know.

"I told you last night," Reb answered, widening her brown eyes. "This big box fell off the back of a truck, right in front of me. The truck kept on goin', so I could have either walked on by or helped myself to a few things." With a shrug, Reb ended, "I needed this stuff—needed it *bad*. So I took it before someone else did."

"The back of the truck had no doors?" Morgan asked.

"They were open," Reb stated, looking too innocent to be believed. "Don't ask me how they were open, they were just open."

"Did you open them?" Morgan pressed.

Reb put a hand on her hip, peeved. "A-duh."

"You broke open the doors," Morgan concluded. "And nothing fell out—you stole it."

"I gotta pee," Reb snapped, obviously unwilling to discuss it further. She marched to the door and opened it, as Morgan dropped the package of wool socks.

Quickly, Morgan found her black Converse sneakers and shoved her bare feet inside. In the stronger light of the hall she saw Reb walking away.

Curious about the light, Morgan paused a moment and searched for the source, then spotted a group of narrow windows on the other side of the building. The hallway wasn't even enclosed, as only the struts remained. It looked as if someone had sledgehammered the drywall out to make way for the natural illumination.

"Reb, wait," she called.

Using her long stride to advantage, Morgan jogged around several crates and ran until she reached Reb's side. As she fell in step with her, Morgan noticed that Reb was scowling.

"I'm not judging you," Morgan asserted. "I know how it is."

"Oh, you do, huh?" Reb asked sarcastically.

"I just want this to start right," Morgan insisted. "I'm not a kid. You don't have to make up stories for me. Tell me the truth."

With a grimace, Reb faced her. "The truth will scare the shit outta you, Big Girl."

Don't I know it, Morgan thought, running her hand nervously through her hair, then stopping at the back of her skull, disconcerted for the second time this morning to find most of her hair was gone.

Her expression must have been easily read, for Reb suddenly burst into laughter. "Had long hair for a while, huh?"

"Uh...yeah," Morgan answered sheepishly.

"It looked good on you, too," Reb allowed, gazing at her critically. "But this," she raised her hand and sent it deep into the hair, caressing the side of Morgan's scalp, "this is *bad.*"

Riveted by the sensual expression on Reb's face, Morgan just stood there, scarcely breathing.

Moving aside, shaking her head as if to clear it, Reb turned toward the shadowy end of the hall. "God, you get me revved up," she remarked.

Blushing, Morgan couldn't help wondering at her own reaction. She knew she was feeling incredibly susceptible, more emotionally and sexually needy than she ever knew she could feel. *But that doesn't mean you just hop in the sack with the first person who's nice to you, for God's sake!*

Trying to distract them both, Morgan asked, "How long have you been living here, anyway?"

"About three months," Reb answered. "This warehouse is condemned. The whole block is supposed to get leveled in another three months. You know, gotta keep makin' way for the yup condos." She surveyed the dim exterior of the old building. "Once I got past the lock and checked out the basics, I knew I'd probably never find the likes of it again."

Reb's eyes got big and incredulous. "I mean—no electricity, but the water was only turned off at the main line, right in the basement. I just linked up a hose to the sink in the janitor's closet at the end of the hall, went down and opened the valve—and ta-da—runnin' water! And get this—the big gas heater was still hooked up, too. I can take a hot bath without goin' down to one of them sleazy, bug-infested shelters."

Marveling, Reb explained, "The other bonus is that the buildin' roof is still tight as a drum."

Morgan scanned the interior and had to admit there was no sign of mildew or water leakage.

Reb elaborated, "Right away I decided to really be careful with the digs. I knew I was lucky to find it, and I don't exactly want to share it with the crazy vets."

Morgan winced at the description, but remembered her own fear of the homeless men in the shadows, watching her pass. A girl alone was a target, and for all their common experience in suffering, those beaten-down men were not above taking a shot at her, too.

Soberly, Reb explained, "Between the gang-bangers and the crazy vets, there ain't much left for the likes of us. So I only come and go when it's dark, and I make sure no one ever sees me do it." She leaned closer to Morgan, imparting, "You can't ever be too careful, Flynn. Gay girls aren't even really human for most of the men out there. They see us and think, 'free pussy.'"

Morgan thought of the man who had grabbed her at Dick's Hamburgers and blanched. *He almost got me....*

Reb missed Morgan's expression, intent on showing off the crude bench-like arrangement they stood before. "There are two elevator shafts—the one close to the squat, and this one down here. I use the close shaft for gettin' rid of dirty bath and dish water, but I figure I want to stay here a while and I don't want to end up dealin' with...you know...sewage funk." Reb wrinkled her turned-up nose.

Morgan felt a familiar fluttering cross her stomach. *She's not Janet!* she reminded herself firmly, thoroughly shaken by her body's continuing betrayal.

"So this far shaft, I use as a...well...you gotta have a can and at least this means the mess is five stories down." Making a face, Reb motioned Morgan closer.

Next to the yawning black of the open elevator shaft was a wooden board with an oval hole cut into the surface. The board rested on two white plastic five-gallon buckets, with another plastic bucket positioned under the ten-inch hole that was cut in mid-board.

"You made this?" Morgan asked, impressed.

"I helped. There used to be three of us livin' up here. Me, Snakey and Tripper. That's how I got the furniture upstairs. Tripper was real handy with tools. She set up this can for us."

Reb shrugged. "After you finish your business, you just take the bucket out from under the board, step up to the edge of the elevator shaft, and pour the mess down. About once a day, I scrub the bucket out, just so it doesn't get too nasty." She grinned, as if pleased with her resourcefulness.

"Where are Tripper and Snakey now?" Morgan asked.

Reb's elfin face lost its cocky good humor. "Snakey's in juvie hall," she disclosed. "Got caught trickin' in Volunteer Park last August. He wouldn't give the cops his parents' name or phone number, so they locked him up."

"Tricking?" Morgan repeated, raising her eyebrows. She had known some kids did that to survive on the street, but she had never thought that she'd know someone who had a friend who actually did it. For a moment, a great fear rose in Morgan. *Will I end up having to....* She chopped the thought off, unable to finish it.

With the back of her hand, Reb wiped her nose, contemplating Morgan. As if in explanation of Snakey's tricking, Reb mumbled, "He and Tripper got to likin' crack." She dropped her gaze. "A lot."

Decisively, Reb picked up the roll of toilet paper at the end of the bench, and ordered, "Turn your back for a minute."

Morgan turned, ruffling the back of her newly shorn head, feeling where the bowl-cut abruptly ended and the quarter inch that was left began. "What happened to Tripper?" she asked, not really sure she wanted to know.

Over the steady trickle, Reb answered, "She left town."

"Oh." Perplexed, Morgan wondered about the tone of voice Reb had used. She sounded both angry and despondent.

"Your turn," Reb prompted.

Who was this Tripper to her? Morgan wondered, brushing past Reb and undoing the waist string of her sweatpants. *Why would Tripper's leaving upset Reb so much, unless...they were lovers?*

"I'll meetcha down in the squat," Reb announced, moving away.

"Okay." And then, feeling suddenly very frustrated, Morgan continued to stand there, frowning down with distaste at the sharp stink of the bucket.

"What am I getting myself into?" she whispered.

Much later, after Morgan had eaten and then promptly fallen asleep again, she awoke a second time. Hearing a guitar, and a girl singing somewhere in the distance, she blinked against the utter blackness all around her. She wondered if she was dreaming. Then, one of the cats meowed and she knew she was still in Reb's squat,

Rubbing her eyes, she sat up and swung her feet to the floor. She felt around with her bare feet until she found her sneakers, then wondered where her letter jacket was. The chilly dampness of the morning had taken on the penetrating bite of true cold. She stumbled to the crate near the bed, knowing there were matches and a candle there.

With a ghostly, haunting lilt, the singing continued, filling the dark with a strange melancholy.

Once Morgan lit the candle, she held it up, scrutinizing the room. The brave flame illuminated the cross above the bed, and Morgan stepped closer to examine it. She'd never have guessed that Reb was religious. Then she saw that Jesus's face had been pasted over, covered with what looked like a color cutout from a magazine photograph. It was a vaguely familiar face. Morgan frowned, wondering who it was, then turned her gaze on the rest of the room.

Reb had cleaned up a bit. The cardboard boxes full of what Morgan suspected to be stolen goods were gone. The assortment of discarded laundry had been removed from the recliner and the stuffed chair across from it. On the other side of the room, the scarred table and three wooden chairs gleamed as if they had been recently scrubbed. And six to eight cats sat in various places, watching Morgan watch them.

Me and the other strays, Morgan mused. *Washed, fed, and given a place to sleep. So now what? I'm not a pet. I'll probably be expected to earn my keep.*

The voice in the distance seemed to weave a spell around Morgan, pulling her toward it.

She shivered and remembered the jacket. Unable to locate it on the chair back where she had seen Reb hang it last night, she looked around until she noticed a scuffed-up black motorcycle jacket hanging from a nail on the wall. Quaking, she pulled it on, picked up her candle and went in search of the singer.

She followed the voice out of the room and along the outer corridor. An errant draft blew her candle out as she came to the section where the drywall had been knocked away. Beyond the struts and remnants of the walls, a faint light glowed, illuminating only a portion of the empty floor that stretched all the way to the far side of the warehouse. In the middle of that vast area, Morgan could see Reb in a small circle of candle-light.

She was wearing Morgan's letter jacket, sitting cross-legged on the floor. In her arms, she cradled a banged-up acoustic guitar, which she strummed as she sang. The voice issuing from that petite, thin frame was surprisingly clear and strong. Morgan didn't recognize the song, but she knew right away that she liked it.

She also knew she liked the way Reb looked as she sang it. Her brown eyes were soft and her cheeks were radiant with color. It was as if her entire being had been given over to the song.

"Hold me close against you," Reb was singing. "I want to get deep inside your warmth...."

The slight rocking motion of her body was entrancing. Slender fingers shifted from one chord to another, swift, capable and certain.

"But if you reach for me, I'll run, you know," Reb sang. "I'm the fox, I won't be tamed."

Reb broke off in the midst of the song. She leaned over, grabbed a pencil from the floor and jotted something into the notebook at her feet. Then, as if she felt Morgan's gaze, her head snapped up and she searched the dark space beyond her candle.

Morgan was amazed by the fear on Reb's face.

"Who's there?!" Reb demanded.

"Me," Morgan answered, walking forward.

Embarrassed, Reb seemed to consciously pull herself together. "Hey," she called softly, watching Morgan approach. "Cut me a break and say somethin' next time."

"I didn't want to interrupt," Morgan offered. "That was really good, Reb."

"Yeah, right," Reb scoffed, but her brown eyes lit up, revealing how pleased she was.

Morgan sat down beside her. She reached for the notebook and scanned the page, noting the chords scrawled below the lyrics. Sections of crossed-out lines and heavily erased areas confirmed her guess. "Your own composition, too," Morgan stated, curious now.

Reb shrugged, cradling the guitar in her arms. She watched Morgan return to reading her lyrics, then asserted, "I want to do rock 'n' roll—form my own band. Like Kurt Cobain and Nirvana—only with girls."

Remembering the cross she had wondered about in the room, Morgan nodded. Jesus was wearing Kurt Cobain's face. *What exactly does that mean?* Morgan reflected, then, puzzled, looked up from the notebook.

"What you were just singing sounded more like a love song than progressive rock."

"So?" Reb asked, immediately defensive. "I felt like writin' somethin' mushy."

"Oh." Morgan met Reb's hostile stare, mystified by the rapid shift in mood. *She's acting like I'm reading something into this.*

"I know it's dumb," Reb allowed, hugging the guitar to her small frame. "I'm not makin' any money at music—so what good is it, right?"

Morgan watched her, suddenly aware of Reb's vulnerability. "I think songwriting is the most important thing in your life," she said softly.

Brown eyes flashed up, then down again.

"It would have to be," Morgan stipulated, "for you to be this good at it. I think I understand why you play and write, and money has nothing to do with it."

Reb slowly lifted her gaze. Morgan felt the fawn brown eyes resting on her, warily.

"Wish I could make money at it, though," Reb confessed. "I busted into a truck and jacked sixty bucks a coupla days ago, but I had a debt to pay. There was a kid up on the Ave who kinda took me under her wing when I first hit town a few years back. She's got AIDS, and looks too sick to trick now, so she's been havin' a rough time."

Reb shrugged. "I only kept enough for some grub for me and the cats. Which meant, by yesterday, I was broke again. Just before I met up with Moon and Leper, I hadda jack the smokes from somebody's coat pocket on the street." Remembering the scene, Reb snickered. "Almost got caught."

"Do you steal a lot?" Morgan asked quietly.

"Enough," Reb stated. There was no apology or shame in her eyes. "I told ya. I don't whore and I don't beg. I got a skill, see? I'm like this modern-day version of Jesse James. Only I ain't got no horse."

Reb laughed at her joke and reached for the nearby box of Marlboros. She shook one out and proceeded to deftly go through the lighting-up process.

Uneasily, Morgan stretched her legs out in front of her. "Am I supposed to steal, too?" she finally asked.

"Not yet," Reb replied evenly. "I'll show you the moves, check what kind of talent you are. Then we'll see."

"What if..." Morgan stopped, wondering if she dared to say this. "What if I don't *want* to steal anything."

"You think I *want* to steal shit?" Reb asked, her voice very soft. She took a drag on the cigarette, narrowing her eyes at Morgan. "You think I *want* to creep around in the middle of the tit-freezin' night, bustin' into cars, hopin' there ain't some alarm ready to go off—breaking my damn eardrums and signaling the cops?"

She gave Morgan a scornful look and her voice rose. "You think I *like* dippin' my hand into other people's pockets? You got any idea what kinda crap people keep in their fuckin' pockets? Booger rags and shit like that—it's unbelievable—let me tell you!"

Morgan tensed and went perfectly still. When her father began yelling, it usually meant the hitting was about to start.

But Reb merely continued smoking her cigarette and staring at her. Finally, she muttered, "You don't gotta do nothin' you don't want to. Okay? And stop lookin' so scared. You make me feel like I'm turnin' into my stupid mother or somethin'."

They sat silently for another few minutes, then Reb began probing. "I told you about me—even about bein' a musician and all. But you ain't told me nothin' about you."

Feeling apprehensive, Morgan debated whether or not to answer truthfully. There was an edge to the way Reb had spoken.

"I write, too," Morgan admitted.

She saw Reb's face change, reflecting her interest.

"What do you write?" Reb asked quietly.

Morgan perceived Reb's demeanor shifting once more. In the yellow light of the candle before her, those brown eyes were soft.

"Journals. Stories." Then Morgan dared to name her dream as she confided, "Someday, I want to write a book."

"Huh," Reb responded, looking at her as if pieces in a puzzle were falling into place. "You were on your way to college, weren't you?" She crushed the cigarette into an upside-down jar lid.

Morgan lowered her head, feeling lanced by the sudden reminder of all she had lost in the past few days. Her throat grew painfully tight.

"Thought so," Reb commented. "You sound like you was one of them kids that gets straight A's in school. You speak good English...but you don't know much about the real world yet."

Stung, Morgan swallowed hard and glared at Reb.

Amused by Morgan's reaction, Reb leaned forward. "'I understand why you play and write, and money has nothing to do with it...'" she mimicked. "Ain't that what you said?" She sat back, disgusted. "Girlfriend," she warned, "in America, you gotta have money or you're gonna be dead real quick. Money is *it.*"

Stubbornly, Morgan folded her arms across her chest and turned her face away. *I'm not turning into a thief,* she thought.

"What made you run?" Reb prodded, a mean tone creeping into her voice. "Must've been bad to make you bail when you were so close to going off to college." She had made a disagreeable singsong of the last five words.

It was bad, all right, Morgan silently acknowledged, trying not to think about the night before last.

"Who beat you up like that?" Reb persisted.

For an instant, Morgan was back on the front lawn, being pummeled unmercifully with hard fists. Ice-cold terror ripped through her. Involuntarily, her knees snapped to her chest and she buried her face in her arms. She heard the frightened, gut-level sound that escaped her as she moved, and one part of her mind was appalled that she had been reduced to this.

"Flynn—I'm sorry!"

She meant to hurt you! an inner voice warned. *You should've known better! Don't trust her!* She burrowed her face into the cool leather of the jacket arms, humiliated.

"God, I can be such a bitch," Reb confessed, annoyed with herself. "I can tell you were a preppie, and I'm sorta prejudiced against 'em."

Trembling, Morgan took a deep breath, trying to push the disjointed memory of her father's latest attack on her back into the other buried memories. Her heart was slamming hard within her chest and the cold sweat of fear was breaking out on her brow.

"You okay?" Reb asked.

Biting her lip, Morgan nodded and stayed there, hunched over. She was desperately trying to convince herself that she was far away from him and finally safe.

"I know that scene," Reb muttered. "My mom tried to smack me around, but she was usually too loaded to catch me."

Morgan sighed. *So you know, but you still had to bug me?*

"Hey," Reb enthused, obviously trying to distract her. "The motorcycle jacket looks cool on you." When Morgan ignored her, Reb proposed, "How 'bout you keep that one and I'll wear yours? No one will ever think a jock jacket is really mine—and it will keep off the questions that you'd get wearin' it. Whatta ya say?"

Morgan raised her head and cleared her throat. "Keep it. I don't want it anymore." She didn't know that the grief on

her face as she said it made Reb feel even worse about tormenting her.

Bitter and restless, Morgan let Reb talk her into getting
dressed and then going out on the street. They were both hungry and there was nothing left to eat in Reb's squat.

Back in the room, Morgan changed into her last set of
clean clothes. Grimly, she mulled over what had happened. *Who
would have thought that the first real gay person I meet would be
such a callous little creep! Putting the make on me in the morning,
mocking me at night! She must think I'm a total fool!*

She decided she just wanted Reb to show her how to
survive without money. As soon as she could manage on her
own, Morgan resolved that she would get away from Reb.

A short time later they were using the flashlight to de-
scend the stairs. Unfamiliar with the narrow passage, Morgan
stumbled a few times. When Reb reached out a hand to steady
her, Morgan made it a point to shake off Reb's hold on her
arm. If she couldn't be friends with Reb, then she certainly didn't
intend to tolerate that incredibly unnerving touch. By the end
of the journey down five flights of stairs, Reb seemed to have
gotten the unspoken message and stayed well away from her.
Morgan wondered why that didn't make her feel any better.

They stepped through the door and Reb knelt in the
alley to lock it behind them. Then she gripped Flynn's hand,
ignoring the renewed attempts to fend off the contact.

With a finely developed stealth, she led Flynn through
the velvet blackness that surrounded them. One hand brushed
along the brick wall, as she followed the rough surface to its
end at the edge of the sidewalk along Eleventh Avenue. There,
she let go of Flynn's hand, and pushed her back against the
wall. Carefully, Reb peered around the corner and checked the
street.

In the pool of yellow below a street light at the end of the block, Reb could see two boys smoking cigarettes.

Flynn abruptly tried to move away from the wall, and Reb leaned into her, hissing, "Stay there."

"Why?" Flynn whispered.

"I got people after me!" Reb whispered back. "We gotta snake around out here, okay? Now stick with me!"

Quickly, Reb set off at a run, and within seconds, Flynn was beside her. They ran across Eleventh Avenue and made it to the dark alley on the other side. Reb began a fast walk.

"Stay beside me," Reb ordered. "I'm not sure if they saw us."

Flynn said nothing, only shoved her hands in her jeans pockets, and slouched along, her gait slower than Reb's but her long strides covering just as much ground.

Uneasily, Reb noted the defiant body language and cursed herself. *She's pissed,* Reb reflected, acutely aware that Flynn had withdrawn from her. *Why did I have to get on her case like that? Why did I kiss her this morning? I'm all outta control, here. Christ, she makes me nervous.*

Sighing, Reb concentrated on keeping her senses sharp. They were walking through a derelict section of Capitol Hill. And even though Flynn was tall and broad-shouldered, and from a distance probably looked enough like a teenage boy to pass for one, they were still going to attract attention. Kids who were out on the street this late—almost eleven o'clock— were usually runaways. And Reb knew there were monsters out there who fed on runaways.

With a glance over her shoulder, she verified that the alley behind her was clear. Still, she wished she dared carry a knife, like many of the Trolls did.

Carry a knife long enough and you'll use it, she reminded herself. *And no juvie court is gonna cut you any breaks, no matter what you were protectin' yourself from. You don't need no jail time, and that's that.*

She studied Flynn again. *If she hadn't stopped Leper and Moon last night, I'd be the one covered with bruises.* Reb shuddered and moved closer to Flynn. *Gotta do better by her. Don't want to be out here alone anymore.*

As if feeling Reb's regard, Flynn looked down at her. Reb smiled. Deadpan, Flynn looked away.

She sure looks good in that motorcycle jacket, Reb couldn't help but note. *Makes me want to try for another kiss.*

Forty-five minutes later, they were behind the Quality Food Company, on Broadway, raiding the dumpster. Reb stood on a precarious perch, one hand grasping the edge of the opened dumpster lid, while both feet tightrope-walked the top edge of one metal side. She was leaning down into the dumpster, rooting through the piled-high trash. Below her, on the blacktop parking lot, Flynn waited, her arms full of slightly foul-smelling possibilities.

This is taking forever, Flynn thought irritably. "Are you sure any of this stuff is even edible?" she asked, grimacing.

"No," Reb replied, laughing. "Don't get excited," she added, seeing that Flynn was readying to throw the whole armload of fruit, vegetables, and cellophane-wrapped sandwiches back into the dumpster. "We're gonna sort through it and select only the best in borderline freshness."

Flynn didn't join in Reb's laughter. She leaned against the dumpster, hungry and cantankerous.

"Look at this shit," Reb went on, clearly feeling the need to deliver a lecture. "How can people be hungry when there's good garbage, just waitin' to be harvested? 'Course, in the summer, you gotta watch out for maggots and you get food poisonin' every once in a while, but this time of year it's a regular dumpster deli."

Still chuckling at her own wit, Reb hopped down from the rim, landing as sure-footed as a cat on the blacktop of the parking lot.

She grinned up at Flynn. "The politicians planned it this way, you know. Kids like us, deviant no-goods, are forced to go scroungin' around in dumpsters and end up providin' a public service. See, this is garbage recyclin' and welfare combined." Reb gave a hoot, then hammed up her finish with a little tap dance. "The ultimate 'Life Skills Program'!"

"Can we just eat something?" Flynn growled. "I'm starving."

"Okay, okay. Spread the stuff out on the ground."

Flynn crouched and carefully released her goods. Quickly, Reb's hands traveled over the vegetables and fruit, rubbing and squeezing. She began deftly tossing some of the produce back into the dumpster, while she shoved other pieces into a small plastic grocery bag she produced from her jacket pocket. With a brusque superiority, she motioned Flynn to move closer to her, and then pushed a banana and three limp carrots into Flynn's jacket pocket.

"Fruits and vegetables are really important," she informed Flynn. "If you were a junk-food junkie before, plan on givin' it up. You can't get by out here eatin' shit like that."

Nodding, Flynn immediately pulled out the biggest carrot and took an enormous bite. She moaned softly as she chewed it; never had a carrot tasted so good to her.

Reb moved on to the cellophane-wrapped sandwiches, opening and examining each one in the light from the loading dock. Flynn watched her lift the bread, sniffing the contents. Some she re-wrapped and slipped in the plastic bag with the vegetables and fruits she had selected earlier. Others were dropped unceremoniously at her feet. One particular sandwich elicited an excited smile, and she shoved it inside the red-and-white letter jacket she wore.

Then Reb handed Flynn the plastic bag and began launching the rejected sandwiches back into the dumpster.

Finally, Reb walked around, scrutinizing the area carefully, pointedly picking up any remaining garbage and tossing it into the open trash container.

"Always clean up after a dumpster raid," Reb instructed. "Or the next time you stop by for a meal you'll be competin' with the true recyclers—the rats."

Flynn choked on her carrot. Small orange bits flew out of her mouth, and Reb placed a hand on Flynn's back, rubbing it soothingly until she stopped coughing.

"Boy, you're so easy to shock," Reb commented. Grinning, she pulled the special sandwich from her coat, unwrapped it, and handed half of it to Flynn. "Ham and cheese with mustard —my fave."

Flynn shifted the plastic bag to her other hand, sniffing the sandwich suspiciously.

"Don't be such a wus, Flynn," Reb teased, then stopped, her gaze riveted on something beyond Flynn. "Oh shit," Reb muttered, her cockiness gone.

Quickly, Flynn turned to see what had caught Reb's attention.

Three boys were strutting around the corner of the building. "Just who we was lookin' for," one of them crowed, and the other two laughed. It was a grating, mean noise that sounded very little like real laughter.

Flynn already knew that the loading dock and L-shaped design of the store walled off two sides of this deserted area. An empty parking lot stretched out to the right, the only possible escape route. She automatically scanned the distance.

"Don't even think about it," the blond boy warned, pointing a gleaming pistol barrel at her.

A gun! He's got a gun!

The blond gave another malicious laugh, then addressed Reb. "Can't resist making a midnight QFC dumpster raid, no matter what, eh, Reb? Got you some new pussy, but you still—"

Reb cut him off. "Aw stuff it, Dwarf-Dick!"

As the boys moved closer, Flynn recognized Leper and Moon, the two fourteen-year-old thugs she had fought last night. And judging by the hate-filled looks on their faces as they came closer, they certainly remembered her. But the blond one with the gun was someone new; he looked about a year or two older, and far more dangerous.

She dropped her untouched sandwich. Nervously, she eyed the gun, her breath coming fast.

"You just *chill*, baby," the gunman crooned to Flynn.

"What do you want?" Flynn demanded.

"Call me Flash, sweetness. My boys was tellin' me all about you. New, fine girl in town, dissin' them 'fore they was even properly introduced." He laughed softly.

Flynn did not respond. He was boldly inspecting her, and the lascivious shimmer in his eyes made her feel slightly sick.

"Yeah, you're a real looker, even with that black eye. I got some fellas I think you should meet," Flash invited, licking his lips. "Future business associates, you might say...."

"Don't listen to him, Flynn," Reb cautioned.

"Shut up, cunt!" Flash snarled.

"It's gang shit," Reb continued, her eyes burning with anger. "The Ghouls are dealers. Crack, coke, heroin—a real choose-your-poison shoppin' network. They just want another whore. They'll get you hooked and use you like they used Tripper and Snakey."

Her throat tight, Flynn stared at the gun and nervously gripped the heavy plastic bag she still held. She had absolutely no idea how they were ever going to get out of this.

"I said shut up!" Flash yelled, moving closer to Reb, who promptly retreated from him. "The Ghouls took care of them two! We was family! The *only* reason you wasn't a member was cuz you was too chicken-shit to take the beatin' in!"

Then the way he was looking at Reb changed. Rage shifted into a sly sort of lust, and as Reb moved closer to Flynn, Flash casually pursued her. "Too bad Tripper up and disappeared while she still owed us money for that last vial of crack. You're the only one left to pay the bill." He looked her over, grinning in anticipation. "Why don't we arrange a little party with my homeboys here...." It was not a question.

Moon and Leper giggled viciously.

Flynn saw Reb's face as Flash seized the smaller girl's arm. As frightened as Flynn was, it was nothing compared to the fear in Reb's round brown eyes. Yet, without hesitation, Reb bent, quick as a terrier, and savagely bit the hand that held her.

Flash gave a strangled cry and snatched his hand back, while Reb continued to take the offensive. Cursing him, Reb placed two hands on his chest and shoved. The boy staggered backward and landed on his rear end. Reb surged away from him. Flash fought to regain his balance, already beginning to swing the gun up, trying to aim at Reb's back.

And in those brief seconds, while everyone's eyes had shifted to Reb, Flynn acted. She whipped the bag of foraged groceries forward, flinging it at the gunman's head. Fast and stunningly accurate, the bag hit him square in the face, causing him to belatedly fling his arms up in self-protection.

With a roar of noise, the gun went off, but Reb kept running. Flash had missed.

Recovering, the boy started to turn the weapon on Flynn, but she was already charging him. Her foot met his wrist in what was essentially a vicious soccer kick. She drove through the motion with all her might and saw the gun fly out of his hand. With smooth precision, she sidestepped, physically following the weapon as it sailed upward and out to the side. The gun clattered as it landed on the blacktop about twenty feet away, and then Flynn was there, scooping it into her hand.

Astounded, Flash sat gripping his wrist, paralyzed. Leper and Moon were shouting hysterically at Flash, unable to decide for themselves whether or not to rush Flynn.

Flynn, meanwhile, only wanted to get rid of the cold steel pistol she gripped in her hand. *I don't want this damned thing, but I don't want them to have it either!* She glanced about and saw only one solution. All in one motion, like Willie Mays in the World Series films, she turned, snapping her arm forward and throwing the gun. It rose higher and higher, then disappeared onto the QFC roof.

"No!" Flash screamed. "You fuckin' idiot!"

The next thing she knew, she was sprinting across the empty parking lot. The soft scuff of sneakers hitting the blacktop behind her spurred her on even faster. A glance over her shoulder told her that Leper and Moon were already in pursuit, though only Moon was close. Increasing her pace, she hurdled the thigh-high fence that formed the perimeter of the parking lot. She landed on the sidewalk, danced between two parked cars, and then glimpsed Reb dashing into the deeper shadows farther down the street. Wondering where Reb was going, Flynn instinctively followed her.

She passed by three-story brick residences with ten-foot front yards and noticed the large bushes that crowded up to the sidewalk. *Good places to hide, but those guys are too close.*

She sped through an intersection. The next block yawned before her, and it seemed to be much darker. Not knowing what else to do, Flynn kept running. She could no longer see Reb, and now that she had left behind the halogen lights that surrounded the parking lot, she knew the boys chasing her were going to have trouble seeing her, too.

Use the dark—just like Reb does, she thought, and turned abruptly into a driveway. Holding in her labored breathing with some difficulty, she flattened out against the darkened wall of a house. Unsuspecting, the boys flew past her, down the street. After a quick check to make sure the ruse had worked, she jogged quietly away, heading for the opposite end of the street.

Where's Reb? she wondered, desperate to know if the girl was safely away from those creeps.

At the end of the block, she turned the corner and began to run west. How dark this section of the city was, dominated by tree-lined streets and clusters of old apartment buildings.

The few street lights she passed hung above her in the night like tiny moons. She stopped and surveyed the next street, vainly searching one more time for some sign of Reb. Then, worried, she began running in earnest.

Though she knew it was the last place she should go, Flynn yearned to go back to the squat. She wanted to collapse on the bed under Kurt Cobain-on-the-cross and hold that smart-ass Reb safe in her arms. Yet she knew she could not do it, not just yet. If Flash, Leper or Moon were following her, she would only end up leading them straight to the only place Reb thought of as safe.

Instead, Flynn kept to a steady pace, running through the dark, until her lungs were burning. The running didn't bother her; what bothered her was having no idea where Reb was.

CHAPTER 6

Chris opened her eyes. Golden sunlight was slanting through her bedroom window. *It's Sunday. And Joyce isn't downstairs making coffee. We won't be lazing about in bed, reading the Sunday newspaper, talking and touching and loving each other.*

Pushing the memories away, she lay there listening. *The house is so empty, so deafeningly silent. Another Sunday with hours and hours of being alone stretching out in front of me.... Is this hell? Shit, it must be, because every Sunday it rips my heart out.*

Impatient with the enduring anguish, she threw the covers back and made for the shower. *Thank God there's work to do outside.*

On this first Sunday in October, the sun was warm and the sky a vivid blue. The yellow leaves of the alder trees at the back of the property were whispering with every breeze. Chris dutifully spent the morning muscling the retractable aluminum ladder around, washing window exteriors. By midday she was mowing and then fertilizing the lawn. As long as she was busy, she felt in control. Her habit of keeping her mind occupied with one task after another had become a routine.

For some odd reason, though, today she was not as successful as she usually was with this mental maneuver. She often found herself thinking of the woman next door. Remembering the sudden, candid conversation she'd fallen into with Jennifer at Allison's house party, Chris intuited that she probably had needed to talk to someone. Yet it was disconcerting to find herself repeatedly thinking about Jennifer, and even more so to realize she wanted to talk to her again.

She was being kind to you—so what? she warned herself sternly. *Last thing you need to do is get involved with your next-door neighbor!*

Late in the afternoon, Chris was splitting wood and then stacking it in the firewood stand near her back deck. She realized that she hadn't seen Alf in a while, and stopped chopping and whistled. When the springer didn't show, she hefted her ax and started to walk up the gravel driveway to look for him.

"He's here with me," someone called.

Across the drive, sitting on the last step of her back stairs, was Jennifer. Alf was happily stretched out at her feet, on his back, getting his belly rubbed.

"I thought you didn't like dogs," Chris smiled, moving closer.

"You thought wrong," Jennifer returned, very serene. "How's that cut finger?"

Chris obligingly held up the grimy Band-Aid on her index finger. "Okay. Thanks."

Without consciously meaning to do it, Chris swept her gaze over the woman before her. In blue jeans and a red pull-over sweater, her light brown hair pulled back from her lovely face in a French braid, Jennifer was enchanting.

And then Chris realized that Jennifer was repaying in kind, looking Chris over with a frankly considering eye. Embarrassed, Chris glanced down at her torn, faded jeans and nondescript blue denim workshirt. Trying to brush off stray bits of wood, she muttered, "Guess I'm pretty much a mess."

Jennifer countered softly, "Clothes are all in the way you wear them...."

Now what should I make of that? Chris thought, unable to read anything in Jennifer's carefully expressionless face.

Alf rolled right side up and smiled at Jennifer in his goofy, adoring way. Jennifer scratched his ears, and on an impulse said, "I've got a roast in the oven. You two care to join me for dinner?"

Alf whined, making Jennifer smile.

Chris's stomach did a slow flip. "Uhh...okay," she responded. A heartbeat later she realized that she had just completely reversed her prudent strategy about being friendly but distant. Hastily, she clarified, "But this isn't a date, okay?"

Jennifer gazed at her, eyebrows raised.

"Because," Chris rushed on, "well, I think it might be...kind of complicated...if we were neighbors and dating."

With a slight shake of her head, Jennifer replied gruffly, "I'm just trying to avoid leftovers til doomsday, Olson." Flicking a testy glance at Chris, and then away, she finished, "You're not exactly my type, you know."

I'm not? Chris thought, feeling piqued. *What is your type, then?* Blushing, comprehending, all at once, that she had insulted Jennifer by bluntly setting up a condition, Chris tried to finish gracefully. "What time do you want me to come over?"

"In half an hour," Jennifer supplied, then added, "You can provide the wine." She looked as if she already regretted extending the invitation.

Giving a nod, Chris turned and walked back to the wood pile. With a fluid swing, she planted the ax in the center of the old stump there, then strode over to her own back steps. She turned and was annoyed to see that Alf had stayed with Jennifer.

His nub of a tail wiggling, his worshipful brown eyes fixed on Jennifer's face, Alf clearly felt no need to obscure his feelings.

Sighing, Chris took the steps two at a time. She crossed the deck and once again braved the oppressive silence of her empty house.

Later that evening, after a sumptuous meal of roast beef, mashed potatoes and gravy, fresh salad and broccoli in cheese sauce, Jennifer let Chris help her clean up. The meal had been a fairly silent affair, but then Chris had been eating and sighing as if she hadn't eaten so well in months, and Jennifer had found that in itself very gratifying.

Once the leftovers were stored in the refrigerator and the dishwasher was loaded, Chris seemed vaguely reluctant to go. She poured them both another glass of red wine, then corked the bottle, and proposed, "Let's sit and talk a while."

Confounded, Jennifer led Chris from the kitchen, through the dining room, to the old-fashioned parlor. Darkness filled the large windows of the comfortable room they entered, but the remains of a cheery hearthfire kept the shadows in the far corners.

Alf tried to jump into the overstuffed armchair near the fire, but a firm "Down" from Chris sent him to the carpeted floor, grumbling.

Smiling, Jennifer commented, "He almost talks, doesn't he?"

"A real wise-guy," Chris agreed gruffly.

With a loud "harumph," Alf lay down, his back toward Chris.

Impervious, Chris took a sip from her wine glass and surveyed Jennifer's living room.

Jennifer watched the tall, lean blonde. She looked very appealing dressed in loose, off-white chinos and a colorful plaid flannel shirt. The amber light of the fading fire highlighted the high cheekbones and strong jaw of her Nordic face, making her look so tempting that Jennifer had to turn away. She went to the small pile of wood stacked next to the large stone fireplace, reminding herself that she still wasn't sure how she felt about this often-abrasive woman.

She's got a million barriers and all that unresolved grief! You're out of your mind to even consider starting something!

With slow deliberation, Chris sauntered around the back of the sofa, pacing the perimeter of the room. Jennifer placed a log on the fire, then went to the sofa, wondering where Chris would decide to park herself.

Moving closer, Chris ran her gaze around the room. "I like what you've done with the house."

"Thanks," Jennifer replied. "You were friends with the former owners, right?" When Chris nodded, Jennifer asked solicitously, "Is it hard for you to be here?"

"No," Chris answered, her eyes growing thoughtful, as if she were surprised by her answer. "Someone had to buy the place. Joel and Frank just flat out needed the money." Shyly, Chris finally looked at her. "And it will be nice living next door to you."

Cradling her wine glass, Chris walked over and sat beside Jennifer on the sofa. Jennifer noted that the earlier tension had left that handsome face. Now, the bright eyes that stared into the dancing flames were content.

Satisfied, Jennifer leaned back and savored her third glass of wine. *I'm drinking too much of this,* she mused. *But I never dreamed she'd have a bottle of something so good on hand.*

Jennifer ventured, "Tom told me you helped Joel nurse Frank, right up until they placed him in that hospice three months back."

Baffled, Chris asked, "When did he tell you that?"

"At Allison's the other night," Jennifer informed her. "While you were talking with Allison. How is Frank, these days?"

"He's very...peaceful," Chris answered. "Which amazes me."

"Why?"

"When the news about Frank having AIDS began to spread," Chris recounted, "a lot of his former friends vanished." She faced Jennifer, her eyes intense. "Gay men and women, some of whom we'd known for years, just abandoned Joel and Frank. Tom says they're scared. He says we can't blame people for being afraid of a plague, afraid of seeing death right there in the room with them."

"And what do you say?" Jennifer asked.

"Well," Chris said slowly, "I just don't get it." She frowned. "Frank and Joel are good men. That first year after Joyce died—between Tom and those two..." She finished by shaking her head. "I don't think I would have made it without them."

"Special guys, huh?" Jennifer remarked. Watching Chris trying to rein in her emotions, Jennifer felt a tug on her heart.

But Chris's pained reverie was brief. With a glance that was half compassion, half curiosity, she turned her gaze back on Jennifer. "The other night, you said you had lost someone," she probed gently. "Would you mind telling me about it?"

Jennifer could only blink at her.

In one long swallow, she finished her wine. For several moments, she debated answering, all the while feeling Chris's need and expectation. *Here you were accusing her of carrying a ghost around with her...as if you're any less haunted....*

"I'm sorry," Chris apologized. "You don't have to...."

Without conscious thought, Jennifer interrupted her. "My kid sister, Laney, died six years ago next week." She was dismayed to hear her voice quavering, despite her best effort to master it.

Talk about walls! she thought. *I've got a God-damned fortress constructed around this little parcel of misery. You can't expect her to do what you can't manage to do yourself.*

She stood and walked to the hearth, placing her empty glass on the mantel. Abruptly, she picked up another split log, then dropped the wood on the fire. Sparks flew and the flames licked hungrily over this new offering.

"My mother caught Laney and her girlfriend, Delia, in bed together," Jennifer began. "Both girls were sixteen. My parents, especially my father, just lost it. He called her names, ordered her to break it off. Laney refused and continued to see Delia on the sly. My parents tried to make her see a psychotherapist, threatened to throw her out, the whole ugly scene."

She kept her back to Chris, but knew she was unable to hide the bitter disgust she felt. It was in her voice, and Jennifer knew if she herself heard it, then Chris heard it, too.

"Then, Delia's parents sent Delia off to some boarding school in Maine and gave orders to the school personnel that no contact with Laney was to be permitted. That pretty much ended their involvement.

"At the same time, at Laney's school, the rumor had gotten out about what was going on—why Delia was suddenly gone and why Laney was so upset about it. You know the power of teen cliques and the general intolerance—downright hate— towards most gay kids. The ones who weren't tormenting her with verbal put-downs just dropped her cold. She went from popular athlete to school pariah almost overnight."

At last Jennifer turned, made herself look at Chris. Fingering her French braid nervously, she found she could barely meet Chris's eyes. "Laney withdrew from everyone and gradually went into this prolonged depression. My parents and the school counselors all assured each other that she'd get over it. You know, the old 'just ignore it, she's going through a phase' theory."

More than a little wildly, Jennifer laughed. "And I was thirty miles away, pursuing my doctorate at Penn, so immersed in my teaching career that I didn't even know any of this was going on. *Me*—her older sister by ten years, who had never thought it worth mentioning to anyone in my family that I was a lesbian. I just accepted my mother's reports that Laney was 'being difficult.'"

How could I have been so oblivious, so self-centered? she asked herself for the millionth time since it had all unfolded like some horrid Greek tragedy.

Some of her inner turmoil must have shown on her face, because Chris stood up and moved across the room, coming to a halt directly in front of her. Chris's clear blue eyes were pools of commiseration. "Go on," she urged.

"My father found her in the basement," Jennifer stated, and she made a small, involuntary gasp as the reality of it found her and pierced her heart, yet again. "She'd rigged up a chair and a nylon rope. My bright, gorgeous little sister hanged herself, and left a note saying, 'I'm sorry I'm not who you want me to be.'"

Jennifer felt Chris's arms slide around her, felt Chris drawing her close. "I'm all right," she protested, even though she knew she was crying. "I'm all right."

"Sure," Chris whispered, moving a hand to Jennifer's hair, stroking errant strands back from her hot, tear-streaked face. "You're fine."

Wondering at herself, Jennifer gripped the sides of Chris's flannel shirt, trying to regain control. "Gosh, I'm sorry, Chris. I haven't talked about it often, and it still seems so... *awful.*"

"I understand," Chris murmured.

"I miss her," Jennifer stated, trying to explain. Then, fervently, she repeated that truth, "*I miss her.*" She leaned into Chris and clung to the strong, lean frame.

Silent, Chris held her.

"I believe," Jennifer choked, "that th-there are m-moments of great karmic opportunity that come once or twice in a lifetime." She swallowed, hoping she wasn't sounding completely crazy. "We enter these moments and set off so many possible outcomes, just by what we dare to risk, what we dare to reveal.

"I thought that by appearing to conform, by being discreet, I could avoid the prejudice and trouble that being gay often entails. I was so damned closeted—hell—I still am! I keep trying to slide through those little prisms of fate. Six years ago, my moments of opportunity came and went and I just never bothered to tell Laney who I was. In shielding myself, I l-lost her. She thought she was alone, and she wasn't. If only I had told her...."

"She knew you loved her," Chris whispered, her voice very low.

"In the end," Jennifer rasped, "I think she came to doubt it."

Sheltered in Chris's warm, comforting embrace, she was suddenly dissolving into harsh, tearing sobs. She clutched Chris, adrift in pain and memories.

After what seemed like a long while, Chris steered her to the sofa, and they sat down together. One arm still around her, Chris handed her tissues from the box on the end table and Jennifer blew her nose repeatedly, sniffling like a child. She hunched over, feeling helpless and sad.

Somehow, her head ended up in Chris's lap, and Chris slowly unbraided the back of her hair, then filled her hands with it. With firm, tender fingers, she massaged Jennifer's scalp until the headache the tears had brought gradually eased.

Neither of them spoke.

The fire crackled, filling the room with light and warmth. Alf lay on the carpeted floor, legs twitching, in the midst of a series of dreams.

Time slid by, and the radiance of the hearthfire gradually dimmed. And still Jennifer stayed in Chris's lap, too comfortable to move. The hands in her hair went on slowly massaging her head and neck, and bewildered, Jennifer lay there, allowing it.

Finally, Jennifer sat up, croaking lamely, "Aren't you glad this isn't a date?"

Chris simply laid a consoling palm against Jennifer's cheek. At that touch, a warm wanting spread through Jennifer. Lowering her eyes, she sighed. She was bewildered, her emotions were raw. *I like her...need her...more than I thought possible,* she at last admitted to herself. *But she's still loyal to Joyce—even now. There's no hope of anything deep developing between us....*

"It means a lot to me," Chris finally said, "that you were willing to share what you did. Please don't be embarrassed."

Agitated, Jennifer stood and moved to the end of the sofa. "Well...it's late," she muttered, her eyes on her black loafers.

Chris took the hint. Without a word, she rose from the sofa and came toward her. Jennifer made herself raise her head.

And as she did, she caught the hurt, searching expression in Chris's eyes.

Far off, down on the Sound, a foghorn called.

Lying in the darkness of her third-story bedroom, Chris watched the fog drift by her window. The blue-gray mist was glowing faintly with the diffused light of the street lamp that stood at the edge of her front yard.

She was physically exhausted from her frenzy of chores throughout the day. Her hunger was satiated with the wholesome food Jennifer had made her for dinner. And yet, at two o'clock in the morning, she was lying in bed, wide awake.

In bed next to her, Alf interrupted his snoring to give a series of soft, sleepy woofs. Distractedly, Chris laid a reassuring hand on his hindquarters and his dream-hunt ended.

What happened to me over there tonight? she wondered. *I was holding her in my arms, trying to be decent, doing what any friend would do for another, and then...* Her thoughts drifted. She was suddenly remembering the feel of Jennifer lying across her lap, remembering the sensation of loose, silken hair skimming through her fingers.

I nearly kissed her! she finally admitted. *I can't believe it, I nearly kissed her!*

Marveling at this unexpected realization, Chris took a deep breath and exhaled, relaxing. The frantic circles her mind had been racing in just expanded, looped outward, extending into a cosmos of possibilities.

Quieting, she closed her eyes again and remembered Jennifer lying in her lap, exhausted and sniffling and utterly trusting. It dawned on Chris that she was completely enthralled by the image.

She recalled how Jennifer had escorted her to the front door. Her eyes and nose endearingly red from crying, Jennifer had been apologizing the entire way. Chris had been saying, "It's okay. I don't care," but Jennifer had not seemed to register it.

Alf had stood by the door, his tail wagging, anxious to go home.

And then Jennifer had murmured, "Maybe we can try this again some other time...."

Deciding that the remark was an opening, Chris had proposed, "How about tomorrow night?"

Surprised, mouth partially open, Jennifer had gazed up at her.

"See you around 5:30..." Chris had stated decisively, then dared to embrace the woman.

Releasing her quickly, Chris had opened the door and raced Alf down the front porch stairs. It had been a rather hasty retreat, but she couldn't deny the exultation she felt.

Across the driveway, snuggled beneath blankets in her own bed, Jennifer was dreaming.

It's raining. I feel the cool mist collecting on my face as I walk along a street with Chris, talking. We come to a little bar and grille on the corner and as I pass her, I glance at the girl standing in the recessed doorway. She's tall, with short dark-red hair, wearing a battered motorcycle jacket and mud-spattered jeans. The girl's head is down and she's leaning against the window as if she's terribly weary. Somehow I know she's both very young and a runaway.

I follow Chris through the door, into the cafe, but then I feel oddly compelled to go back and talk to that girl, to make sure she is at least not hungry. And as I retrace my steps, the girl in the doorway turns and looks at me. Inexplicably, she is shorter now, and her face has changed.

Why...it's...my sister!

"Laney!"

Jennifer stared around herself, breathing hard, then realized she was sitting up in bed. The room, even in the dark, was unmistakable. There were the large windows, eerily aglow with the signature Seattle fog outside.

"Laney," she whispered, wrapping her arms about herself.

The dream had seemed both incredibly real and laden with meaning. Anxiously, Jennifer wondered what it signified.

Is that how Laney would have ended up? she asked God, forgetting yet again that she no longer believed in Him. *If Laney had chosen to fight, to live, would she have become one of those nameless, scruffy street kids?*

Sighing, Jennifer wished that Laney had dared even that, the most desperate and dangerous escape a teenager could make. *Anything would have been less final than that rope in the basement,* she raged inwardly. *Anything!*

That night, beneath the Olive Way highway overpass, Flynn was huddled against a concrete bridge abutment. The ever-constant truck traffic passing below on Interstate 5 created an unceasing roar. Noisy as it was, this was the best she could do. All the quieter bridges had been staked out by other Trolls.

While she shivered with cold, the events of last night were churning through her fevered brain in endless replay.

In the half-dark before dawn, she stole back to Eleventh Avenue and hid next to an old cement loading dock. She was fairly certain that Reb had come back to the squat, but she still remembered that fearful phrase Reb had used: "I got people after me!" Flynn sensed that someone already had a general idea about where Reb lived, although they didn't know the exact building.

Carefully, Flynn peeked over the edge of the loading dock, using the faint dawn light to check the alley that led to the warehouse's locked door. She was hoping that Reb was watching for her, or else would hear her if she knocked loudly enough on the steel door. At last, reassured that no one else was around, she was about to leave her hiding place when she suddenly smelled cigarette smoke on the breeze. Seconds later, Flash, Leper and Moon were swaggering into the alley, all of them smoking, all of them looking around. Looking for her.

Terrified, she pressed into the corner, where the dock and wall met, hoping that there was enough of a shadow to conceal her. The boys passed on by, oblivious to her thundering heart.

Long after they were gone she remained crouched there, tired and hungry and frightened. And then, deciding that if they saw her and came after her, at least she would lead them away from Reb and the squat, she simply stood up. Boldly, she walked through the alley, following in the direction they had gone. Instead of turning into a decoy, she walked unseen, through the misty dawn hour, all the way back to Olive Way. As daylight began to penetrate the fog, she sought out the noisy, hidden environs of the I-5 overpasses.

Flynn had spent the last twenty-four hours alternately snoozing and waking, hiding beneath this overpass, lulled by the continuous roar of traffic. At times she was consumed with hunger—a hunger that gnawed straight through to her backbone. The food Reb had stuffed in her pocket on Saturday evening was long gone. She had found nothing else edible that night, though she had rooted through countless trash cans on her way to the overpass.

The Sunday sunshine had come and gone. In the evening, as the cold fog moved into the city, Flynn began to realize how grim her situation had become. She was shivering violently, and there was a strange tightness in her lungs. As the hours of darkness slowly passed, she heard her breathing take on a rasping sound. Soon, she felt too weak to stand, and she knew beyond a shadow of a doubt that the worst was happening. She was getting sick.

Oh, God! I'm messing this up, she thought, feeling completely defeated. *I left home Thursday night and it's not even dawn on Monday morning and look at me! I need to find Reb. I need to eat and get warm—soon—or I'm going to end up in even worse shape than this!* With an angry surge of will she swore at herself, *Well, you're not dead, yet! Get up and do something!*

She pushed herself off the muddy ground and stumbled to her feet. For a moment, she stood, swaying, one hand anchored to the concrete wall. The dizziness settled into a general sense of weakness and Flynn walked out into the fog, intent on finding Reb.

Reb peered through the window, into the restaurant, reading the large red-and-black clock on the wall. *Almost three o'clock in the damn mornin'. Where the hell is Flynn?*

Sneaking back to her hiding place behind the evergreen bushes, Reb licked the last of the teriyaki sauce from her fingers. She had discovered the ample remains of a takeout order in a carton at the bottom of a trash can on Broadway. She was being reckless, she knew, leaving the squat this soon. But the food had been worth it, even if she did have to brave the main streets to find something.

The gang boys who had chased her Saturday night, only to lose track of her around Tenth Avenue, were still searching for her. In the last day, from a dirty window high in the warehouse, Reb had watched Flash, Leper and Moon marching around, blatantly staking out Eleventh Avenue. They had wandered the area, trying to break into various warehouses for almost twenty hours. Just when Reb had thought they would never leave, they finally disappeared.

Unbelievable, Reb thought, still amazed. *Flynn and I have totally trashed their rep, and by now everyone on Capitol Hill probably knows it. Those guys want our asses.*

Worriedly, from her post by the warehouse window, Reb had scanned the street. She had hoped that Flynn would see the boys first and know enough to stay away. Although where she would go, Reb had no idea. For sure, Flynn was the biggest country bumpkin she had ever met. *Clueless about how to get around the city! She even had a map in her back pocket that first night, when we met on Broadway! I mean, what a giveaway that she was fresh meat!* Stuffing the teriyaki carton deep into the bush she hid behind, Reb reconsidered, remembering. *Yeah, and that was another time she saved my know-it-all ass, so why don't I just shut up and find my girl?*

And so, here she was, hiding behind an evergreen bush in front of the Boston Market on Olive Way, using this perfect pea-soup fog to search for Flynn. She wasn't exactly sure when she had started thinking of Flynn as "my girl," but she knew she got a warm rush every time she did it. Ahead, the traffic light at the intersection turned from red to green, but in the dense fog, Reb could see little else.

She had a feeling that Flynn had gone underground in the network of cement tunnels and overpasses near the Convention Center. Many of the kids spent their first Troll days down there—suffering the nonstop boom of traffic in order to be alone. Trying to break into a group of strangers who had already set themselves up beneath a nice quiet road seemed daunting at first. Reb remembered it well, though it had been several years ago for her. If Flynn was down by the Interstate, where Reb thought she was, it meant she would be walking up Olive Way when she eventually decided to emerge and return to Capitol Hill. Reb was prepared to wait for her.

Just then, the fog shifted and she caught sight of a figure at the corner. Whoever it was stumbled as she lurched away from the support of a telephone pole. Reb instantly recognized the black leather jacket.

With a soft curse, Reb slipped out from the behind the evergreen bush and ran. She was closing in, slowing down, when Flynn swung around on her, striking out with her foot. Reb was just far enough out of range for the kick to miss, but it scared her so much she shrieked.

Recovering, Reb hissed, "Dammit, Flynn! It's me!!"

Flynn staggered. "S-sorry," she rasped, her teeth chattering madly. "Never c-could stand up to my dad...b-but now it's like I c-can't stop f-fighting."

From where she stood, roughly five feet away, Reb could hear Flynn wheezing with each breath. Concerned, Reb stepped up to her and smoothed a hand across her forehead.

"You're burnin' up!" Reb said. "How'd you get so sick?" She grabbed Flynn's arm possessively. "You go crash at one of them shelters after I told you not to?"

"No," Flynn replied. "I remembered what you s-said about the bugs...."

"And the sickness," Reb added. "There's old sick guys in them places. Tuberculosis-sick guys!"

"I was down there," Flynn mumbled, gesturing toward the highway. "I got s-so hungry and c-cold. G-guess I'm not much g-good at this." She weaved over to the curb and abruptly sat down.

"No, Flynn," Reb coaxed, taking hold of an elbow and trying to pull her back up. "I'm sorry I yelled at you. Now, c'mon. Don't give in to it. We gotta get back to the squat while the fog lasts."

"Please," Flynn murmured. "Just let me rest for a sec."

"You gotta help me," Reb pleaded. She tugged on Flynn's arm, a fierce desperation entering her words. "You're my girl and I'm takin' you home. Get up!"

"Your g-girl?" Flynn asked faintly, her eyes closing.

"Shit, yes! I'm fallin' for you, you big dope!" Reb hissed.

Flynn opened her eyes, looking very perplexed. "Me?"

"Yes, you. Now, stand up," Reb entreated. "Before a cop car, or worse, some of the Ghouls come by."

"Okay," Flynn sighed.

She coughed a little, then rose to her feet. She was unsteady, but with an arm slung around Reb's shoulders, she began to walk. They passed out of the range of the intersection's bright street lights, into the dark and swirling fog.

Oh God, don't let me lose her again, Reb prayed. Her confession of love had been a risk she had never dared with another soul. *This is the one I want. Just let me have this one for keeps and I'll quit stealin' so much. I promise!*

As they walked, Flynn croaked, "I missed you, Reb. Kinda surprised me." Then she laughed, and the laughter abruptly turned into a hacking cough.

Worried, Reb tightened the arm she'd slipped around Flynn's waist, holding the sick girl closer against her.

CHAPTER 7

On Monday afternoon, a steady rain began to drum on the streets of Seattle.

Chris and Tom were working on the exterior of their latest project, a turn-of-the-century house on Tenth Avenue, near Volunteer Park. They needed to get the exterior work completed before the autumn rains moved in to stay, but after ignoring the first smattering of drops, they realized that the weather was against them.

Tom pocketed his scraper and pronounced, "Too wet to do this safely now." Decisively, he descended the ladder.

Knees creaking as she rose from her crouch by the porch railings, Chris turned off the electric sander she was using. Alf, who had been investigating and diligently marking every other foot of the front yard, came scooting up the steps. With a sigh, he lay down beneath the shelter of the porch roof.

Though she knew it was really too early to quit, Chris hurried to unplug the sander's electrical cord. Nonchalantly, she told Tom, "Think I'll call it a day."

Tom asked, "How's that finger you cut at Allison's house?"

"It's okay," Chris answered.

"Hmmm. Must be the scraping, then," he commented dryly, watching Chris gather up the sander and the long extension cord she'd been using.

Too preoccupied to catch the sarcasm in his remark, she carried her equipment across the front porch. As she passed through the open front door, Tom followed with an armload of various-sized metal scrapers and the wire brushes.

Chris dropped the cord, then packed the sander away in its protective metal case. Absently, she asked, "What's that?"

Gently unloading the scrapers and brushes next to Chris's toolbox, Tom explained, "It's only a quarter after three. I have never seen you go home before five in the afternoon, no matter how hard it rained." He regarded Chris with a skeptical eye. "When it rains, you usually work on some indoor project."

Chris responded, "Oh."

"So, what gives?" Tom quizzed, returning to the porch for a moment and then bringing the ladder he'd been using into the house. "What's the rush? Or do you have a hot date?"

She glanced at him, feeling her cheeks getting hot.

"You're blushing like a virgin, Chris," Tom teased, his voice hushed. He placed the ladder aside and came closer. "Am I right? Do you have a date?"

"Sort of. Not formally a *date* date. It's a friend...but I like her," Chris said, her voice very quiet.

"Well, honey, congratulations," Tom said, smiling. "So who *is* she?! Dish, girl, dish!"

"Jennifer Hart," Chris mumbled, then gasped, as Tom seized her and spun her around in a bear hug.

"Girl, Girl, Girl!" Tom crowed. "You *do* have a brain—and a libido—after all!"

"Down, boy!" she yelled, and he dropped her with another infectious laugh.

Chuckling, Chris knelt down and grabbed the extension cord she had carried inside earlier. Using her elbow and the palm of her hand, she efficiently began wrapping the cord into a storable coil.

Tom knelt beside her. "So how did this get started?"

"She asked me over for dinner last night, then mentioned maybe we could do it again...." Chris finished, "And tonight is again."

"Sounds like she's been doing all the asking-out stuff. Are you going to be the femme to her butch, or what?" Tom again teased.

Nettled, Chris ignored him.

"This is a big step. You must be pretty nervous, huh?"

"What big step?" Chris asked, frowning. "Just because I don't cruise the bars every weekend, and jump into bed with one new young thing after another—like you do—doesn't mean I'm absolutely hopeless at this."

"Chris, you've spent the last five years alone," Tom countered.

"I didn't *want* to be with anyone else," Chris stated, exasperated that she had to explain it to him.

Tom shook his head. "Joyce has been gone a long time, now, and girlfriend, you may as well have gone into a convent and taken the vows. Forgive me for being dense, but I can't quite figure out your no-sex lifestyle."

Eyeing him, Chris retorted, "Ever hear of solo?"

"Oh, puh-lease," he snorted, then laughed outright.

"How is that worse than sex with strangers?"

"Divine strangers," Tom purred. "Like we tell the straights—don't knock what you haven't tried."

"I just hope you're being safe," Chris mumbled, glowering as she looked away. "You worry the hell out of me, sometimes."

"I'm a good little scout," Tom assured her. "Always prepared."

"Well, it only takes once," Chris felt compelled to point out.

There was a long pause and Chris knew she'd gone too far.

"Do you have any idea how patronizing that sounds?" he said quietly. "*I'm* the one who lost a lover to AIDS. *I'm* the one who sewed Albert's name on a damn six-by-three-foot quilt panel, and then sent the thing off to travel around the country." He sighed. "Stupid 'Names Project.' I mean, after seven years together, what a hideous way to come to terms with the end of a relationship. Adding your beloved's name to a never-ending quilt."

Feeling awful for hurting him, Chris pushed her hand into one of his and squeezed. "Tom, I'm sorry."

But Tom had turned reflective. He listened to the rain lightly thrumming on the porch roof. Softly, he said, "Sometimes, now, the only concrete reminder I have that Albert even existed is that panel in the quilt."

Rain filled the silence.

"I love you, Tom," Chris offered resignedly.

"Me too. I didn't mean to bug you," Tom returned. "Guess I sorta catch myself wishing I was a lesbian, sometimes."

Perplexed, Chris asked, "Why?"

"Oh, no meat-market dating scene. No obsessive worship of youth and physical beauty. No AIDS carving away at the ranks of your friends." He gave her a sober wink and tugged on the sleeve of her oversized workshirt. "To say nothing of being able to publicly cross-dress, day in and day out."

Chris laughed, but was still left wondering if he really meant what he'd just said. *God, he's been through so much.* She fumbled with her toolbox, straightening up the contents. She darted an assessing look at him, wondering if she dared pursue the topic further.

"Are you scared of caring for someone, again, Tom?"

Tom pursed his lips, thinking. Then deliberately answered, "Terrified."

Nodding, Chris conceded, "Me too."

They didn't dare look at each other. In all the years since Tom had lost Albert and Chris had lost Joyce, they had never discussed this.

"I keep thinking," Chris admitted, "that I could never get hurt like that again and live through it."

"But gay folks are gutsier than most people," Tom commented. "We have to be, just to be who we are in this Holy Christian Age." He grinned at Chris. "I keep wanting to write a play. Title it, 'The American Inquisition' or, 'Fuck Right, Dammit.' I'll just string together actual quotes of Pat Robertson, Newt Gingrich, Pat Buchanan and Jesse Helms, and there's the script! All we'll really need is lots of cosmetics and sequins for the queens!"

Preoccupied, Chris only managed a faint smile. *Can I do this? Do I have the guts to try again?* And then a sudden thought hit her. *What if Jennifer doesn't want me?* She frowned, stunned by the possibility. *But she has to....*

"Hey, don't worry," Tom was saying. "It's all serendipity, anyway, you know."

"What is?" she asked.

"Love. Finding it, making it, keeping it."

From the corner of her eye, Chris watched him moving gracefully beside her. With a clean, soft rag, he wiped raindrops off the scrapers and wire brushes, then sorted the implements into her open toolbox.

All at once she realized how accurately he read her.

He's right. Arranging to do something with Jennifer tonight is an incredibly big step and I'm freaking out about it.

Feeling chagrined, Chris confessed, "I'm not even sure if Jennifer likes me. I think I get on her nerves, sometimes."

"Hmmm," Tom murmured. "I can see how that might happen...."

Mildly exasperated, Chris faced him. "Oh, you can?"

Ignoring the question, he closed up her toolbox. "You're cooking for her?"

"I'm taking her to the Wildrose," Chris replied, and found Tom saying the last three words with her.

He rolled his eyes in disgust. "Lesbians!" he proclaimed to the chipped ceiling. "I take it all back! I would *die* if I had to live such a culturally deprived existence."

"They have great veggie burgers!" Chris insisted, then couldn't help laughing as Tom expounded, "Haute cuisine, to be sure."

Toenails clicking on the hardwood floor, Alf padded in from the porch and watched Chris expectantly.

"You're *too* predictable," Tom told Chris. "See that you at least pick up the tab, or I'll lose all respect for you. So far, Jennifer seems to be out-butching you at every turn."

"Maybe I've just grown more accepting of my feminine side," Chris cracked.

"Next thing I know," Tom responded, "you'll be decked out in come-fuck-me pumps."

"I don't think so," she remarked serenely. "You've got all the high-heel action cornered in this town." Chuckling, Chris grabbed her toolbox and strode toward the door. Alf hustled to stay in front.

"And don't forget it!" Tom called after her. "And hey— at some point tonight, you *might* consider kissing the lady!"

From the front steps she protested, "I'm not as fast as you!"

"Well then speed up!" Tom exhorted. "Because I'll bet Miss Jennifer can kiss like a house on fire!"

The sweet thrill of hearing those words stayed with Chris all the way home.

If only the Ghouls would quit hanging around Reb's ware-house, Flynn thought. *I just want to go to bed and stay there.*

Tired beyond belief, Flynn followed Reb through the rain. She ached all over and she was sweating, even with her motorcycle jacket open. She wished that they had been able to get into the squat this morning, instead of having to spend the day wandering from one coffeehouse to another.

Sitting inconspicuously at small tables, or in hard booths, never buying anything, they had both repeatedly fallen asleep. Eventually, at each place, they wore out the counter help's bored tolerance and were asked to leave.

Reb stopped in front of a quaint-looking restaurant. Above the door hung a neon sign, but Flynn felt too weary and sick to lift her head and read it.

"You wait in here, out of the rain," Reb instructed firmly, pulling her into the vestibule. "I know somebody who works in the kitchen. Former street kid who made good," Reb explained, then laughed softly. "I'll see if I can hit her up for some soup." Her eyes moved over Flynn's face, more tender than Flynn had ever seen them. "You look like you could use it."

Flynn nodded, then shivered as she watched Reb go through the entrance.

Jennifer was on the passenger's side of the truck cab, Chris was behind the wheel. In between them, Alf was sitting up straight, looking around with all the presence of royalty.

I hadn't expected that the dog would be coming along, Jennifer thought. *But he really is kinda cute.*

As if aware of her thoughts of him, Alf looked over at her with a panting-smile. Satisfied that she was paying proper attention to him, he returned his gaze to the scene beyond the windshield.

Chris was competently navigating the truck through a series of puddles at the edges of the wet street. A light rain had been falling for the last few hours. It had slowed the Monday-night flow of rush-hour traffic as Jennifer drove home from the university, causing her to arrive home later than usual. When she had finally turned into the drive and parked her black Saab, Chris had jogged over and met her on the front porch.

Is this a date? Jennifer wondered, gazing over Alf's head at the circumspect woman behind the wheel. She frowned, confused. *I keep telling myself that I don't want to get involved, and yet here I am, having dinner with her for the second night in a row.*

Chris glanced over at her and smiled. "Have you ever been to the Rose before?"

God, what a smile... "No. What's it like?"

"Oh, it's sort of a beat-up little cafe with a jukebox and a couple of pool tables and all these lesbians hangin' around."

"Good food?"

"The best," Chris enthused. "The Wildrose offers it all, from vegetarian fare to cheeseburgers. And there's a wide selection of micro beers, as well as great espresso drinks." Diverting her eyes from the road for a moment, Chris flashed that quick, disarming grin. "But what I really like is that it's always lively in there. I like the energy level."

With one hand, Chris turned the steering wheel right and Jennifer noted that they were traveling onto Pike Street.

Scanning the street, Chris said, "Between the Rose and the Cafe Paradiso, this block looks all parked up. We're gonna have to park farther down the street and walk. Is that okay?"

"Sure," Jennifer murmured. After a brief silence, she ventured, "Do you come down here often?"

"Tom and I have dinner at the Rose once in a while," Chris explained. "He raves about the Reuben sandwiches they serve, but I think he does it just to get me out of the house. It's a little too timberjack for him," she said, her eyes twinkling.

She pulled into a parking space and turned off the truck engine.

"Timberjack?"

"Yeah," Chris admitted, blushing. "You know, rough around the edges. Like a timber town bar. Only the local toughs are all dykes." Chris laughed. "Like me."

"You're rough around the edges?" Jennifer asked ingenuously, studying Chris's denim jacket, faded jeans and cowboy boots.

"Don't you think so?" Chris responded.

Jennifer waited until Chris pocketed her keys and made eye contact. "No," she replied, scratching Alf's ear. "I think that you like to give the impression that you're tough, but anyone who has seen you treating this dog like your child knows that's not true."

"And you've seen me treat Alf like my child?" Chris asked.

Jennifer thought she spoke a little breathlessly.

"I live right next door to you," Jennifer mentioned. "I see plenty." And then Jennifer just couldn't say anything more. *God! That sounded like you were coming on to her!* She nervously looked away from Chris. *Am I coming on to her?*

All at once, the truck seemed stifling, and she had to get some air. Impulsively, she opened the door and jumped out.

On the other side of the vehicle, Chris exited, too. As Jennifer moved to the sidewalk, she noticed that Chris had left the driver's window partially open at the top for Alf. The springer spaniel had shifted into Chris's seat, behind the wheel, and he was watching them mournfully.

"I'll bring you a burger," Chris told him. "I promise."

They fell in step, walking side by side in the fine, soft drizzle. Chris's black cowboy boots clicked on the sidewalk, and Jennifer felt the cool moisture gathering on her face.

It was close to six o'clock, that period of the day when the long twilight begins, and even with the overcast skies, it is still light enough to see. While Pike Street was just ten blocks from the upwardly mobile neighborhood where they both lived, it primarily featured rundown warehouses, restaurant-bars, and secondhand clothing stores. This was clearly an area of the city which had seen better days. Except for the group of scruffy-looking boys standing at the corner, the street was deserted. Yet, as they walked, Jennifer had an odd sense of déjà vu, as if she had done this before, and recently.

She glanced over at Chris and found the keen blue eyes lingering on her. "What?" Jennifer laughed.

"You look...wonderful," Chris offered, seeming very pleased.

Self-consciously, Jennifer looked down at her open tan anorak, forest-green corduroy shirt, and khakis. *Back in Philadelphia, Gail used to accuse me of looking like a slob whenever I dressed like this.* "Thanks," Jennifer managed to reply.

"Here we are," Chris announced, as they slowed before the old-fashioned storefront on the corner.

Jennifer immediately noticed two high, broad, showcase-style windows on either side of a vestibule, which led to a recessed door. Then her eyes were drawn to the colorful neon sign which hung overhead, proclaiming "The Wildrose." Rich aromas of delicious food suddenly permeated the cool evening air. And a faint but recognizable song could be heard on the jukebox. K.d. lang's "Constant Craving" filtered out to the rainy sidewalk.

Chris led the way into the vestibule, where they passed a tall girl in a black motorcycle jacket. Head down, shoulders hunched, the girl with auburn hair was leaning against the window, obviously seeking shelter from the wet weather. Smoothly, Chris opened the door and waited for Jennifer to walk into the warm, vibrant cafe.

Instead, Jennifer stopped, her eyes shifting irresistibly back to the girl in the black leather jacket. She took in the guarded posture, the grimy, baggy jeans, the muddy black Converse sneakers. Suddenly, her breath coming fast, she thought, *It's just like the dream....*

"Jennifer?" Chris asked solicitously.

Without attempting an explanation, Jennifer stepped up to the girl and dared to place a gentle hand on her shoulder. The youngster raised her head, startled, but allowed Jennifer to turn her around.

Glassy, denim-blue eyes focused on Jennifer. It was an attractive face, even with the blue smear of a fading bruise dominating the crest of one cheek. Still, the flush on her face wasn't quite natural and she looked exhausted.

It's not Laney, Jennifer thought, torn between dismay and relief.

The girl coughed into her hand, a harsh, congested sound, then croaked, "I'm waiting for my friend. She's talking to someone." Nervously, she motioned with her thumb toward the inside of the Wildrose. "I won't stay here long. Honest. I'll be gone soon."

For some reason, that last part echoed in Jennifer's mind. *I'll be gone soon.* It was the plea of the streets, a phrase Jennifer had heard in Philadelphia, in New York City, in Washington, D.C. The incessant promise to move on, made to those who owned property by those who did not. Hearing it from this tall child made Jennifer feel as if, somehow, in her striving toward personal success, she had missed recognizing and performing some important duty, some true reason for her being alive.

"Do I know you?" Jennifer asked, feeling a great, pressing familiarity at the back of her mind.

The girl eyed her, a trace of fear entering her expression, though she was probably trying with all her might to hide it. "No," she uttered, subtly moving away from the window.

Chris let the door close and came to Jennifer's side. They both watched the girl shuffle away from them, out into the rain. She stood on the sidewalk, uncertain, watching them watch her. Then, apprehensively, she peered down the street. With another harsh cough, she shoved her hands into her jeans pockets and lurched into an unsteady walk. Chris and Jennifer moved forward to watch her travel slowly down Pike Street, heading in the direction from which they had just come.

"Look at the way she's walking. Must be a druggie," Chris surmised sadly.

"Maybe," Jennifer differed. "Or maybe she's ill."

"Well," Chris sighed, "whichever, there's not much we can do about it. No one can save these kids from themselves." She turned and went back to the door, then held it open for Jennifer once more. "Like Allison says, they ought to just stay home."

With one last glance at the figure retreating down the street, Jennifer yielded to Chris's unspoken summons and entered the cafe. *I feel as if I should help that kid. She's obviously afraid of anybody who's too interested in her, and I certainly don't know her...but still....*

Plagued with an odd sense of guilt, Jennifer followed Chris to a table by the window. *What on earth is the matter with me?* she wondered, irritated with herself. *I actually expected that girl to be Laney! Laney's been dead six years now. I ought to be further along in dealing with it by now!*

She sat down heavily in the chair Chris pulled out for her. Oddly depressed, she turned toward the window and stared out at the row of sleek, wet motorcycles parked by the curb.

Minutes later, Chris was staring at the menu, feeling uneasy. *I could've done something for that kid. Bought her a sandwich or given her a few bucks.* She glanced over her shoulder at the door. *Instead, I decide she's on drugs and walk right by her.*

Suddenly, a brash, young voice cut through the crowd noise.

"Did anybody see where my friend went?"

The Wildrose quickly quieted.

A short, reed-thin girl in an oversized red-and-white high school letter jacket stood just inside the front door, holding what looked like a bowl of soup. "The kid in the black leather?" the girl prompted impatiently.

Women began murmuring among themselves.

The teenager quickly moved to an empty table and set the steaming bowl aside. "C'mon, c'mon! It ain't that hard a question!"

What's she doing in here? Chris wondered.

Nearby, a young woman with glasses scraped her chair back and replied, "The good-looking babe in the doorway?"

When the teenager responded with a curt nod, the woman pointed over at Chris and Jennifer. "I saw those two hassling her a couple minutes ago."

"What?" Chris blurted out, incredulous. "We weren't hassling her. My friend thought she recognized her, that's all."

In seconds the short girl in the red-and-white letter jacket was planted next to her chair. Chris wrinkled her nose at the distinct body odor emanating from the girl's clothes.

"Hey," the girl hissed, "whatever you thought you were doing, you scared her off and she really needs me right now, okay?" With a monitoring eye on Jennifer, the street kid went on, "Just tell me which way she went."

"She's ill, isn't she?" Jennifer asked, her voice earnest.

"Yeah! Now, which way?" the girl demanded.

"I'll help you find her," Jennifer volunteered, then had her coat half on as she headed for the door.

The girl hustled to follow Jennifer out of the restaurant. Chris shook her head, a little amazed at how fast her plans for the evening were changing. *What the hell...* she thought, and grabbed up her faded denim jacket.

Outside, Chris was jogging through the rain to catch up with them, when she heard a dog—a dog that sounded like Alf—barking hysterically. Intuitively, Chris accelerated to a full sprint. Jennifer and the unknown girl with her also broke into a run, but as the sense of dark foreboding seized Chris, she flew by them.

From a block away she could see her white pickup truck. The driver's side window was broken and the door was thrown open. Her heart pounding, Chris searched for Alf as she ran, and then finally saw him.

A boy came from behind her truck, staggering onto the sidewalk. He was using a thin rope looped around Alf's neck to drag the springer away. Leaping and pulling against the crude leash, Alf was wild-eyed, and began barking louder when he saw Chris racing toward him.

The boy kicked at the dog, shouting, "Shuddup!" while struggling to keep a grip on the rope.

And then, from the opposite side of the pickup, a form in a black jacket hurtled into Chris's view. Diving recklessly at the boy holding Alf's leash, the black-jacketed figure tackled him, literally slamming the dognapper to the wet pavement. The two bodies rolled across the sidewalk and Alf struggled against the rope, yanking himself free. Still barking, the frightened springer spaniel dashed for Chris. Two more boys suddenly emerged from the other side of the truck and tried to grab the short rope trailing behind Alf, but they both missed.

One boy followed Alf's headlong flight with his eyes and spotted Chris approaching. The boy's nose was streaming blood, and Chris instantly knew that this scene had been well under way before they had ever heard Alf's barking. Though he grabbed his blond friend by the arm, the boy was shaken off; his friend was busy landing a series of blows to the back of the kid in the black leather jacket.

Chris slowed to a trot, scooping up Alf's rope. The dog reared up on his hind legs and leapt at her, clawing and whining.

The boy who was staring at Chris easily read her rage. He shouted, "Flash, Moon, run! It's over, you assholes!" before he spun about and fled down the street.

Undeterred, the other two boys continued to pummel the person who had dared to intervene on Alf's behalf.

A red blur went tearing past Chris, shrieking, "Get off her!"

It took Chris a moment to realize it was the girl in the red letter jacket. Like a tiny human torpedo, she plowed into the sturdy blond boy, hitting him at top-speed and causing him to stumble backward before he grabbed her by the arms.

As Jennifer came to a gasping stop beside her, Chris turned and thrust Alf's makeshift leash into her hands.

"Hold Alf for me," Chris ordered.

With a huff, Jennifer said, "I don't think so!" She hustled Alf closer to a parking regulation sign and swiftly tied him there.

Fighting to get free of the boy, the street girl was raging, "Dammit Flash! Let her alone!"

"No fuckin' way, Reb!" he snarled.

Reading the vicious intent in his eyes, Chris was moving, running at the boy. In the same second, Flash unleashed a vicious punch, catching Reb in the stomach and physically lifting her into the air with the force of it. Mouth open, soundless, Reb fell to the wet sidewalk and curled into a ball. Flash raised a booted foot, preparing to stomp her.

Furious, Chris barreled into him, taking him to the ground. They rolled on the rain-slick cement and Flash ended up on top of her, raising his fist for a punch. Then, instead of striking, the boy's fist simply jerked to a stop in midair. Above them, Chris saw Jennifer, clenching the boy's upraised arm in both hands.

Roaring in frustration, Flash struggled to free his arm. Finally, he threw himself off Chris, onto his back, and Jennifer abruptly lost her grip on him. Swiftly, Chris scrambled away and leapt to her feet.

Nearby, his buddy, Moon, continued to curse and grapple with the black-jacketed figure. Glimpsing red hair, it finally registered with Chris that the fighter in the black jacket was the girl who had stood in the doorway at the Wildrose.

"Hey, pretty lady," Flash was crooning to Jennifer.

Jennifer was backing up, and instinctively, Chris moved to shield her.

"You gonna fight me, bitch?" Flash jeered at Chris.

For an instant, Chris was held by the coldest eyes she had ever seen. The fact that those eyes leered at her from a face too young to manage a beard made Chris's stomach churn.

Warily, fists up, Chris prepared herself. Nervous sweat formed on her brow and trickled down her back. She was so awash in adrenaline that she was shaking.

Laughing, the boy began to taunt her. "Cunt-lickin' lezzie! Pussy-eater! Queer!"

From the corner of her eye, Chris saw the figure in the black jacket blast a punishing knee into the bigger boy's groin, then roughly push him aside. The girl was determinedly rising from the sidewalk. She swiped the back of her hand across a bloody lip, then squared off against the big blond teenager taunting Chris.

Flash took one glance at the girl and did a comic double-take.

The tall girl crouched slightly and sidestepped closer to him. Without saying a word, Chris and Jennifer flanked her on either side.

"Stupid dykes!" he yelled, then backed up a bit, focusing on the tall girl. "Man, you're gonna pay for this!"

The girl said nothing, only gave her head a little shake, as if trying to clear it. Chris felt a twinge of concern, for a goose-egg was easily visible on the girl's forehead when the straight, wet chestnut hair shifted.

"Flynn, be careful," the smaller girl gasped, arms still wrapped helplessly about her stomach.

With a weary, acknowledging wave of her hand, Flynn followed Flash into the street, and Chris and Jennifer stayed right beside her. The girl was wheezing, squinting into the rain as if it was hard for her to see. But her single-minded pursuit caused the small hairs on the back of Chris's neck to stand up.

A police siren sounded in the distance. *Someone called the cops,* Chris thought. *Thank God.*

"Fuck! The cops are comin'! Help me, Flash!" the boy on the sidewalk whined. "She damn near broke my balls!"

"Help yourself, Moon, you asswipe!" Flash growled back.

He stabbed a finger at Flynn, declaring, "I ain't done with you!" Then he took off at a run. In seconds he had rounded the corner and was gone.

Moon groaned as he got to his feet. Slowly, he began to hobble away from them, then turned into the first alley he passed, disappearing from view.

Hearing Alf's bark, Chris glanced at the parking sign to verify that he was still safely tied there. Jennifer saw her worried gaze and said, "I'll go get him."

The police siren was growing steadily louder.

With a slight moan, the small, dark-haired girl rocked into a sitting position, her eyes fastened on the tall one who was still standing alone in the street. "Flynn," she called. "Flynn, c'mere."

The big girl turned and strode back toward the smaller one. "Reb, I had to," she began hoarsely, touching a finger tentatively to the large bump on her forehead. "I saw them break the window. They were stealing him...the dog...and he was so scared...." Suddenly, her legs wobbled and she was down on one knee.

Reb and Chris both surged toward her, and Reb just managed to catch the girl as she rolled to the pavement. Kneeling next to Reb, beside the fallen redhead, Chris found her sensitive nose registering the sharp stench of stale perspiration.

Lights flashing, siren screaming, a patrol car screeched around the corner. Chris looked up at it with relief, but did not fail to catch the panic on Reb's face.

"Shit!" she cried. "Get up, Flynn! Get up!"

"It's okay—I'll tell them what happened," Chris said, trying to reassure her. "She'll probably need to go to the hospital...."

Fiercely, Reb interrupted her. "No! They're just gonna pin somethin' on us and lock us up!" She leaned over her unconscious friend, and with a trembling hand tenderly wiped blood from her face. "Flynn, please, wake up!"

The police car skidded to a stop twenty feet away and two uniformed officers quickly emerged. A man came rushing out of a store across the street, shouting that he had been the one who had called them. Pointing at the little group of women, he began giving an excited account of the disturbance that had just broken up.

"Really, it's okay," Chris reassured Reb. "I owe you two. I won't let them do anything to you...."

Her frightened eyes on the policemen, Reb half-stood, looking for a moment as if she were going to run. Then, tears in her eyes, she sank back on her heels. A heartbreaking despair swept over her face. "I can't leave her. I *can't!*"

The small, thin cop broke away from his partner and the shopkeeper, running into the alley down which the injured boy had disappeared.

Jennifer moved to Chris's side. As Alf wiggled with joy and licked Chris's face, Jennifer whispered in Chris's ear, "Tell the police the girls are your nieces."

"What?" Chris asked, pushing Alf aside long enough to get a look at Jennifer's tense face.

Flynn opened her eyes just then, looking up at them as they huddled over her. Reb gave a deep sigh of relief.

Jennifer continued to whisper in Chris's ear. "Don't let them call an emergency medical vehicle or do anything else that ends up with the redhead getting taken to a hospital."

"Why not?" Chris asked, baffled. "The kid's a mess! It's obvious that she needs medical attention."

"Parental consent laws," Jennifer hissed. "These two are runaways. She'll end up in the custody of Social Health Services. They'll either track down her real parents or she'll be consigned to a foster home. Trust me on this"

"Is that so bad?" Chris whispered back.

"Jesus, lady," Reb interjected contemptuously. "How long you been on this planet?"

Annoyed, Chris stared at her. Then she remembered reading a newspaper account of a recent court case. Physical and sexual abuse had been taking place over a period of years in a local state-run home for teenage boys; the twelve-year-old concerned had reported the crimes, and no one had believed him. At age nineteen, he had gathered the irrefutable testimony of countless other victims and was successfully suing the state for not protecting him.

Shit! What the hell is happening to this country? Chris despaired. *Why doesn't anything work the way it's supposed to anymore?*

The heavyset policeman left the shopkeeper and began to approach them. Watching him apprehensively, Flynn began struggling up to a sitting position.

Jennifer slipped closer to Flynn, supporting the injured girl around the shoulders while Reb glared at her. "You ought to lie down," Jennifer told Flynn.

The girl looked over at Jennifer and stammered, "I-I think I j-just fainted." She leaned her head on her knees and drew a tremulous breath. "Reb? That guy hit you, right? You okay?"

The hostile expression on Reb's face changed, and Chris marveled at the loyalty and love in the smaller girl's gaze. "Yeah," she retorted. "Worry about your ownself."

The small, thin officer came out of the alley alone and jogged over to join his partner. He gave a shake of his head and muttered that the boy had gotten away. A moment later, both men came to a stop next to Chris.

Gruffly, the heavyset one barked, "The shopkeeper gave us a rundown on things. Want to file a complaint?"

"Yes!" Chris began heatedly. "Those hoods broke into my truck and tried to steal my dog—"

Smoothly, Jennifer interrupted, "Well, they got away, all the same, didn't they, Chris? What's the use of making a big thing out of it?" Before Chris could reply, Jennifer continued, "Shouldn't we get your nieces home now?"

The officer frowned. "Lady, I know these girls are street kids. They're probably Ghouls, too, and were meant to serve as a diversion. We'll take them off your hands now."

Beside her, Chris saw the fear on Reb's face intensify. With her large brown eyes fixed helplessly on the officer towering over her, the formerly smart-mouthed punk was suddenly just a scared kid.

Making a great effort to appear reasonable, Jennifer addressed the officers in a jesting tone. "Street kids!" she laughed. "Hey, I know they look the part—we can't get either one of them to dress like they have more than a dime in their pockets." Smiling charmingly, Jennifer explained, "But they aren't street kids and they certainly are not part of that gang. These girls live with my friend and me over on Sixteenth Avenue."

"Sure, lady," the shorter officer chuckled. "And I'm married to Demi Moore." While the other officer laughed heartily, the small, narrow-eyed one stated, "Sorry. I know your heart's in the right place, but we gotta take these girls in for routine questioning."

"Flynn," Reb whispered, so quietly that Chris barely caught it. "Can you stand?" The big girl gave a slight nod. Reb informed her, "We gotta bail."

Both girls stood and the tall one immediately swayed.

Impulsively, Chris stepped close to her, lifting one long arm and ducking under it. *There's no way this kid can run. And the other one won't leave without her. They're helpless.*

Gathering her wits, Chris stated, "The *real* criminals high-tailed it out of here before you arrived, and that's the sad truth. Now, you and I both know you're just following procedure. There are better ways to spend your time than going any further with this."

Reb gaped at her.

Looking bored, the heavyset cop opened his mouth to protest.

Chris cut him off before he even began. "They're going home with me," she asserted, then immediately thought, *What am I saying?*

The big policeman stepped forward and placed a hand on Flynn's other arm. In that instant, Chris turned and saw the dazed, hopeless expression on her face.

"Sorry, lady," the big cop reiterated, pulling Flynn toward him.

Furious, feeling like a grizzly protecting her cub, Chris tightened the arm she had wrapped around the tall girl's waist. "Get your hand off her," she snapped.

The cop glared back.

"My name's Chris Olson and you can check me out with Mayor Rice and Chief of Police Stamper. We worked together during this summer's Habitat For America program."

The officers looked unimpressed, until Jennifer added, "Or contact Officer Dorothea Jance. She can vouch for Chris."

At that, the narrow-eyed cop put his hands on his gunbelt and remarked to his partner, "I heard dispatch on the radio a little while ago, calling Jance's number. She's close by. We could ask her to take this detail off our hands."

"Do it," the heavyset officer barked, releasing Flynn's arm and eyeing them silently while his partner retreated to the patrol car.

Six minutes later, another patrol car pulled up and Thea climbed out of the driver's side. After a brief discussion with the other policemen, Thea motioned Chris away from Jennifer and the two girls. Quickly, Reb slipped in to replace Chris's supportive arm under Flynn, then steered her friend over to the curb where they both sat down.

As soon as the three older women were alone together, Thea supplied, "They tell me you want to take these kids home with you."

Chris nodded, scowling at the other officers. Rapidly, the rainy evening was getting darker. Already hungry, and wet, she was also thoroughly fed up with this low-level bureaucratic foot-dragging. Irritated, she muttered, "What's the big deal? No one even cares that the big kid can barely stand up! They care more about following police procedure than the fact that these kids didn't commit a crime—they stopped one!"

With a puzzled grin, Thea inquired, "You going into social work, Olson? Or just growing a conscience?"

"Do you want to hear what happened or not?" Chris demanded.

"Go on," Thea answered, her voice mild.

"While Jennifer and I were at the Wildrose, some hoods broke my truck window, then tried to steal Alf." Genuinely puzzled, Chris broke off and asked, "Why, Thea? Some sort of new malicious mischief, or what? What do they want with a dog?"

"They sell stolen animals—dogs and cats, both—to fronts. The fronts are usually adult couples who check out as law-abiding citizens." Frowning, Thea purposefully looked away from Chris. "These upstanding citizens then up the price and resell the pets to the University of Washington's research labs. They use the animals in medical experiments."

"Shit!" Chris yelled, grimacing as she realized how close Alf had come to a grisly, forlorn death. "Why don't you arrest these people?"

"They're hard to catch in the act. And dogs and cats can't exactly testify against anyone, now can they?"

"Well, someone caught them tonight!" Chris hollered.

"Calm down, Olson," Thea coaxed. "These are street girls, and the law says we gotta run a check on them."

Angrily, Chris told Thea, "That tall girl stopped three boys and got the crap beat out of her in the process. I'd say I owe her more than standing by while some official police response gets her hauled before a judge and consigned to our gloriously inept Social Health Services system."

Hands on her hips, Thea moved to one side and studied the two girls near Jennifer. The tall one was hunched over, her eyes closed. The smart-mouthed short one was smoking a cigarette and talking to Alf. Thea watched her telling him to "bite those guys next time." She even demonstrated by growling and snapping her teeth. Thea shook her head.

"That little one sure looks like trouble to me," Thea rumbled. "And I think your pugilist is the one that bowled me over at the YWCA last week. Looks like someone gave her a haircut since then, but I remember that black eye. I don't forget a face. Especially after an assault."

"You said it wasn't an assault. You said she was just afraid," Chris contended.

"Chris, honey," Thea chuckled, "every runaway in this city is afraid. And unfortunately, it's made some of them damn mean. They'll do whatever it takes to survive."

Stubbornly, Chris asserted, "I have to do this, Thea. I'm taking them home. They can stay with me for a while."

"Chris, pardon me for being obnoxiously frank," Thea explained, "but you have no absolutely idea what you're taking on here. These girls are probably practiced thieves, maybe prostitutes as well. They may be infested with lice or crabs. They may even have AIDS...."

"Shit," Chris breathed. "Just because someone is having a bad time doesn't mean they're not human beings any more."

She glanced over at the girls and made herself lower her voice. "They're not invisible, dammit! I *see* them." Taking a deep breath, she ran a hand through her hair. "I admit that I've been very involved with myself and my own problems for a long time now. But something happened tonight and these two kids did the right thing and ended up getting beaten right before my eyes. I can't pretend that the system works and just hand them over to it." Meeting Thea's eyes, Chris finished, "In my gut I know what's right and I've got to do it. They're sisters, you know."

"I thought so," Thea answered. "The little one keeps giving Jennifer that 'touch my girl and die' look."

Chris laughed, and Thea joined in, slapping Chris's denim jacket with her hand.

"Girl," Thea said, sobering, "you're letting yourself in for some major gray hair."

Shrugging, Chris allowed, "It's turning gray, anyway. May as well have it from caring as from not caring."

"Humph," Thea answered. She put an arm around Chris's shoulders and squeezed. "Welcome back to the community, girlfriend. This town needs all the big, strong Amazons it can get." Then she pushed Chris toward the three waiting for her on the curb. "Go on home now. I'll have to call in some favors, but the official report will say that everyone ran off."

She started to go, then turned back. "I'll have Molly roust out Jane Harada and stop by your house later on. Give your new children a medical." Thea shook her head and laughed softly all the way to her patrol car.

Good-naturedly, Chris stuck out her tongue at Thea, and went to tell the others the news.

Minutes later, Chris, Reb, and Flynn climbed into the truck cab for the short trip to Sixteenth Avenue. Thea and her partner followed close behind in the squad car, giving Jennifer and Alf a ride home in style.

CHAPTER 8

I need a smoke, Reb thought nervously.

Unfortunately, she had chain-smoked several cigarettes in a row back on Pike Street. Fidgeting beneath the gaze of three cops and two yuppie dykes, waiting for them to decide what to do, had driven her into a nicotine fit. Now the box of Marlboros in her pocket was empty, and though she and Flynn had somehow avoided getting hauled down to the station, she still wasn't sure that the alternative would be any less hazardous.

She surreptitiously studied Chris Olson's profile as the older woman drove. *Oh, shit! This is the truck I broke into! And Flynn's wearin' the jacket I stole! And now here's this lady takin' us home with her. When's she gonna ID that jacket and start raisin' hell?*

Unaware of Reb's covert scrutiny, Chris made a right turn, leaving Fifteenth Avenue and slowing down the vehicle. They were entering a quiet residential neighborhood on the east side of Capitol Hill. Reb silently checked out what the streetlights illuminated: large, older homes, surrounded by spacious lawns and tall, thick-trunked trees.

Rich-people territory, Reb told herself.

Chris made another right turn, and the pickup truck rumbled into a narrow street. Then Chris braked beneath several big maples, her hands pulling the steering wheel left this time. The pickup truck bounced softly over the lip of the driveway and coasted to a stop on the gravel strip that divided two grassy lawns.

On either side of the driveway stood two huge Victorian houses, each one half-hidden in the murky shadows at the edge of the streetlights' reach.

She's got money! Amazed, Reb nudged Flynn with her elbow.

With the barest wisp of a cry, Flynn lifted her head and squinted at Reb in confusion.

Man, she's really hurtin', Reb fretted. "Hang in there, buddy," she whispered, taking her friend's hand.

Chris hopped out of the truck and came around to the passenger's side. Opening the door, she stepped back to allow Reb to slip out, then moved in and reached for Flynn.

Firmly, Reb announced, "*I'll* help her," and wedged herself in front of Chris's lean frame. A surprised, faintly amused expression crossed Chris's face before she gave way.

In the back of her mind, Reb reminded herself that she had to resist being blinded by whatever wealth and comfort this stranger had to offer. It was up to her to be the responsible one here. Flynn was ridiculously inexperienced and her rocky state of health had been further eroded by that wild fistfight. And more than one street kid had ended up on someone's sexual menu at a fancy address such as this.

"C'mon out, Flynn," Reb coaxed.

"Where are we?" Flynn asked, moving clumsily off the edge of the passenger seat and into Reb's arms.

The full weight of her five-foot-nine-inch body transferred to Reb and only Chris's sudden intervention kept Reb from crashing to the ground with Flynn on top of her.

Plucking one of Flynn's arms off Reb's shoulders, Chris casually draped it around her own. She paused to ask Reb solicitously, "Okay if I help, now?"

Just keep your hands where they belong.

The police car that had been following them most of the way pulled into the driveway behind them. From her position beneath Flynn's other arm, Reb felt her friend's entire body stiffen with trepidation.

"Chill, Flynn," Reb whispered. "It's gonna be all right."

The black female officer climbed out of the driver's side and then opened the back door. Quickly, the brown-and-white spaniel and Jennifer emerged.

The dog bounded up to Chris and proceeded to repeatedly jump up on her, while Chris asked him, "When you gonna start guarding that truck, huh?" Alf wiggled his little stub of a tail so hard that his entire hindquarters shimmied.

He's nuts about her, Reb discerned. Since she had great faith in the abilities of pets to judge human character, Reb began to relax a little.

Chris fished in her jeans pocket, then held her keyring out to Jennifer. "Would you mind doing the honors?"

With a nod, Jennifer came forward and took the keys, then turned back to the police car. "Good night, Thea," she called. "You were wonderful. Thanks for everything."

"No problem," Thea acknowledged. Then she fixed Reb with a hard stare. "Do wrong by these folks and you better not stay in this town long enough for me to find you."

Knowing a hollow threat when she heard one, Reb simply smirked and replied, "Yeah, right."

She glanced up to find Chris gazing at her with a faintly puzzled expression. Feeling vaguely nonplussed by that steady regard, Reb dropped her eyes.

Chris shifted her attention. "Ready, Jen?"

Reb looked up again in time to see Jennifer nod, and then casually toss back her shoulder-length, light brown hair.

She's awful pretty, Reb reluctantly decided. Quickly, she glanced up at Flynn to see if she had registered this fact, yet. But the redhead's eyes were closed, and her head sagged forward, as if she were nearly asleep on her feet.

Seeing Reb's concerned gaze, Chris called good night to her policewoman friend and began to turn. Reb hustled to stay in step with her, as they followed the dog and Jennifer up the drive and then across the lawn to the front porch.

Wearily, Flynn staggered between Chris and Reb as they helped her up the steps, across the gleaming white paint of the wooden floorboards. Jennifer opened the front door and went in to turn on a light.

Chris told Reb, "It might be easier to get through the doorway with her if you turn sideways and lead the way inside. We can probably do the same to get her upstairs for a bath."

Reb nodded. *Be ready for anything,* she told herself. *Flynn and me ain't gonna do tricks, no matter what.* A moment slid by, and lights in the house went on.

They crossed a blue-gray carpet, and Reb's eyes swept over a comfortable-looking room. These were belongings that were well-cherished, as evidenced by the neat, homey arrangement of furniture, the faint scent of lemon wax emanating from an array of polished wood surfaces. There was a stereo in the bookshelves by the fireplace, a big-screen television across the room, a grandfather clock in the nook by the wide staircase. Reb tried to nonchalantly take it all in before anyone noted the impact it was having upon her.

Shit! These people are livin' in fuckin' Heaven!

At the edge of the staircase, Reb turned slightly, leading the way upstairs. Chris continued to support Flynn from the opposite side, but most of the effort of climbing the steps was on Reb's shoulders. Exuberantly, the dog charged by them, intent on getting in front of the impromptu parade.

"Whoa, Alf!" Chris called, but the dog had already knocked Reb off balance.

She paused on the fifth stair, straining to regain her stability. Suddenly, her vision darkened, and she began to sink under Flynn's limp weight.

"I have her," Chris was saying, though it seemed from a far distance. There was a jarring thump and then Reb found herself sitting on the stairs. Jennifer was in front of her, one hand on each of Reb's shoulders, peering anxiously into her face. Reb turned and saw Chris carrying Flynn up the rest of the stairs.

"You nearly fainted," Jennifer said. A tender hand cupped Reb's cheek. "Are you okay?"

Distressed to find herself losing it like this, Reb nodded. *You have to watch out for Flynn. Get up!* Carefully, she stood, ignoring Jennifer's steadying hand on her back.

Reb hustled up the stairs to join Chris and Flynn in what had to be the largest bathroom she'd ever seen in a private home. The room was at least twelve feet by twelve feet, and was dominated by gleaming white fixtures and a subtle, silver-blue design on white wallpaper.

"Wow!" Jennifer commented from behind her. "This is immense." Her head swiveled back and forth as she gazed about her with wide hazel eyes.

Confounded, Reb considered her. "Don't you live here?"

"No," Jennifer returned, then glanced over at Chris and a deep rose blush spread from her neck up to her face. "I live next door," she clarified. "Chris and I are neighbors. I guess we're a little late in making introductions. I'm Jennifer Hart." She reached out and shook Reb's hand.

Neighbors, Reb mused apprehensively. *Maybe I'm wrong to trust them. This could turn into a swingin'-singles party after all.*

"Chris Olson," the curly blonde one disclosed, as she settled Flynn on the old-fashioned Shaker bench along the far wall.

Toenails were clicking busily on the ceramic tile floor, and though distracted, Reb noticed that Alf was continuing to oversee events. The dog sniffed Flynn's jeans for a moment, then sat down next to her and leaned his shoulder into her knee.

A second later, Reb looked up to find a pair of keen blue eyes resting on her. "And you two are...?" Chris asked expectantly.

Reb hesitated, then figured, *Aw, what the hell.* "They call me Reb." She motioned at her friend. "This is Flynn."

Both Chris and Jennifer looked down at the girl in the chair. She sat slouched over, her elbows planted on her thighs. Her ultramarine eyes were half-lidded and fixed uncomprehendingly on Chris's black cowboy boots.

Worried, Reb moved forward. "Flynn, I think we're about to get you washed up. Think you can deal?"

Flynn nodded, then closed her eyes. She mumbled something Reb couldn't quite hear, but Chris, who was closer, bent down to listen.

Whatever she heard, Chris straightened up, looking stunned.

"What did she say?" Jennifer asked.

With an angry grimace, Chris stepped back and swung around to the oversized bathtub. She set the drain stopper and twisted the faucets, letting the water drum hard and fast into the shining porcelain tub. She moved about the room, gathering washcloths and shampoo and several towels, and placing them near the tub. The flurry of activity only ceased when Jennifer caught her by the arm as she passed.

"What did she say?" Jennifer repeated.

Stiffly, Chris reported, "She said...'Please don't throw me down the stairs again.'"

There was a moment of tense silence, as both women turned to stare at Flynn.

"My God," Jennifer finally whispered.

Reb flicked a resentful glance at them, embarrassed for Flynn, embarrassed for herself. *She's out of her head with fever or she never would have said that. When I went dizzy on the stairs and nearly dropped her, it probably brought it back. She's lost track of where she is, and what's goin' on.* Pierced with anguish, Reb moved to her friend's side.

"If you don't mind," Reb asserted, "I can take it from here, I think."

Both women began protesting. "You're not in much better shape yourself," Chris began forcefully. "Let us help you," Jennifer persuaded.

"I think she'd want it this way," Reb said, standing fast on her decision. "She's real shy."

"This is dangerous," Chris insisted. "What if she falls?"

Jennifer, however, was backing out of the room, taking Chris's hand as she passed her. With firm authority, she tugged the unwilling Chris closer to the door. "Go ahead, Reb," Jennifer pronounced. "We'll be getting a room ready for you both. But give a shout if you need help, okay?"

"Okay," Reb agreed, watching them go.

Alf hurried to trot after them.

The door closed softly. Reb could hear Chris carrying on, still arguing the point as they went down the hall.

Reb placed a hand on Flynn's shoulder. "Help me get you undressed, buddy."

A short while later, Chris knocked on the bathroom door. "I've got a couple of terrycloth robes here," she called.

From inside, a muffled voice instructed, "Put them on the floor by the door. We'll be right out."

Grumbling to herself, Chris did as she was told and then retreated to the doorway of the room across the hall.

Seconds later, the bathroom door cracked open. A hand reached out, grabbed the two robes, and dragged them inside. In another few minutes, the door opened fully, and the two young women appeared, swathed in white terrycloth. Reb was dwarfed in Chris's robe, but on Flynn the same size left at least two inches of the taller girl's wrists exposed. Their identical, freshly washed, bowl-cut hairstyles gleamed in the overhead hallway light.

Then Chris noticed that Reb was studying her suspiciously, her eyes hard and her feet set in a combative stance.

One's sick as a dog and the other has a major chip on her shoulder, Chris thought, feeling overwhelmed. *Still, they both look more human now, and they certainly smell better.*

"Flynn needs to lie down," Reb told Chris.

"Right this way," Chris said, and turned, gesturing at the well-lit bedroom behind her.

As Reb helped Flynn cross the hall, Chris walked into the bathroom and shook open the plastic trash bag she carried. Quickly, she began tossing the clothing they'd been wearing into the bag.

"Whatcha doin?" Reb called from the bedroom door, and Chris turned to meet an accusing stare.

"Your clothes will need a couple of cycles in the washing machine," Chris stated, depositing the bag by the hamper. "In the meantime, I've put some socks, T-shirts and sweatpants out on the dresser for the two of you, so you'll have something to wear."

Nervously glancing at the fresh clothes, Reb seemed skeptical.

Chris retrieved the jackets the girls had been wearing, and left the bathroom.

Reb visibly tensed.

"And yeah, I recognize this," Chris confirmed, examining the black motorcycle jacket she carried. She walked by the girls, into the bedroom, then casually placed both jackets on a chair by the window. "Guess my sixty dollars is long gone, though, huh?"

Reb stared back at Chris, mute. Beside her, Flynn's glazed, dark-blue eyes focused on the double bed. Blinking wearily, she seemed oblivious to the tension between Reb and Chris.

Softening, Chris said, "Go ahead, Flynn. Have a seat."

Flynn broke free of Reb's light grip on her elbow, weaved over to the bed, and sank onto the mattress gratefully.

"We can't stay, Flynn," Reb began, and Chris came to her side, interrupting her. "You *can.* Just don't steal from me again."

After a brief silence, Reb agreed. "It's a deal, lady."

Downstairs the doorbell rang.

"That's probably Molly, and Doctor Harada," Chris explained.

Reb huffed. "No doctors!"

"Oh, come on, Reb," Chris insisted, irritated. "Look at Flynn! Jeez—look at yourself!"

"Doctors gotta report shit! I shoulda known better than to trust a couple of damned yups. Next thing I know you'll be tryin' to get us to phone our stinkin' parents or somethin'!" With a quavering breath, Reb tried to yank Flynn to her feet.

She's panicking again. You're the adult here—take control of this before she starts heading for the street. Chris forced a laugh, placing a hand on the bewildered Flynn's shoulder and firmly pushing her back down to sit on the bed. "Reb, honest, this doctor won't be making any reports. Jane's doing me a favor."

"We don't need no favors!" Reb shouted.

"And here I thought *everyone* in the state of Washington wanted free medical advice," Jane joked from the doorway..

Chris and Reb both turned toward the door and watched Dr. Jane Harada enter. She set her black bag down, knelt on one knee and appraised the flushed girl sitting quietly on the edge of the bed.

Flynn's fever-bright eyes narrowed. "Don't send me home," she stated, her husky voice barely audible.

"I promise I won't," Jane replied. "I want to help you. Okay?"

Flynn nodded slowly.

Looking contentious, Reb reluctantly sat down beside Flynn.

"I'll be taking your blood pressure first, then listening to your heart and lungs, then taking your temperature."

Satisfied by Flynn's nod of assent, Dr. Harada asked, "Any allergies to medications?"

"No," Flynn croaked.

"Are you taking any drugs?"

"No," Reb snarled.

"That's quite a black eye," Jane said to Flynn, studying her face. "By the discoloration, I'd say you didn't get that tonight. You've had it for a few days now. Want to tell me how it happened?"

Flynn coughed nervously and looked away.

Taking the hint, Jane let the question go unanswered. After taking a blood pressure reading, she put on her stethoscope and slipped her hand inside Flynn's robe. Reb sat forward to see better, and the doctor winked at her. After listening for a few minutes to the left and right sides of Flynn's chest, Jane stood and slid her hand and the stethoscope down Flynn's back, beneath the terrycloth robe.

Jane gave a slight gasp. Then, gently, she peeled Flynn's robe down off one shoulder.

Chris moved closer to see what Jane had found. The girl's skin was mottled with fading, yellow-green contusions, a virtual smear of discoloration that covered most of the visible area of Flynn's back and shoulders. Chris couldn't believe her eyes.

Reb jumped up and grabbed the edge of the robe, jerking it back in place. "It's none of your business!" she declared angrily.

Unperturbed, Jane lifted Flynn's auburn bangs and studied the lump on the girl's forehead. Holding up two fingers, she asked, "How many?"

Flynn squinted. "Two," she mumbled.

"Any prior head injuries?" Jane quizzed.

"I...fell down some stairs last week."

"Fell, huh?" Jane murmured.

Reb threw a warning look at Chris.

Jane picked up the generic medical form and began recording information. "Are you nauseous?"

"Yes."

Jane turned to Chris. "I'd really feel better about this if we could get a CAT scan and some x-rays."

"No hospitals!" Reb retorted loudly.

Unfazed, Jane faced Reb. "Did you two eat today?"

"Hey, I been on the street two years, Doc," Reb replied. "Missin' a few meals don't kill ya."

Jane raised an eyebrow at Reb, but didn't dispute it. Gently, she slipped a small digital device into Flynn's ear. A moment later, Jane peered at the thermometer readout. "Temperature of one hundred two," she announced. Bending to meet Flynn's downcast eyes, she asked, "How long have you felt sick?"

Flynn asked, very slowly, "What day is it?"

"Just since last night," Reb volunteered.

Jane nodded. "I'd like to draw some blood so I can run a few standard tests," she told Chris, then reached into her medical bag and brought out a large syringe.

Flynn saw the needle and her eyes widened. "I won't do it anymore." Her voice grew louder, breaking with emotion. "Don't lock me up—please don't lock me up! I'm not crazy. I'm not queer."

"Whoa," Jane exhaled, returning the syringe to her bag. "Sounds like someone's on the run for good reason."

Reb put her arm around Flynn, whispering, "Chill, buddy."

Flynn ran a hand over her face, then turned to Reb, slowly calming down. She mumbled, "Can I go to sleep now?"

"Soon," Reb answered soothingly.

Chris watched in amazement as Reb tenderly held her.

"I'm only going to draw some blood," Dr. Harada told Flynn.

Sighing, Flynn nodded.

A few minutes later, Dr. Harada was dismantling the syringe and storing the vial of blood in her bag. "Flynn, I think you may have a bad case of respiratory flu," she stated.

Flynn mumbled, "I won't do it again...."

"Shhh," Jane soothed. "Let's get you in bed."

Jane peeled back the covers. Flynn made a childlike sound as she crawled in and nestled her head into the pillow.

"Sleep tight, buddy," Reb whispered, as Flynn immediately dropped into an exhausted slumber.

Jennifer looked up from the pot of chicken noodle soup she was stirring as Chris walked into the kitchen. Beside her, Alf leapt to his feet, his tail wagging. Nearby, in the narrow pantry visible off to one side, Molly Webster was sorting through Chris's meager food stores and scribbling away on a notepad.

Chris called hello to Molly, then addressed Alf. "I might have known you'd be down here mooching." With a slight smile, she finally rested her eyes on Jennifer. "Need some help?"

"No, it's all ready, thanks," Jennifer returned. Concern was clear in her eyes as she asked, "What'd Jane say about Flynn?"

Wearily, Chris pulled out a chair and sat down at the table. Alf parked himself right beside her, his head in her lap. Chris idly stroked him as she relayed Jane's diagnosis.

"Jane's still up there, giving Reb a routine checkup," she concluded, reaching for one of the sandwiches Jennifer had arranged on a plate placed in the center of the round oak table. "And I think I might ask to have my head examined before she leaves."

There was a muffled chuckle from the pantry. "Chickening out already, Chris?" Molly called.

"No, just seeing things a little more clearly," Chris told her. "I don't regret bringing them home with me. After all, Flynn *did* save Alf...." She stopped and took a cautious peek at the door, as if making sure what she was about to say was not

overheard by the wrong person. "But that little one—Reb—
jeez! Ornery as hell. And she's acting like I've got some sort of
kinky sex angle going on here—like I'm just waiting 'til she lets
her guard down to whip out a pair of handcuffs."

"That's probably exactly what she thinks," Molly agreed,
coming out of the pantry. "And rightfully so, Chris. She's probably received a proposition or an unwanted pass with every
handout she's ever gotten."

"But I'm a *woman,* for God's sake," Chris objected. "And
a lesbian to boot!"

"And if she obviously knows that," Molly reasoned, "and
still doesn't trust you, the girl must have met some predatory
lesbians."

Chris frowned. "I find that a bit hard to believe."

Uneasily, Jennifer thought of Gail. After their breakup,
Gail had often jested about driving through Philadelphia on a
cold winter's night, cruising for a good-looking street girl to
take home and use as a bed-warmer. *Only for some reason I never
really thought she was joking....*

"It doesn't matter what you believe," Molly told Chris,
pausing beside her. "What matters is what *she* believes."

"Jeez," Chris groaned. "No psycho-babble, please."

Alf grumbled and nudged Chris's leg, anxious for a piece
of the cheese sandwich Chris held.

Molly grinned good-naturedly. "Think of her as a stray
pup and you'll get the gist of what's going on." She made a
note on her pad of paper, then elaborated, "You're going to
have to be patient and win her trust. Kind of like taming a pet
that was forced to live wild for a while."

Her brow furrowing as she thought that over, Chris took
a bite of her cheese sandwich.

Half an hour later Jane came into the kitchen, put her
medical bag on the hutch in the corner, then walked over to sit
in the chair next to Chris.

Taking her cue, Jennifer began ladling chicken noodle soup into bowls.

Meanwhile, Molly tore a sheet of paper from the note-pad she held and set the paper in front of Chris. "Your pantry is a disgrace, Chris...."

Shrugging, Chris mumbled around her mouthful of food, "Don't eat here much."

Taking a sandwich, Jane commented, "You're under-weight."

Chris muttered, "Am not."

Once more, Alf complained that he had no cheese and Chris told him to lie down. Harrumphing, he threw himself down by her chair, obviously disgusted with her.

Moving around the table, Jennifer placed a bowl of soup before Chris and Jane. They thanked her, while Molly sat down, leaning over to tap the grocery list in front of Chris.

"The point is," she went on, "you need to go to the store and stock up on some nourishing provisions." Molly, too, helped herself to a sandwich, saying, "You've got two half-starved young'uns on your hands now, and believe me, once they start recuperating they are going to eat like you'll not believe."

"Jane, if you don't mind my asking, what's their overall state of health?" Jennifer asked. She went back to the counter by the stove and retrieved two more bowls of soup.

Irritably, Jane replied, "You mean, what's wrong with them besides the debilitating effects of poor nutrition, lack of shelter, brutal physical abuse and chronic exhaustion?" She blew out a breath, then asserted, "Well, the good news is I didn't find any track marks, so they're not heroin addicts...."

In the hallway which led to the kitchen, Jennifer spotted Reb standing and listening, eyeing Jane coldly. One by one, all the women followed Jennifer's gaze. Reb's proud, youthful face took on a sort of bitter resignation. Jennifer wanted to take her into her arms.

"Since I've already met Flynn," Molly announced, "you must be Reb." With a warm smile, she encouraged, "Come on over here and have something to eat."

Reb's big brown eyes fastened on the plate heaped full of sandwiches.

Jennifer brought two more bowls of soup to the table and set one down in front of Molly. The other bowl, she placed before an empty chair. When Reb advanced as far as the doorway and then stayed there, looking unsure, Jennifer walked slowly over to her.

Standing with her back to the others, Jennifer murmured, "Sorry. Jane probably needs a caffeine boost...."

Reb's mouth twitched up, as if she was barely managing to suppress a laugh.

"Besides, I made all this for you and Flynn, and now these characters are the ones pigging out on it."

Subtly peeking around Jennifer, Reb considered the food on the table.

Jennifer enticed, "I hope you like ham and cheese."

"On wheat?" Reb breathed, her face suddenly wistful.

"With mustard," Jennifer affirmed.

Reb's hands darted into the pockets of her robe, and she straightened up to her full height.

Moving aside, Jennifer returned to the table, saying, "Chris, would you please get Reb a glass of milk to go with her sandwich?"

And then she plucked the ham and cheese on wheat bread from the plate of sandwiches and placed it on the plate before the empty chair. Seconds later, Reb slid into the seat and grabbed it.

Alf promptly moved to Reb's side and adoringly dropped his head in her lap. After a few gentle pats, Reb tore off a piece of cheese and gave it to him.

"So, Chris," Molly asked, her eyes on Reb as the girl took an enormous bite, "let's be fair to Reb and talk about parameters. What do you have in mind? An overnight? A stay till Flynn is over the worst? A possible visitation policy so the girls can come and go in the future—maybe do some laundry or take an occasional bath?"

By the refrigerator, Chris flicked a surprised look at Molly, then at Jennifer. She opened the milk carton and filled the glass on the counter with deliberate care.

She hasn't planned any of this, Jennifer thought. *Poor Chris. She invited them here out of impulsive gratitude and she's just now understanding the magnitude of what she's done.*

But then Chris shocked her by saying, "What parameters? Reb and Flynn are welcome to stay as long as they like."

Reb, who had been pretty much wolfing the sandwich, stopped chewing. Her cheeks were gorged with the load she'd crammed into her mouth and her brown eyes were wide. Stunned, she watched Chris carry over the glass of milk and then place it in front of her.

"Is that realistic, Chris?" Molly intoned, all at once very professional. "It isn't fair to give the girls false hopes."

"Screw realistic—is it sensible?" Jane Harada asked.

"Like I said, you're welcome to stay," Chris said to Reb, altogether dismissing Molly and Jane. "It's a big house and there's plenty of room. I'll ask you to work, of course. If not at some outside job you get on your own, then with me and Tom in the construction business. What do you think? Is it a deal?"

Vigorously, Reb nodded her head. She studied Chris with a trace of bewilderment.

"Just so we're clear," Chris continued, her eyes locked with Reb's. "Certain things are out—like drugs or stealing or lying. Other than that, I won't try to be your mom...but I'll be here for you if you need me." She stopped and thought a moment, then shrugged. "We'll work the rest out as we go along, I guess." With that, Chris sat down and returned to eating her sandwich.

No one spoke for a moment, and then Jane remarked, "Chris, some of these kids aren't exactly the young victims they seem...."

"Jane," Chris said quietly, "Reb is a guest in this house."

Looking very serious, Jane gripped her sandwich. "Some of them are junior con artists...."

"That's enough," Chris said emphatically.

The icy gaze that accompanied that last phrase made Jane sit back and fall silent. For a few minutes, a heavy quiet hung over the table.

Jennifer sat down and nibbled her food, watching the others. As Reb finished her sandwich and slurped spoonfuls of soup, she remained stoically withdrawn. Delighted with the cheese Reb had given him, Alf stayed by his new friend's side. Molly continued scribbling new items on the list of supplies Chris would need.

Throughout the deafening silence, Jennifer found her eyes returning, over and over again, to Chris. The tousled blonde hair still showed the effect of the exposure to the wind and rain earlier. She looked tired, but her cheeks and eyes were aglow with something Jennifer had not yet seen in them.

Chris looked over at her and caught her gaze. She managed a sheepish grin before dropping her eyes to her empty plate. Deep within, Jennifer felt her pulse quicken in response.

Stern-faced, Jane Harada finished quickly, rose and took her dishes to the sink. "I'm outta here," she announced, then went for her bag. "Come on, Molly. I've got early rounds tomorrow."

Without waiting, Jane strode out of the room.

Slower to leave, Molly tore off several pages of notes and placed them before Chris. Then she turned and favored Reb with a concerned smile. "I hope you'll forgive Jane. She lost a boy she really cared about today. A heroin overdose."

Reb murmured, "Yeah, I get it," though she seemed perplexed by Molly's attempt to smooth things over before she left.

Chris stood and companionably walked Molly out of the kitchen and down the hall. Alf trailed behind them, as ever, keeping an eye on what Chris was up to. Jennifer could hear

Chris sincerely thanking her friends as they lingered by the front door.

Left alone with Reb, Jennifer regarded the girl for a moment, then asked, "Will you promise me one thing?"

Reb grinned like the Cheshire cat. "Sure. What?"

"Don't confuse Chris with all the other adults who've used you and hurt you."

The grin gone, Reb looked away.

In a soft, persuasive tone, Jennifer added, "She's had her share of rough times...you know?"

Reb got up from the table. "I'm real tired."

"Promise me, Reb," Jennifer coaxed.

Sarcastically, Reb asked, "You want my word?"

"Aren't you a woman of honor?" Jennifer returned, purposefully answering the question with a question.

Frowning suspiciously, Reb demanded, "What are you— a teacher or somethin'?"

"Will you promise to give Chris a chance?" Jennifer pressed. "And not take revenge on her for the mean things other people may have done to you?"

Reb stood there, deep in thought. "Yeah," she said at last, her voice sounding very young.

Jennifer and Reb contemplated one another. The front door closed and a moment later Chris and Alf entered the kitchen.

"Where do you want to sleep?" Chris asked Reb. "You can have your own room if you want it. With Flynn being so sick, you might sleep better alone."

Casting her a disparaging look, Reb retorted, "Right." She patted Alf and then walked past Chris, out of the room.

Halfway down the hall, she stopped, then turned. "Oh...um....thanks." She stood there a moment, fiddling with the ends of the terrycloth belt that secured her robe. "Thanks a lot. You won't regret this, lady." She met and held Chris's eyes.

Then she shoved her hands in her robe pockets and quickly made her way down the hall.

Chris looked at Jennifer incredulously and silently mouthed, "Lady?"

Clapping a hand over her mouth, Jennifer smothered a laugh.

Shaking her head, grinning, Chris meandered over to the kitchen table and began collecting dishes. Alf sighed contentedly, then lay down under the table. Jennifer moved to the sink and began rinsing off the plates and utensils already waiting there.

Quietly, efficiently, they eased into working as a team. While Jennifer finished wiping off the table, and then the countertop, Chris began slipping the few remaining sandwiches into small cellophane storage bags.

Watching Chris, Jennifer at last brought forth the question that had been skimming through her head for hours. "Um...I have to know, Chris. Did you do this because of...what I told you last night? Because of my sister Laney?"

Chris's fair brows furrowed. "I'm not sure," she said. She didn't look up from the small stack of bagged sandwiches she carried to the refrigerator. Thoughtfully, she opened the door and placed them on a shelf. "Something happened...out there on the street, tonight. Something inside me...." She stopped.

Moving closer to her, Jennifer asked softly, "What happened, Chris?"

Carefully, Chris closed the refrigerator door and stood there, her blue eyes down. The soul-searching underway was apparent in her solemn face. Though close enough to touch her, Jennifer did not. Instead, she waited nearby, until Chris raised her head and met Jennifer's gaze.

"They were so...brave." Chris confessed, "It kinda made me ashamed of the way I've been living. Always protecting myself."

Jennifer nodded, understanding. Reaching out, she tenderly pushed an errant curl back off Chris's forehead. "But if these girls stay here with you..."

Distracted, Chris watched Jennifer's hand retreat from her hair.

"Have you ever been around teenagers for any length of time?" Jennifer asked. "Are you sure you know what you're in for?"

"Don't you think I can handle it?" Chris asked pensively.

"Well," Jennifer equivocated, "I don't want to see you hurt."

Utterly silent, Chris stared at her. Then, slowly, she closed the space between them, leaning down. "Why are you so concerned about me?" she quizzed, her voice low.

"Um...I...I...."

Mesmerized, Jennifer felt the hand slip around her waist, felt the gentle pull into the kiss. And then, with that first brush of lips on her own she was lost. She felt herself being enfolded, being gradually, delectably consumed by the sweet mouth moving over her, kissing her, claiming her. With this one kiss she knew something monumental was beginning.

Oh, my God....

Amazed at herself, amazed at the soft power of Jennifer's responsiveness, Chris at last stepped back from her. Her arms still around Jennifer, she whispered, "I don't want you to go home."

Jennifer searched Chris's eyes. She looked flustered, but answered steadily enough, "Thanks, but I think you've made enough life-altering decisions for tonight, don't you? Why don't you just walk me home, instead."

"Okay," Chris managed, wondering if this meant that she was being rejected. She'd been sure she had sensed interest in Jennifer, even concern.

"Don't look so worried," Jennifer murmured, leaning forward to kiss her cheek. "I'll be back tomorrow. As soon as I'm done at the university, I'll come over and help you with your nieces." And then she chuckled, in a rather breathless way that made Chris narrow her eyes.

And suddenly Chris understood. Jennifer was leaving her for the night, but it was not an easy thing for her to do.

Later, after she'd escorted Jennifer home and then stood in the backyard while Alf did his nightly business, Chris went about her own routine. She walked through the house with Alf by her side, locking up and turning off lights. And as she moved through the habits of years, her mind was in chaos.

What a night. First, I bring two strange kids home with me like they were a couple of abandoned kittens. And then I up and kiss Jennifer—just grab her and kiss her—like I go around kissing women in my kitchen all the time!

She climbed the stairs, thinking about the commitment she was making to the girls in the bedroom across the hall. Anxiety over this new responsibility made her throat close so tightly she could barely breathe. She had to stop at the top of the staircase and remind herself of the anger she had felt when she saw the fear and hunger on those youthful faces.

Stop asking "what's wrong with this country?" Stop acting like it has nothing to do with you! she scolded herself. *It's your country! What's wrong with you that you're willing to look the other way while gay kids are treated like excess garbage—just thrown out—dumped?* For a moment she stood there, gripping the banister, fuming. *If gay people won't look out for their own, then who else will? The Christians? Ha! Like they looked after all the guys who got AIDS!*

Sighing, Chris leaned down and stroked Alf. "Well, it looks like we've got some unexpected company, huh, boy?"

Together they moved across the hall. Deciding to take a chance on offending Reb, Chris pushed open the partially closed bedroom door. She needed to check on Flynn one more time in order to put her mind at rest. In the light cast from the hall, Chris could see two forms beneath the bed covers.

Stealthily, she moved forward.

Flynn was on her side, facing Chris, and behind her, eyes closed, Reb was spooned against the bigger girl's back.

Cautiously, trying not to frighten Flynn, Chris gently placed her hand against the girl's cheek. Flynn's face was hot and moist. Feverishly, she turned from Chris's touch, muttering something Chris couldn't understand.

Worried, Chris went into the bathroom, fetched a clean washcloth and ran it under cold water. She wrung it out, then brought it back to Flynn and placed it on the girl's forehead. Quietly, she brought a chair over to the side of the bed. She sat down, deciding she'd better stay up for a while.

Alf, who had been following her around, curious, tried to get up on the bed. When Chris wouldn't allow it, he lay down on the floor, groaning, feeling woefully sorry for himself.

A short while later, feeling as if someone were watching her, Chris squinted through the darkness. And there were Reb's sleepy, distrustful eyes, fixed on her.

She couldn't help wondering how long Reb had been monitoring her every move.

CHAPTER 9

Flynn rolled out of an embrace. She knew it was an embrace, knew in some part of her mind that it was Reb even before she opened her eyes and saw her.

A faint, golden light painted Reb's heart-shaped, elfin face. Her eyes were closed, her face was utterly relaxed. Sleep had transformed her. For once, the gutsy, cagey street punk looked sweet, innocent, childlike. An overwhelming surge of affection rose in Flynn, startling her.

My friend.

She recalled Reb holding her, whispering things to her, while the room seemed to contract and expand around them in a surreal dance. Puzzled, Flynn silently began taking stock of herself, wondering what had happened. She found she was wearing a half-open robe and nothing else. Her hair felt damp, so did the robe. And then she remembered that at one point she'd been sweating, had in fact been covered with sweat. Reb's voice had offered the quiet explanation, telling her that she was fighting a fever, but that everything was going to be okay. While Reb had held her, someone else had wiped her face with a cool, wet cloth.

Time had passed since then.

How much?

She knew she was no longer alternately burning up or shivering violently. But there was a wheezing sound accompanying each breath she took, and her thoughts were a fuzzy, disjointed muddle.

Where am I? What's wrong with me?

Feeling sluggish and uneasy, she pulled the robe closer around her and pushed herself up on her elbows. She frowned against a mild headache, determinedly surveying what she could see of the dimly lit bedroom. Relieved, she at last decided that the vague outline of colonial-style furniture meant she was not in an institution.

Not yet, anyway.

Beside her, in the glow of a nightlight, a middle-aged woman with short, curly hair was sitting in a chair, watching her.

"Go back to sleep," the woman said.

"Who are...?" Flynn ventured, and stopped, surprised by how hoarse her voice sounded. Then she saw the springer spaniel who peeked over the side of the bed. *Oh yeah.* "He's your dog?"

"That's right," Chris whispered. "You've been pretty sick. The fever broke just a few hours ago. My doctor friend, Jane, says it's a respiratory flu. You're supposed to get plenty of rest. And Reb will skin me alive if I let you wear yourself out talking to me."

Flynn nodded, oddly pleased by that last remark. Feeling incredibly groggy and tired, she eased down into the warm bed.

For some unknown reason, she impulsively reached out and stroked Reb's cheek. *Janet Belden never cared for me like this.*

Reb stirred, murmuring, "'S'okay Flynn," as she moved into her arms and burrowed closer.

Flynn's last conscious thought was of how good it felt.

In the morning, Chris showered, changed clothes, then stumbled downstairs to phone Tom. Not feeling energetic enough to tell him the whole tale, she merely told him that something had come up and she wouldn't be at the job site today. He immediately launched into a series of innuendos about her date with Jennifer. So sleep-deprived that she was incapable of refuting it, Chris instead dissolved into an incredibly silly snicker.

"What's so funny?" Tom demanded, sounding intrigued.

"Well—as yet, there's no Mama Bear, but I've got two hungry Baby Bears upstairs waiting on some porridge, so excuse me, but I've gotta go." And with that, she hung up the phone and started making breakfast.

No more than twenty minutes later, Tom arrived at the back door, dressed in his work clothes. Laughing, Chris let him in and returned to readying the breakfast tray. He glanced at the plate of buttered toast, the three glasses of juice and the three bowls of oatmeal, then fixed Chris with a look filled with consternation.

"You go without sex for years and then you throw yourself into a ménage à trois!"

"Oh sure. You just missed the contortionist. She wanted to stay, but the circus leaves town today...."

Tom interrupted. "If you don't tell me what's going on, I'll scream!"

Chris gave him a brief rundown of events. By the end, he was staring at her in disbelief. She ended with an embarrassed shrug, then muttered, "And I swear if you call me 'Mother,' even just once, I'll brain you."

In answer, he grabbed her and delivered a bone-crushing hug.

"God, I love you, you big, beautiful dyke!" he enthused. Just as Chris realized no more air could be forced from her lungs, he released her and grabbed the tray. "Now, put a hustle in that bustle, Flo Nightingale."

Chris followed him out of the kitchen, down the hall. "So you don't mind helping? Maybe providing a positive male role model...or even letting me bring them into the business as apprentices?"

Tom laughed over his shoulder. "Don't tell me! We'll start their training with a variety of paint-scraping techniques!"

"No," Chris insisted, so intent on setting out her tentative thoughts that she didn't even register his teasing. "I want to *really* train them, give them a marketable skill, so that from here on out they have a means of supporting themselves. I also want to try to get them to finish high school, maybe try for college, if they want to...."

He turned at the foot of the stairs, studying her. "Ah, Chrissie. Don't get too far ahead of yourself here." Ever the realist, Tom asked, "What if they're already corrupted? What if they're already so skilled at living outside the system that they can see no reason to try living within it?"

Chris frowned, thinking of Reb. "One is quite a smart-ass. She may be hard to bring around," she admitted with a sigh. "The other one, I don't know. She's very sick—although from what I saw last night, she can fistfight like Mohammed Ali."

"And that's probably fueled by huge amounts of suppressed anger," Tom surmised. "She may be harder to deal with in the long run than the smart-ass." He gave Chris an encouraging wink. "But we got sledgehammers in the renovation business, and many's the day I have vicariously pounded someone's head to smithereens while tearing out drywall!"

"Don't I know it," Chris acknowledged. "Molly Webster was over last night, with Jane Harada. They've volunteered their future services, too. That's a social worker and a doctor...and with Jennifer we have an educator...so we seem to be acquiring a panel of experts." Worriedly, Chris rubbed the back of her neck, wondering for the hundredth time if she was up to this task.

Tom was looking around, perplexed. "Where's your slobbering beast? I have food in my hands and he's nowhere to be seen."

"Alf's upstairs, in bed with the girls," Chris said, breaking into a smile, "He's very busy getting belly-rubs."

"Oh, God," Tom groaned, taking the steps two at a time while Chris hurried after him. "Can he possibly be more spoiled than he already is?"

Reb liked Tom immediately.

He told Flynn and Reb that they were gifts sent from Heaven, since Olson, Morrissey & Wheeler had all these construction jobs lined up and Chris was, of all things, falling in love and fast becoming a shirker.

While Chris made faces and loudly denied this, Tom went on to remark on how thin Reb was. In a confidential whisper, he informed her that any self-respecting dyke had to be at least two hundred pounds in order to properly fill out the required flannel shirt.

Chris swatted him and told him he was, as usual, a great argument for the separatist lesbian lifestyle. He, in turn, told her that he was very sorry to break the news, but the capacity for multiple orgasms did not mean that lesbians were the most highly evolved life form.

He managed, in less than five minutes, to fill the room with laughter.

As Reb laughed at his banter, another part of her mind remained serious. For the first time, she began to weigh the possibilities. Could this really be a safe place for Flynn and her, a place where they might dare to linger? At least for a little while?

While Tom entertained them, Chris ate quickly. Moments later, she excused herself, saying that if anyone in the house was ever going to eat another thing, she had to go grocery shopping.

Tom volunteered to stay with "the girls," as he called them, while Chris was gone. He took Chris's place in the chair by the bed, and began flipping through a several-months-old copy of *Curve* magazine.

"I know—I'll read you a story," Tom announced magnanimously.

Alf settled himself happily at Tom's feet as Tom began reading aloud from an interview with Melissa Etheridge. Listening to his deep baritone had a soothing effect on Reb. Her suspicions about these people and what they really wanted were gradually subsiding. However, another more troubling worry was presenting itself.

After only a few spoonfuls of oatmeal and a bite of toast, Flynn's hand markedly shook as she returned her breakfast to the tray on the bedside table. Reb watched, feeling helpless, as her friend covered her mouth and barked a series of alarmingly harsh coughs. When they at last ended, she dragged in a desperate breath.

"Hey, you okay?" Reb asked, smoothing her hand over the back of the T-shirt Flynn wore.

Nodding wearily, Flynn stretched out.

Reb pulled the covers up over her friend, studying her pale features with concern. *She'll never make it on the street while she's this sick. And she's got enemies now...my enemies....*

Flynn closed her eyes.

"That lady left out some aspirin for you. How about sittin' up and I'll getcha a glass of water to take them with?"

Flynn groaned a sleepy refusal, but Reb bounced out of bed and went to the bathroom to fill her empty juice glass. When she came back, she cajoled Flynn into sitting up and swallowing two pills from the small bottle Chris had set on the nightstand. Then Flynn began coughing again, so Reb made her take the cough medicine Chris had also left.

At one point, as Reb was deflecting Flynn's softly spoken yet undeniably crotchety responses, Reb looked up to find Tom observing her. He had the most empathetic look in his eyes, as if he knew what it was to be so worried about someone. She shook off her initial annoyance about being spied upon, and turned her attention to taking Flynn's temperature.

The digital thermometer read 98.6° Fahrenheit, and Reb felt a wave of relief that at least the fever seemed to have abated.

Flynn was on her back, her eyes closed. Quietly, she murmured, "Reb? Would you...lie close to me? Like last night?"

Tom kept his eyes carefully on the page and went on reading.

Feeling very special, Reb set the thermometer aside and crawled into bed. Gently, she settled her head on Flynn's shoulder.

Flynn was soon asleep, and Reb lay beside her quietly, staring at the ceiling, allowing herself to savor the luxury of lying in a warm, clean bed. The background comfort of Tom's deep voice eventually ceased, but she could hear him turning pages every once in a while. The house was quiet, and Reb couldn't fight off the unexpectedly drowsy feeling of bliss. Against her best intentions, she, too, fell asleep.

She woke with a start.

The sunlight in the room had shifted; a clock on the dresser told her that it was a little past noon. Though initially guilt-stricken, she was encouraged to find that nothing much had happened during her lapse in guarding her friend. Flynn was still right next to her, buzzing a congested-sounding snore. When Tom saw her sit up, he reported that Chris was downstairs, unpacking groceries.

A short time later, Chris stopped by the bedroom to say she would be on the third floor, in her room, taking a nap. Tom waved her on and quickly enlisted Reb's help in making lunch.

While Flynn continued to sleep, Tom and Reb descended to the kitchen.

While rattling pans and talking a mile a minute, Tom coached Reb in the preparation of a meal full of tasty, soft foods to tempt Flynn's palate. Soon they loaded the tray again and marched upstairs with an assortment of tasty foods. Even so, Reb had to coax Flynn into finishing the plate of scrambled eggs, buttery, steamed squash, and chilled applesauce. Once again, the minor effort of sitting up brought on a prolonged coughing spell. Afterwards, Flynn snuggled beneath the covers and within minutes fell asleep again.

Reb shoved her hands in the robe pockets and followed Tom as he carried the tray of dishes downstairs. "Is she gonna be okay?" Reb asked, trying vainly to keep the anxiety from her voice.

"Sure," he answered soothingly, then waited for her on the stairs. "Chris and I are expert nurses, you know." As she came even with him, he reached out and put a big arm around her shoulders.

Reb froze, alarmed at being touched by a man—even a gay man—and he instantly recognized her fear. The arm fell away as quickly as he had placed it on her.

Tom continued down the stairs and after unconsciously hesitating, Reb once more trailed after him. *I gotta quit freakin' over everythin'. I haven't even properly cased the house. There could be tons of stuff lyin' around, just beggin' to be jacked.*

"How come you're expert nurses?" Reb asked, trying to fill in the heavy silence. "I thought you were carpenters or somethin'."

She had the feeling that Tom was reading something into the way she'd reacted to his attempted hug, and she was afraid of where that might lead. She had a set-in-stone policy of not answering anyone's questions about her past. It wasn't so much that she was afraid to reveal what had happened to her as it was that she was reluctant to confront the events by talking about them. It just seemed so much easier to cope by living each minute, with no thought of past or future.

Tom strode down the hall, toward the kitchen, talking over his shoulder as he went. "Chris and I learned to take care of people because we had to. My lover, Albert, got AIDS. Toward the end, Chris, Joyce and I nursed him in shifts. You've heard about Joyce? Chris's partner?"

Reb shook her head.

"Oh," Tom said. He placed the tray on the counter and opened the dishwasher. "Well, anyway, Jane Harada—who was Joyce's former girlfriend—drilled us in medical techniques until we were awesome." He smiled fondly at some memory.

"So where's this Joyce?" Reb prodded. "They break up?"

Looking miserable, Tom began rinsing dishes and loading the dishwasher. "Joyce died five years ago, and soon after, so did Albert. With Albert, we at least knew, had time to accept it—if you can ever accept the fact that someone you love is dying." Carefully, he placed the plates and glasses on the racks.

"But Joyce... God, she was here one day, gone the next. Some drunk killed her. He used his car, so that made it an accident, not murder. He got two years in jail." He gave a bitter laugh. "The jerk is out now, and he's probably still driving drunk."

Reb watched him shut the dishwasher and turn to face her. She was stiff with righteous indignation, remembering the man in the alley, remembering the smell of whiskey on his breath as he pinned her beneath him. She was suddenly smoldering with rage.

Tom came closer to her. "Reb?" he asked quietly.

She bent her head, incapable of speech. *The bastard raped me—then tossed ten dollars at me to satisfy his conscience. He was drunk and horny and I was there for the taking. Just a stupid little runaway, with no daddy, no brother, no boyfriend to keep him offa me... All I did was make the mistake of sleepin' in an alley, like a man would.*

"Reb, honey?" Tom reached out to comfort her, but she shrank from him. He instantly pulled his hand back.

"Hey—you like to read?" he asked, obviously trying to distract her. "Since Flynn and Chris are both down for the count, we'll probably have to entertain ourselves all afternoon. Let me show you what has to be the largest private collection of lesbian books in Seattle."

Tom led the way into the large, sunny living room. He headed for the floor-to-ceiling bookshelves. Reb got as far as passing the huge stereo unit, and the shelves of compact discs beside it, before stopping.

With effort, she closed the door on her sudden rage, forcing it back into that corner of her mind where all the bad memories were confined. Here was something much more interesting.

Enthralled, she ran her eyes over the CD player.

"Oh," Tom pronounced, grinning. "So it's music you like."

"Yeah." Reb breathed. "Can you put on somethin'? Anything's fine."

"Well, you may not like most of this," Tom confided, coming to stand before the shelves of compact discs. "Joyce was into that mellow, New Age stuff and Chris collects classical and jazz. Not much current here, unlike at my house."

"Play anything. I just want to listen...." She didn't add what she was thinking. *Without standin' outside the Wildrose, gettin' soaked in the rain while I'm strainin' to hear the jukebox.*

Tom regarded her with a beneficent smile, then turned on the unit, selected a disc and loaded it. "This is Chris's favorite."

There was an acoustic guitar lead-in and seconds later Joni Mitchell's smooth-as-silk voice was singing, "I am on a lonely road and I am traveling...."

"My mom used to play this record for me," Reb confessed, then pressed her lips together, disgusted with herself. *Go ahead, Stupid! Tell him all about yourself!*

Nervously, she glanced up.

Tom was chuckling. "Be sure you tell that to Chris," he stated. "The fact that she's old enough to be your natural mother is priceless! I need someone to get some licks in for me.

Here I've already gone bald and she hasn't even gotten decently gray! Most hideous and unfair, believe me."

Reb nodded absently, trying to focus on the music. *These yups. Always whinin' about gettin' old.*

Seeing that she wasn't interested in talking, Tom moved back to the bookshelves. Privately, she told herself, *I may not have the biggest collection in Seattle, but thanks to the used book stores in this town, I own the classics.*

For a moment she felt a twinge of homesickness, missing her own cold, damp squat high up in the warehouse on Eleventh Avenue. She missed her books and her guitar. She particularly missed her Kurt Cobain crucifix. She felt unlucky without it. *And the cats are goin' hungry.*

More than anything else, though, she dearly wanted a cigarette. Everyone in this place seemed so damned health-conscious she had not even dared to bring up the topic.

Joni Mitchell continued to sing and that intimate, yearning voice washed over Reb like a tropical ocean surf. Slowly, Reb sat down on the carpet and gave herself up to the exquisite sound pouring out of the speakers. Warmed in a shaft of sunlight from a large window, she reveled in the music, and barely even noticed when Tom left the room.

It wasn't long before she was stretched out on the blue-gray rug, feeling incredibly contented. She was well-fed, and for the first time in over a month, not one part of her body felt wet or cold. There was music flowing around her and through her and Flynn was upstairs waiting for her, a lover-to-be if ever she had met one. This was certainly a day of riches.

I don't hafta steal anythin' here. Shit, they're just givin' me whatever I want.

But most priceless among all these gifts was the awareness of just being safe. She was protected here—more and more she was accepting it, cherishing it. *When was the last time I felt so safe?*

Reb fell asleep before she could think of an answer.

Just after six o'clock, Jennifer crossed the wooden deck, then hesitated under the porch light by Chris's back door, trying to restore some order to her windblown hair. *Why am I agonizing over how I look?* she asked herself sternly. *I'm just dropping by to see how Reb and Flynn are.*

She knocked loudly on the back door. Moments later the door opened and Chris was there, waiting for her. Suddenly bashful, Jennifer could barely meet her eyes.

"Hi," she murmured as she stepped inside.

Chris, however, was blessedly assertive and intercepted Jennifer's attempt to step past her. Jennifer found herself moving into Chris's arms, into a kiss, as a matter of fact. It was brief and yet strongly given, so much so that when Chris released her mouth, Jennifer found herself off-balance. She stumbled a little, involuntarily leaning into the taller woman. Chris caught her by the elbows and steadied her. Their lips ended up mere inches apart.

They kissed again.

This time, their lips brushed in an exquisite appreciation. Then gradually, Jennifer's self-consciousness evaporated and the kiss shifted into something deep and arousing. There, in the cold draft of the open doorway, she gave herself up to the lips gliding away from her own lips, down across her jaw to her neck. Simultaneously, she felt hands sliding beneath her open anorak and across her sweatered ribs. It rocked Jennifer to the very core. Then Chris pulled her in close, a low, growling noise emanating from her throat, and Jennifer felt her trembling.

Across the room, something clattered as it hit the floor.

Flustered, Jennifer pushed Chris back. She looked to the arched threshold of the hall and saw Reb kneeling down to pick up the compact disc case she had dropped.

"S-sorry," Reb muttered, then jumped up and began to back down the hallway. She looked rested and refreshed, and an impish grin quickly replaced the startled expression Jennifer had first seen on her face.

After sending Reb an answering smile, Jennifer turned and closed the door behind her, moving past Chris and into the kitchen.

"She's just discovered Nina Simone," Chris divulged, grinning sheepishly. "Now I'm showing her how to load the multiple tray and program the song selection, so the CD player will play all through dinner. Shit, it will probably play until the year 2,000."

Jennifer laughed. There was a slightly harassed, yet genuinely affectionate expression on Chris's face, and it was so endearing that Jennifer felt unnerved.

Boldly, Chris took her hand, leading her toward the hall. "I'm really glad you came over, but I gotta warn you, it's a crowded house. Tom's been here all day, helping me get things together. Jane just arrived and is upstairs now, checking on Flynn. And Molly's in there with Reb, helping her sort through a couple of bags of secondhand clothes that Molly brought with her." Shrugging helplessly, Chris finished, "I think everyone's staying for dinner."

Jennifer sniffed the tangy scent of tomato and oregano in the air and asked, "Is that spaghetti sauce I smell?"

"Yep," Chris answered. "Want to join us? Tom and Reb started the sauce from scratch about two hours ago. As soon as Jane and Flynn are finished I'll start the spaghetti and garlic bread."

"That'll make—what—seven people? Can we all fit at the table?" Jennifer turned in the hallway and looked back at the round oak table in the center of the kitchen. "I don't want to just barge in on you."

"Eight. Thea Jance is coming over, too. I can insert the leaf in the middle of the table to make it bigger. And there will always be a place at my table for you, Jen," Chris murmured, shooting her a significant glance.

"Oh, there will, huh?" She said it in jest, grinning mischievously.

Chris tightened her loose grip on Jennifer's hand and gave her a dead-on serious gaze. "Yes."

Lord, Lord, this is happening fast, Jennifer thought, staring into those blue eyes, noticing how the outer edge was darker than the field of the inner iris. Her heart was racing and she could feel her face flushing. *Do I want this? Do I want to fall in love with her? I hardly know the woman! What if she's some kind of sociopath—like Gail? Cunning, self-centered, remorseless—just a facade of gentility that has no substance?* At the mere memory of the pain she had experienced loving Gail, Jennifer found herself wincing.

Chris caught the instinctive flinch. Perplexed, clearly not understanding Jennifer's inner turmoil, she lowered her eyes.

Jennifer walked along beside her, thinking, *I promised myself that I'd never be hurt like that again. But does that mean I'm never going to give anyone else a chance?*

They were at the edge of the living room, now. Nina Simone was singing *"I loves you, Porgy..."* Feeling extremely vulnerable, aware that she had been floundering for self-control since she had walked in the back door, Jennifer determinedly freed her hand from Chris's grasp.

She fastened her gaze on Reb, who was across the room, holding a long-legged pair of blue jeans up in front of her.

"I bet these Silver Tabs will fit Flynn," Reb declared.

"I thought so, too," Molly replied, waving a hand at Jennifer, and then exchanging a few pleasantries with her.

Tom was folding clothing into two separate piles. "How do, Professor?" he teased.

"Nicely, thank you," Jennifer returned, hoping she appeared more composed than she felt. "Your tomato sauce smells divine."

"Wait till you see the salad Reb made," Tom enticed. "For once, a dyke that's trainable in the culinary arts."

Reb threw the blue jeans at him.

As Tom peeled the Silver Tabs from his head, Jane Harada came into the living room and placed her medical bag on the end table by the sofa. She greeted Jennifer matter-of-factly, but cocked an eyebrow at Molly as she turned away. Jennifer suddenly intuited that her developing friendship with Chris was being discussed in private.

"Hey, Reb," Jane began, "Flynn says she'd like to take a shower. Care to help her?"

"Sure, Doc," Reb answered, her eyes very earnest. She immediately turned to Molly and asked, "Okay if we change into some of these?" She held up a stack of folded clothes, her face carefully blank, as if she was desperately trying to downplay how excited she was by this sudden wealth. However, her adolescent face was radiant, and Jennifer knew that there wasn't a person in the room who couldn't read Reb's joy.

"That's why I brought them," Molly assured her. "They're clean, ready to wear, and all yours."

"Cool!" Reb enthused. She hurried over to Tom and picked up the piles he had made, filling both her arms. Tom draped the blue jeans he held over her shoulder and Reb headed out of the living room at a trot. "We'll be quick. I'm starvin'."

They all watched her charge up the stairs, then heard her shouting, "Wait'll you see this, Flynn," before she'd even gotten into the bedroom.

Quickly, Molly glanced over at Chris and Jennifer, then away, but not before they both saw the shine of tears in her eyes.

Meanwhile, Tom had crossed the room to stand beside Jane. "Is Flynn okay?"

Jane kept her voice low as she answered. "As I told Chris last night, I think it's a current flu bug that's going around."

Turning to Chris, she continued, "She's basically healthy and should recover fast. I don't think she's been on the street long. Reb, on the other hand, is very malnourished and

anemic. I want to give her that B-12 shot tonight before I leave."
With a weary smile, Jane suggested, "I may need some help to
pull this off, since last night she was fairly unreceptive to my
medical offerings."

Molly countered, "Could have just as easily been dope
in that needle instead of vitamins. Reb was just being careful."
Gracefully, Molly scooped the empty clothing bags from the
floor. "I get the feeling this kid has been on her own for a while."

"Two years—she told Jane and me," Chris furnished.

"Christ," Jane whispered, rubbing her forehead. "And
she can't be more than seventeen."

Tom angrily paced before them. "How the hell *does* a
seventeen-year-old kid end up alone and homeless? Somebody
explain it to me!"

"Some say we need to bring back orphanages," Jane
offered, although she had the good grace to appear dubious
when Jennifer faced her.

"Reb's no orphan," Jennifer insisted. "I'm certain she
has parents somewhere—people who are just going on with
their lives, minus one child!" Wrenching herself to a halt, Jennifer stood there, trembling, surprised at the rush of emotion she
felt.

Chris sighed. "This is *my* generation we're talking about.
I was a hippie. We said we were going to change the world. But
look at American society...it's so fucked up. Everyone's working, the kids are parked at daycare centers, or at school all day
long. Little children carry latchkeys to let themselves into empty
houses, then watch TV till someone finally comes home, someone too tired and stressed-out to talk with them. Drug abuse.
Domestic violence. And incest is off the scale... Why is it such
a big shock to find that all these kids are running away from
home?"

Molly agreed. "When did we start rationalizing that
there were other things more important than the fundamental
business of nurturing our children?"

"I'll tell you what happened," Tom fumed quietly. "We've let those nitwit Christian fundamentalists define what family values are. Trust their narrow minds to completely miss the *love* part of the whole concept! I mean—why dwell on love when you can obsess about the sin and punishment part?"

"Oh, let's just cut the shit," Chris demanded. "What good is talk? Let's *do* something about it. That's what counts, right? If gay kids are out on the street, shouldn't adult gays and lesbians be trying to help them? We could raise funds for shelters, maybe even encourage gays to adopt or become foster parents."

Jane frowned. "We'll probably be accused of recruitment."

"As if gays aren't routinely recruited into a hellish attempt at heterosexuality," Tom griped.

"*We* know that you can't recruit troops that have already voluntarily joined the ranks," Jennifer offered, then sighed. "Why do we continue to let homophobes define who we are and what we do? Why do we look for excuses to not help these kids?"

For a moment, they stood together in a small circle at the center of the living room, their faces mirroring one another's despair. Nina Simone's velvet voice rose in the background, singing, *"In my solitude, you haunt me..."*

Finally, Chris broke the silence. "Thanks, Jane, for your medical input," she murmured. "I'll try to talk Reb into that B-12 shot. But I don't know... She doesn't seem to do a thing she doesn't really want to do."

"Hey, I know," Tom offered, glancing at the stairs to be sure he was not being overheard. "Get Flynn to back up the suggestion. I've noticed that Reb will do just about anything for Flynn."

"Sounds like young love," Molly mused.

Jane stretched, suppressing a yawn. "Or lust."

Tilting her head to study Jane better, Molly asked, "How much sleep did you get last night?"

"Save that Mother Hen bit for Thea," Jane retorted. "Now, when do I get some of that famous Tom Morrissey spaghetti?"

"Physicians first, Doctor Harada," Tom replied, grinning and proffering his arm. "Let's leave the problems of modern society behind and console ourselves with a shameless pasta binge."

Molly chuckled and followed Tom and Jane into the hall.

As Jennifer started to leave, she noticed Chris gazing at the stairs, her eyes sadly thoughtful.

"Twenty years ago, that could have been me," Chris muttered.

"What?" Jennifer asked, the tentative smile Tom had left her with slipping away.

"My father knew about me," Chris confessed. "And he hated me. I didn't know I was gay. Shit, I didn't have a clue until years later, when Pam Davis jumped my bones after a softball game and a few pitchers of beer. But my dad—he knew. And he wanted me out of his house—couldn't wait for me to leave. So I did—right after I graduated from high school. Took a job typing in an office, wore a skirt and stockings and was miserable." She shook her head.

"I remember being seventeen years old and forced to live with all that silent, cold disapproval, all those unexplained, malevolent looks. If I was a seventeen-year-old now, and knew about myself, knew why he hated me, I don't think I would stay around to take it. I'd probably clear out, too." Chris sighed deeply. "It's a tough thing, being openly despised. Wears you down. Ends up making you loathe yourself."

Not knowing what to say, Jennifer merely nodded.

The expression on Chris's face was one of incalculable suffering. There was more sadness here than grief over Joyce, that much was evident. Being valued and openly loved were obviously uncommon threads in the tapestry that was Chris Olson's life.

Somehow, Jennifer found it endeared Chris to her even more.

Reb led the way downstairs, excitedly relating how she and Tom had made the spaghetti sauce. Trailing behind her, Flynn concentrated on what Reb had promised her about all those strangers waiting in the kitchen. She'd said, "They want to help us. They're yups, but I think they're really okay." All the same, Flynn's heart was beating hard and fast.

She was frightened. She wanted to run.

Instead she followed Reb, down the stairs, past the luxurious living room, and down the hall. She was feeling strangely disoriented. After the dreary experience of Reb's crude squatter's quarters, the warm, brightly lit Victorian house she was walking through seemed like something out of a dream. Reb led her to the kitchen table and she blinked incredulously at the abundance of food. Slowly, the aroma of good home-cooking penetrated her stuffy nasal passages and awakened her belly.

At Reb's command, Flynn sat down.

The strange, detached numbness which had sheathed her for days began to fade, and recent wounds came shockingly to life again. Janet's betrayal, her father's hatred, the paralyzing terror of being adrift in Seattle, penniless and alone—it all rose to the surface in an undeniable rush of anguish.

Then the one they called Thea arrived. One look at the tall African-American woman in a police uniform and Flynn was breathing in short, panicky gasps. *I remember her from the YWCA! I smashed into her as hard as I could! She's probably here to arrest me!*

She would have run, but at that instant she began coughing and couldn't stop. Helpless, she covered her mouth and turned away from the table, her entire body jarred by an explosion of bottomless, racking coughs.

The adults ceased their last-minute meal preparations and gathered around Flynn, all of them talking at once.

Dr. Harada charged down the hallway and returned with her medical bag.

While Molly was greeting Thea with a distracted hug, Dr. Harada knelt beside Flynn and pressed an inhaler into her hand.

"Take a hit," Dr. Harada ordered.

Flynn moved the plastic mouthpiece to her lips, struggling to stop coughing long enough to use the device.

Reb moved closer and whispered in her ear. "Chill, buddy. You're scarin' me."

Surprised, Flynn gazed up at Reb, and the coughing rumbled to an abrupt end.

Dr. Harada nudged her, urging, "Go on. Do it. Just breathe deeply."

Flynn used the inhaler and the tight congestion in her chest eased dramatically. She sat back in the chair gratefully, unable to do anything but breathe.

Catching Flynn's anxious glance, Thea said with a chuckle, "Relax, Miss Blitzing Linebacker. I'm here in an unofficial capacity. Okay?"

Flynn nodded, mortified.

Dr. Harada stayed by Flynn's side, watching her intently for a few minutes, then finally stood and pronounced, "Nothing wrong with this kid that a plateful of pasta won't cure!"

Relieved, everyone laughed, including Flynn.

After that, they all slid into chairs and a noisy, rambunctious dinner got underway. Jokes and teasing insults were traded with a casual ease. The huge portions of spaghetti, salad and garlic bread began rapidly disappearing. In addition to enjoying the food, the adults all seemed to be competing to make each other laugh.

Flynn sat between Reb and Chris, being steadily encouraged by both to "eat a little more" of this or that. Gradually, the scent and taste of tomato sauce and garlic and buttery bread completely captured her. She was amazed to realize that she was really hungry.

Eventually, too full to manage another bite, she sat silently watching the others. Between the teasing and the long, outrageous stories, their laughter never really stopped. Looking around the table, Flynn realized that the open affection and good fellowship in this kitchen was something she had rarely witnessed.

This is what a home should be, Flynn thought. *This is what family is.*

Feeling Reb's gaze, Flynn turned and found her new friend studying her. As if she read how Flynn was basking in this congenial setting, Reb gave her a happy little smile.

Even in this roomful of people, Reb's expression had an intimacy that made Flynn blush.

Then Reb shot an edgy, resentful glance across the table.

Thea Jance was observing them. The policewoman sat back, appearing rigid and formidable in her light blue uniform shirt and gleaming silver-and-gold badge. Her scrutiny was intimidating.

Thea waited for a pause in the conversation between Chris and Molly, then stated bluntly, "Chris, I'll need to be leaving shortly. We'd better get on with it."

Chris turned toward Flynn and Reb. "I asked Thea to come over and give us some advice on legalities. If you decide to live here, you'll need more than food and a roof over your head. You'll probably eventually want to make some plans about your future."

Flynn glanced uncertainly at Chris, vaguely remembering this woman saying something like that to her last night. *Does she really want us?* Determined not to get her hopes up, Flynn had spent the day convincing herself that last night's conversation was grounded more in fever delirium than in reality.

Chris regarded Flynn with cool blue eyes, then suggested to Thea, "Why don't you fill Reb and Flynn in on the specifics of state law, in case they want to go back to school?"

Incredulous, Flynn blurted, "I can do that?"

Making a disagreeable face, Reb sneered, "Yuck."

Eyeing Flynn speculatively, Thea disclosed, "Washington state law says that at sixteen you can 'emancipate' yourself—declare yourself financially independent of your parents. You have to sign some papers and file them with a state agency, but then you'll be free to live where you wish and enroll in the local public school that encompasses that district."

"No lie!" Flynn demanded, completely shocked.

"Hey—we're free already," Reb commented. "We don't need to sign any stupid papers. Like, who wants to go to school?"

"I do," Flynn asserted fervently, facing Reb. "I was trying for a..." She stopped, feeling exposed and in jeopardy. *I don't know these people—not really. They seem nice, and probably mean well, but what if somehow this only leads me back to Dad?*

Gently, Jennifer encouraged, "Go on, Flynn. What were you trying for?"

In an agony of confusion, Flynn dropped her gaze to her lap. She felt beads of sweat collect on her brow, and coughed anxiously.

"You were trying for a scholarship," Chris guessed, placing a hand on her shoulder. "Weren't you?"

Flynn kept her head down and her mouth closed. The silence in the room was terrifyingly loud. Not a fork scraped, not a coffee cup rattled. She knew they were all staring at her.

"Let Flynn go at her own pace, Chris," Molly counseled.

"If she stays out of school very long," Chris declared, "she'll lose her chance." There was a pause, as Chris pressed her fingers into Flynn's shoulder. "Like I lost mine."

Intrigued by the wistfulness in Chris's tone, Flynn raised her head. She dared to meet Chris's concerned eyes and curiosity began to outstrip fear. "What happened?" Flynn asked.

Chris said quietly, "My father didn't believe in women going to college. He told me I wasn't smart enough." Chris shrugged and lowered her gaze, but not before Flynn saw her wounded pride. "I made the mistake of believing him. I never even sent in the applications."

Reb snorted. "So what?" she demanded. "Look at you. You got plenty now, don't you? Food on the shelf, money in the bank! You own your own house, you run your own business. What the hell did you need college for?"

"It was...a dream, Reb," Chris retorted, her face weary. "I wanted to study architecture. Maybe design buildings."

"But you're rich," Reb insisted, baffled. "You didn't need their fu-uhm—their stupid piece of paper to prove how smart you are."

Chris looked at Flynn meaningfully before she let her gaze return to Reb. "There's a fire in dreaming that lights up a woman's soul, Reb. And something happens when it goes out. Something that makes the rest of your life a lot darker."

Flynn searched Chris's eyes. She believed every word.

"Right," Reb scoffed. She turned to Flynn. "You don't *have* to go back to school, Flynn."

"But I *want* to," Flynn stated, frowning as she faced Reb. "I didn't think it was possible...but if it is...and if I can still qualify for a scholarship, I definitely want to go to college."

"Damn you, you're gonna ruin everything," Reb accused. "We don't have time for a job and school both, and we gotta work to stay here." Obstinately, she challenged Chris. "Ain't that what you told me last night?"

"Actually, I'd prefer you going back to school," Chris admitted. "We can work something out, job-wise."

"Reb, what about your music?" Flynn asked, bewildered by Reb's protest. "You've got ambitions—I know you do. Don't you want to develop your talent?"

Glowering, Reb muttered, "Shuddup about that." She threw a belligerent look at the adult faces around them.

Suddenly feeling stronger, Flynn persisted. "You're a good musician! You want to do it for a living—so why don't you get real, and start making plans on how you intend to pull it off? Or maybe you think you can't deal—so you won't even try."

"They don't teach you how to play rock 'n' roll in school!" Reb snapped, as if amazed that Flynn was even suggesting it.

"Yes, they do," Tom interjected. "There's a Fine Arts program at Jimi Hendrix High School, two blocks over. They even have special classes in electric guitar technique. I know a couple of guys who graduated from there."

Reb maintained a suspicious silence. Alf, who had been lying by Reb's chair throughout the meal, sat up and plopped his head in her lap. Dutifully, Reb tore a piece of garlic bread from the half-eaten slice on her plate and slipped him a bite.

Dr. Harada yawned, then glanced up at the clock above the refrigerator. "It's eight o'clock. Flynn ought to turn in early tonight."

"I feel fine," Flynn said, then found herself yawning, too.

Pushing her chair back, Chris offered, "Why don't you two sleep on this school thing?"

"We'll help clean up first," Reb said decisively. She stood and began circling the table, gathering plates.

Chairs scraped back, and while issuing a series of instructions, the old friends began clearing the table.

As Flynn stood, Jennifer took her by the elbow and steered her into the hallway. In a matter of seconds, Reb was on the other side of Flynn, looking pugnacious.

"That's enough for tonight," Jennifer told them both, leading them along the corridor. "Let those know-it-alls go to it. They love bossing each other around."

Almost grudgingly, Reb seemed to put aside whatever was bothering her and managed to grin.

"You two go on upstairs," Jennifer urged as they paused by the staircase. "If you're not tired, I have no doubt that you could use some time alone to talk things out." And with a deliberate casualness, Jennifer took Flynn's hand and placed it firmly in Reb's palm.

In another moment, she was walking back toward the kitchen.

Flynn was left staring into Reb's chocolate-brown eyes.

At that moment the doorbell rang and Flynn started. The front door opened, and a devastatingly attractive blonde woman in high heels and an elegant business suit sauntered in. She crossed the carpet to stand before Flynn and Reb.

Without preamble, she looked them both over and remarked coolly, "I had to see it to believe it."

CHAPTER 10

"Chris, I think you'd better come here!"

Even though the anxious call was nearly drowned out by the rattle of china and her friends' chatter in the kitchen, Chris heard the voice and knew it was Jennifer. In seconds, she was moving. She loped down the hallway, hearing Allison's derisive laughter.

"So, what's your usual racket? Hooking?" Allison reached out to stroke Flynn's face. "God knows you've got the looks for it."

Chris darted around Jennifer in time to see Flynn scowl and duck away. Flynn's right arm began to snap forward and, seeing it, Allison stepped back. In the space of a breath, Reb leapt forward and caught Flynn's arm in mid-strike.

"No," Reb cried and, shocked at herself, Flynn froze.

Sardonically, Allison said, "Hot-tempered, isn't she?"

"You started it, bitch!" Reb accused, outraged.

"Allison, what...?" Chris began.

"Jane told me what was going on," Allison interrupted. "How ever did you *allow* these brazen little paupers to move in on you?"

Alf parked himself in a stiff-legged stance by Chris's side and warily sniffed the air.

"Chris, we pay taxes, right?" Allison continued. "If you recall, there's a state-run foster care program in place for these sorts of problems."

"I ain't suckin' from your taxes, Blondie," Reb interjected. "I take care of myself."

Allison threw a contemptuous glance at Reb before facing Chris again. "And our production schedule is going to go straight to hell if you and Tom are going to start taking days off like this...."

Chris opened her mouth to reply, but Jennifer was suddenly stepping between her and Allison, smoothly steering Allison away from the girls and into the living room.

"Won't you join me," Jennifer stated, her firm delivery leaving no room for argument.

Chris noticed that Jennifer had grasped Allison's upper arm. She was pushing Allison before her in the desired direction.

Allison twisted her arm about futilely as she tried to rid herself of Jennifer. "Show some sense, Chris." She turned and stated, "They're only going to stay in this house long enough to steal you blind."

Angry and embarrassed, Chris studied Flynn and Reb. "Please excuse her." For several seconds Chris clenched her teeth together, then whispered, "She can be such an ass."

Reb's tightly controlled, impassive face was transfigured by a wickedly pleased smirk. Flynn, however, was staring at the floor, red-faced. Even as Chris spoke, Flynn was edging up the first two stair steps, intent on fleeing as soon as possible. Reb noticed Flynn's wide-eyed, embarrassed expression, and immediately sobered.

Chris remembered Tom's observance that Reb would do anything for Flynn. Watching them now, it was easy to see that tough, self-reliant Reb was highly sensitive to Flynn's moods and needs.

Trying to compose herself, Chris touched Flynn's arm, saying, "I'll take care of this and then come up to see you later, okay?"

Shoulders hunched, Flynn gave another nod, then pivoted quickly and jogged up the steps. Reb followed her, and after an indecisive whine, so did Alf.

Behind Chris, in the living room, Allison was speaking in a low voice, demanding of Jennifer, "Was this your idea? Is that why you're here?"

"No, it was mine," Chris answered, the coldness in her tone enough to bring Allison around to face her. Purposefully, wanting to establish things once and for all, she finished, "And this is a *date*, Allison. Jennifer and I are *dating*. Or is that something else I have to clear with you first?"

From the suspiciously silent kitchen, Chris heard Tom's behind-the-scenes support in a loud, "Yee-haah!" followed by a chorus of "Shhh!"

Her lips drawing into two thin, lipsticked lines, Allison at first did not respond. Then she asked, "So...you're finally over Joyce?"

Chris's determination instantly faltered, and faded into pain. She was speechless with it, unable to think.

Quietly, Jennifer remarked, "I am not intruding on Joyce's home or her relationship. Joyce has been gone for five years now. And I think Joyce would probably be heartbroken to know that Chris has been struggling as much as she has been, just trying to go on without her."

Taking a moment to solemnly study Chris, Jennifer concluded, "Joyce died in that accident and Chris lived. When Chris remembers that life is a gift, not a curse...then maybe she'll be able to explore what that gift really means."

Frowning, Chris considered the words. *A gift, not a curse....*

Darting a look at Jennifer, Allison sniped, "Explore away, ladies." She walked toward the front door, commenting over her shoulder, "Meanwhile, I hope you realize that those two baby-faced thieves upstairs are going to end up giving you a lesson in human nature that you'll never forget."

Under her breath, Jennifer asserted, "They're kids, damn you." She glared at Allison. "They've been living out there on the edge of civilized society with nothing—*nothing*—just trying to survive from one day to the next."

At the door, Allison turned and coolly examined her. "Well, Miss Bleeding Heart Liberal, they're not *my* kids. Whoever had them should've been responsible enough to discipline them—not let them run off from God-knows-what-hick-town so they could roam *my* city streets like packs of wild coyotes."

Firmly, Chris said, "Good night, Allison."

In reply, Allison angrily raked her eyes over Chris. Giving her head a slight shake, she opened the door and left.

Except for the solid, low ticking of the grandfather clock in the corner of the room, the house was totally silent.

Then, from the kitchen, Chris heard smothered cheers and hysterical peals of laughter. "The Wicked Witch is dead!" Tom crowed once, before being roundly shushed. The noise of a kitchen cleanup started up again, amid a barrage of intense, whispery exchanges.

Agitated, Chris rubbed the back of her neck. She was overwhelmed with huge, disorderly emotions. She was furious with Allison, irritated by the gossiping friends in her kitchen, overwhelmed by the enormity of this parenting role she had embarked upon. And yet she also felt strangely, fiercely protective of the young women upstairs.

Meanwhile, she couldn't take her eyes off Jennifer.

Jennifer muttered, "How on earth do you stand that woman?"

"Oh," Chris began lamely, "she's usually a tad more subtle at bullying me, I guess."

There was another pregnant silence.

Hesitantly, Chris inquired, "So, we *are* dating, right?"

Jennifer raised her eyebrows and smiled. "Looks like it, doesn't it?"

Roughly five minutes after the quiet arguing had stopped and the front door had closed, Reb heard footsteps coming up the stairs. There was a knock on the partially opened bedroom door, and then Chris's voice, asking if she and Jennifer might come in.

Man, you own the place, lady, Reb thought, a little confused by the courtesy, then replied, "Sure. Door's open."

Chris and Jennifer entered, looking chagrined. Reb rubbed Alf behind the ears and accepted their apologies, while Flynn sat on the bed, silent and avoiding eye contact. Personally, Reb found herself delighted by how unfailingly nice these two women seemed to be.

They couldn't be an easier pair of suckers if they opened their wallets and told me to clean them!

Soon, however, she spied Jane Harada at the door with her medical bag in one hand and a syringe in the other. Reb's smug satisfaction evaporated. She tensed, and knew by Harada's smile that her apprehension showed.

"Just a B-12 shot, kids," Jane soothed. "You'll feel a lot better for it."

And then Reb noticed that Chris was leaning down near Flynn's ear, discussing something Reb couldn't quite hear. Flynn nodded once and Chris sidled over to Jennifer's side.

Out of the blue, Flynn remarked, "Come on, Reb. Let's just take the shot and get it over with."

Reb had been about to staunchly refuse, but Flynn's brave nonchalance made her feel slightly silly about feeling so paranoid. Disconcerted, she studied her friend. Flynn no longer looked quite so ill and exhausted, but the sapphire-blue eyes were still troubled.

Is she still worryin' about that blonde bitch? Reb wondered.

At the same time, Reb became aware of something she had not been willing to acknowledge during the past few days on the streets. Flynn had come to affect her deeply.

Don't get all stupid over this, she told herself firmly. *You can't afford to care about anyone. It ain't ever worth it, anyway.*

Reluctantly, Reb agreed to the shot and Harada waved Chris and Jennifer into the hall. Alf cheerfully plopped down on the floor by Reb, gazing at her fondly and utterly ignoring Chris's call.

Once the door was closed, it seemed incredibly demeaning to Reb to be told to drop her pants, then even worse to take the needle in the butt. However, a few minutes later, Harada did the same thing with Flynn. When Flynn went comically red-faced, the whole thing seemed suddenly very funny. Hearing Reb's soft chuckle, Flynn threw her a disparaging look.

When it was over, Dr. Harada opened the door and invited Chris and Jennifer back into the room.

The two older women strolled in side by side. Her hands deep in the pockets of her off-white chinos, Chris looked very relaxed. Jennifer's light brown hair was loose on her shoulders, and the rose turtleneck and black slacks she wore clung in all the right places. Pensive, Reb mused that this woman was more than beautiful. Her heart had a way of shining in her eyes. And right now, those eyes were lingering on Chris.

They look at each other a lot, Reb thought. *If they aren't together yet, they soon will be.*

Watching them, Reb couldn't help but wish she was that old and that rich. No one frightened them, no one pushed them around, no one told them they weren't any good. They seemed invincible.

Maybe one day Flynn and I will be like this. Not yups...just nice, dyke ladies. Just regular people....

Flynn walked past her and sat on the bed.

Reb frowned, perceiving how distressed Flynn still was. *Why?*

Misinterpreting Reb's expression, Chris said, "I'm not about to force you into going to school, Reb, so please don't lie up here losing sleep over it."

Quietly, Jennifer added, "Speaking of which, we'd better let them get to bed, Chris. They need rest."

Harada agreed, telling Flynn, "You're not out of the woods, yet. Don't take on anything too energetic, okay?" And as Flynn innocently nodded, the doctor leveled an admonishing gaze on Reb.

Reb snickered. *Like hell. I'm makin' no promises. I'm gonna fuck the girl's brains out as soon as she gives me half a chance.*

Then Chris and the doctor were saying good night and moving toward the door. Chris firmly called Alf, and though he hesitated, as if debating whether or not to stay with his young friends, he finally trotted out of the room to Chris's side.

Nearby, Jennifer brushed her hand over Flynn's hair and bent lower, whispering something Reb couldn't hear. Flynn nodded, then raised her head and watched Jennifer leave.

Feeling resentful and jealous, Reb stood and closed the door smartly behind Jennifer.

"What did she say?" Reb asked, willing herself to appear only mildly interested.

On the bed, Flynn sat perfectly still. Her eyes were glimmering with tears and a barely concealed despair. "She told me not to be so hard on myself," she mumbled.

Baffled, Reb demanded, "What's that supposed to mean?"

Flynn sighed, exasperated with her. "Reb, believe it or not I'm ashamed! I almost hit that woman down there tonight! If you hadn't stopped me I would have!"

"So?" Reb retorted. "Tell me she didn't deserve it? You had every reason to kick her yupped-out ass!"

Flynn scowled at her. "Shit, Reb!" she declared hotly. "I just can't keep going around punching out people! For the past five days—ever since I ran away—I feel like I'm always mad or I'm afraid or I'm running away from something... And I *hate* it!"

"Whadda ya think I feel like all the time?" Reb flung back at her. "The street ain't exactly been a party for me, you know!" Angrily, Reb stomped away from her and began yanking off clothes. "Jesus! Stop beatin' yourself up over it!"

Angry as she was, Reb made herself carefully fold each piece of clothing as it was removed. She placed the clothes on the dresser thinking, *Gotta take care of this stuff...* Moments later, she pulled on the long T-shirt she'd chosen to sleep in.

Across the room, Flynn was sitting cross-legged on the bed. Her elbows rested on her knees and her head was clasped in her hands.

Reb approached her slowly, murmuring, "Flynn, I know that right now, for you, the whole world seems...so unbelievably mean and scary." She gestured helplessly with both hands. "But this is the way it is most of the time! Real fucked up! You just didn't have to deal with it until last week. And even though I act like I've been around and it doesn't get to me...well, it still gets to me. A lot!"

Flynn made no response.

"The only difference between you and me is I learned a long time ago not to show any weakness." Frowning intently at Flynn, she warned, "There are wolves out there, always lookin' over the herd for the weak ones. Know what I mean?"

Flynn gave her a brooding, sideways glance. "No."

"It's simple," Reb stated. "Don't let them know they got to you. Don't let on that you care."

"What if I can't do that?" Flynn asked softly.

"Learn," Reb ordered.

"I want to stay here, Reb," Flynn proposed. "Here in this house. I like Chris and Jennifer. I trust them. They're offering us a way out—a way to get off the street. Can't we just take it?"

Like a mother to her child, Reb hedged kindly. "We'll see."

"Reb, I don't get you," Flynn said angrily, then sighed. "It's like you're afraid of trying to be normal again."

Grinning, Reb approached the bed. "Fuck normal," she joked. "Who needs normal?"

"Maybe I do," Flynn muttered.

Annoyed, Flynn unfolded her legs and stood, turning away from Reb, unbuttoning her plaid flannel shirt. Reb watched her from beneath lowered lashes, stealing covert looks at the bruised back before it disappeared beneath another long T-shirt. Flynn dropped her jeans and Reb continued to watch her, more and more boldly.

Unexpectedly, Flynn turned and caught her.

Embarrassed, the redhead blushed. "What're you staring at?" she demanded, very defensive.

"*You*, Doofus," Reb responded.

Flynn went nearly crimson. For a moment, she froze, as if she didn't know what to do. Then, abruptly, she crossed the room, opened the door and sought refuge in the bathroom.

Reb sat there listening to the distant sounds of the toilet flushing, of Flynn washing her face and brushing her teeth.

I'll bet she even flosses, Reb thought, feeling oddly vexed. *I didn't know she was so into bein' clean. Guess she wasn't a Troll long enough to get used to livin' dirty.*

Seconds later, Reb huffed a small sigh. *Yeah, well, I use ta like bein' clean, too. Maybe I just don't want to get used to it, again. God knows I'm not gonna be able to stay here much longer. I ain't like these folks, and pretty soon they're gonna know it. That blonde bitch saw it—saw me for who I was. In the Real World, these dykes are somebodies. They've made the whole fucked-up heterosexual world back off and leave 'em alone. And I'm just a little cockroach that's learned how to live off everyone else's garbage. I don't think I can take bein' a geek in some school or kissin' up to some nerd of a boss...or any of that supposedly normal shit. I been doin' as I pleased too long.*

When Flynn came back, she still avoided eye contact.

Sighing, Reb went off to take her own turn in the bathroom.

Downstairs, the dinner guests had completed the cleanup and taken their leave. Alf was stretched out on the carpet in the living room, completely exhausted by a busy day of supervising everyone else in the house. Chris and Jennifer sat nearby on the sofa, talking.

Chris was speaking eloquently about her determination to serve as a competent, caring guardian for the two girls upstairs. Though she was listening intently, Jennifer found herself mainly watching Chris's lips. Meanwhile, Chris seemed very nervous. She had managed to meet Jennifer's gaze just once, briefly, during the entire conversation.

Why am I discouraging her? Jennifer thought. *I've become the mask I created to deal with my pain over Gail—the reserved and cautious Professor Hart. Am I never going to take another risk on love?*

"So, what do I do next?" Chris asked quietly. She sat forward, nervously fiddling with one of the CD cases that Reb had left on the coffee table.

Jennifer watched her a moment, then teased, "With me or with the girls?"

Chris dropped the CD case. It bounced on the carpet and disappeared under the coffee table.

"Damn," Chris muttered, and bent over, looking for it.

For once, Jennifer decided, she would be brazen. Abruptly, she leaned closer and sank her hand into the crisp, light-gold curls. Chris turned toward her, surprised, and Jennifer moved that hand to Chris's cheek. Slowly, the uncautious Professor Hart smoothed her palm under Chris's chin. She lifted the handsome face, guided it closer to her own.

Their lips met softly, almost uncertainly. And then, without breaking the kiss, Jennifer leaned into Chris, pushing her back against the couch. Chris made a small, needy sound and slipped her arms around Jennifer. Seconds later they were kissing heatedly. Something within Jennifer opened, like a long-closed door.

Some time later, slightly disheveled, they both came up for air. They sat a moment, dreamily staring into each other's eyes, then ended up laughing at themselves.

"I can't believe we're sitting here making out," Chris observed shyly, then offered. "Would you like to come upstairs? Maybe spend the night? My room is on the third floor at the front of the house. It's pretty far from the girls' room. Very private."

Tilting her head, Jennifer considered the possibility. "Part of me would like to very much, but part of me says no."

Disappointment flashed across Chris's face. "Look, Jen, I'm no good at games," she sighed. "I really like you. In fact, I kind of lose my head when I'm around you." Lifting her gaze to Jennifer's, she finished, "I want to try to figure out what that means."

Amused, Jennifer chuckled. "*I* know what it means."

Chris asked softly, "So, what does it mean, then?"

Feeling as if she'd been dared to explain herself, Jennifer fell silent. *What she's asking is: Are we in lust or in love?*

Frankly, the question frightened her. She didn't want to reveal that she was already harboring a mushrooming infatuation. It seemed too soon, even a little nonsensical to feel all that she did, and so she chose to hide the truth.

Chris must have seen the vulnerability on her face, for she gently drew Jennifer closer and kissed her. Again, the passion burst forth. And a tentative boldness was directing the way Chris's hands roved over her.

Finally, Jennifer pushed Chris back and took several deep breaths. "I'm *not* staying the night with you," she managed, then forestalled Chris's aggrieved reaction by saying, "I want you to be sure about me, Chris. I want us both to take time to get to know each other, and be absolutely certain about what we're doing."

Frustrated, Chris grumbled, "We'll know by the time the night is over, won't we?"

"And what if we don't?" Jennifer asked. "Will we even know how to talk to each other in the morning?"

A pained expression crossed Chris's face.

"Maybe, instead," Jennifer proposed, "we could...court each other. I propose that we agree not to sleep together for at least two months."

"Two months?!" Chris squeaked, obviously stunned.

"Yes," Jennifer continued, "It's only eight weeks, for heaven's sake. That way we'll have a chance to establish some solid bonds between us. We won't take the physical shortcut to intimacy—we'll create *emotional* intimacy."

"Two months!" Chris repeated, her voice rich with dismay.

"Wait a minute," Jennifer stated, perplexed and more than a little surprised by Chris's alarm. "Forgive me if I've got this wrong, but you've been celibate for years now, haven't you?"

Dark-blonde eyebrows lowered and the blue eyes became decidedly frosty. "Who told you that?" Chris demanded.

"Never mind," Jennifer informed her, returning to the topic. "I have it on good authority that you are a marvel at sexual self-control. How is it that two more months is suddenly too much?"

"It was Tom, wasn't it?" Chris went on doggedly. "I saw him stop you in the hallway and then stand there whispering with you while I was seeing Thea, Molly and Jane to the door." She leaned closer to Jennifer, trying to appear menacing. "*Confess!*"

Jennifer recognized the smile playing at the edges of Chris's eyes and laughed. "*Never!*"

With a riveting intensity, Chris leaned still closer.

Jennifer watched helplessly, then closed her eyes and felt Chris invade her space. All along the surface of Jennifer's flesh, a thousand nerve endings were clamoring for touch. Chris's arms were closing around her, cradling her, lowering her until they were both prone on the couch. Seconds later, Chris's lips were softly engaging, then commanding her own.

They kissed until Jennifer was willing to do anything Chris wanted. In some far-off corner of her brain she wondered why she'd ever even brought up the idea of delaying the inevitable result of this incendiary attraction.

Chris leaned back, studying Jennifer's face. "I haven't wanted anybody like this since..."

For Jennifer, the pause said everything. *Since Joyce.*

Ardent, Chris stared into her eyes. "I *really* want to be with you, Jen."

Licking her lips nervously, Jennifer ventured, "I have to know somebody to go to bed with them."

Smiling, Chris countered, "I feel like I've known you all my life."

"Is that a pickup line?" Jennifer accused with mock umbrage. "Are you really a bar-girl, masquerading as..."

She didn't get to finish the jest, for Chris leaned down and kissed her again. Minutes passed and Jennifer was soon thoroughly befuddled. When Chris finally freed Jennifer's lips again, they were both breathless and more crazed than before.

"Oh, Goddess," Jennifer groaned. "I don't think I can hold out for two months."

"Yeah!" Chris crowed, raising a fist in victory.

"Let's make it two weeks," Jennifer offered.

"*What?!*"

Annoyed, Jennifer argued, "Oh, come on, Chris! Don't make me be the only one with good sense! The way we handle this crazy sexual attraction between us is important. We need time to create more than that one, simplistic physical connection! What we do tonight may well be the difference between a one-night stand and a lifetime romance."

"Aw jeez!" Chris complained.

Abruptly, she released Jennifer and then sat up. She turned away and blew out a sigh that was sharp with annoyance.

Jennifer pushed herself into a sitting position beside Chris. "Or maybe you're not interested in a lifetime romance," Jennifer muttered.

She stole a few glances at the flushed face beside her. Just as Jennifer was getting truly angry, Chris surprised her yet again.

"Wow," Chris remarked. "Forgive me. I'm not exactly used to this. Talk about sensual overload. And in answer to your question, I *definitely* want a romance, of whatever length you'll consider." She cast a slow, apologetic smile at Jennifer. "OK, I agree to a courtship, that's fine. Although, I must warn you, you have quite an effect on me."

Amazed and impressed by this sudden turnabout, Jennifer stared at her intently.

"I also want..." Chris hesitated.

"What?" Jennifer urged quietly.

"Maybe we could...be a family. You, me, Reb and Flynn."

"I'd like that, I think," Jennifer stated.

"Not exactly conventional, but it might do us all some good," Chris explained, her face very serious.

"Might?" Jennifer echoed with a chuckle.

Chris grinned.

Jennifer gazed at her, remembering Allison talking on the phone last week. Jennifer had come upon her unannounced and accidentally eavesdropped long enough to hear Allison say, "Five years of celibacy—can you imagine what she'd be like once you got her going?"

Well, now I know. She's...very hard to say no to. Again Jennifer idly questioned herself about why she had wanted to postpone making love.

To Chris she replied, "C'mon Romeo. Walk me home."

Fresh from the shower, Reb sauntered into the bedroom. Flynn went scarlet again.

Reb pulled back the covers and climbed in beside her, saying, "Hell, you blush more than anyone I ever met."

Indignant, Flynn stated, "You make me. On purpose."

"No shit!" Reb dissolved into helpless laughter.

Peeved, Flynn shoved Reb's shoulder. "Don't laugh at me."

Reb laughed harder.

Glaring, Flynn ordered, "Quit it!"

Unable to stop, Reb howled until tears filled her eyes.

Flynn announced, "Oh, I think it's time I got you good!" Seconds later she was tickling Reb below the ribs.

Reb squealed and thrashed, desperate to get away from Flynn's tormenting hands.

"Say you're sorry!" Flynn commanded. She pinned the smaller girl with a muscular thigh over her hips and tickled her sensitive sides.

"No!" Reb shrieked, trying to buck Flynn off her. "Get off me!" she gasped. "Get off, you big jock...."

She was caught in gales of torture-induced laughter, twisting vainly to get away and only exposing more flesh to Flynn's merciless hands. Breathlessly, she heard herself begging Flynn to stop.

Suddenly, Flynn did stop.

Reb gazed into the face hovering a mere six inches above her own. Flynn looked astounded. And in her eyes, Reb saw desire.

Oh, finally...you want me the way I want you....

Before Flynn could roll away, Reb ran a hand behind Flynn's silken neck. Seizing the lead, she pulled Flynn down. Swiftly, she made contact with Flynn's lips and a sensation like the wings of a hundred birds fluttered to life inside her. She felt Flynn tense, as if readying to end it before it even got started.

"Flynn, please...please..." Reb entreated, her voice so quiet and yet fervent that it disturbed Reb to hear the need in it.

Desperate, Reb kept kissing her, softly calling her name between kisses. Flynn made a small, vulnerable sound, like a little cat that was lost. Elated, Reb concentrated on arousing her, kissing her slowly, stroking Flynn's neck and back with her hands. Flynn shivered and they exchanged a series of feverish kisses. Reb knew the seduction was taking hold.

Firmly, Reb pushed on one of the broad shoulders until she succeeded in rolling Flynn over and climbing on top. Determined to control things, she lost no time in strategically positioning her thigh.

That's just to keep your attention....

With expert agility, she moved gently against Flynn, whispering to her. "Yeah, I've got you now, Flynn. I'm gonna do it real sweet...make you so hot and so wet. You're gonna scream for me... Oh babe, you're gonna scream...."

Then she kissed Flynn until they were both gasping. Their breathing became too ragged to keep their mouths together. Their hands were migrating everywhere, coursing under shirts and over skin, finding breasts and buttocks and then the private, fiery spots. Flynn was moaning, a low, intensely vulnerable sound that seemed to come twisting out of her. It was half sob and half hunger, and hearing it completely undid Reb.

More and more she was struggling to hold her focus, to concentrate on what she intended to do. Flynn's caressing, compelling hands were inexorably casting a spell over her. Even as she consciously tried to will herself to resist, Reb was yielding. The sustained brush of those fingertips, sweeping indolently all over her body, was devastating, and Flynn seemed to know it. With astonishment, it occurred to Reb that the woman beneath her was an accomplished lover.

And suddenly, Reb was craving that touch. *This isn't how it's supposed to happen...this isn't...*

"Oh, God, you're makin' me crazy," Reb rasped, closing her eyes.

She was supposed to be seducing Flynn—that was the way it had always unfolded in her plans. And yet here she was, urgently grinding against Flynn's leg, so far gone that she was unashamedly seeking what she needed.

Flynn didn't bother to go slowly now. She didn't pause to ask Reb's permission. She simply lifted Reb's hips and slid a hand into Reb's underpants. Fingers gently delved into the slick, hot center of Reb's universe. Reb groaned, feeling whatever self-control she had left lurch away. She belonged, body and soul, to the exquisitely tender fingers circling her clitoris.

"Come on," Flynn coaxed, her voice so low Reb barely heard the words. "Come on, Reb," she breathed, while her hand lovingly stroked. "I'll give you what you want."

Reb thought she was going to pass out. All she knew was that she was awash in an almost crazed arousal. She was a puppet dangling in midair, writhing at the slightest motion of Flynn's fingers. She desperately wanted Flynn to just take her, fuck her, demolish her defenses. She was yearning for release with every cell in her body. In some urgent, primordial part of her, she was hoping that Flynn would shatter the barriers between her soul and the rest of the world, and carry her back to a time when love was not an impossible risk.

The hand at her vulva went on stroking, relentless, fulfilling Reb's wish. Riding the swell of a towering passion, Reb heard herself whimpering, pleading, "Please, please...."

And then, all at once, lightning streaks of pleasure began blasting through her. She was thrashing, crying out. Vigilant, Flynn kept her there, in the midst of the storm, until Reb's entire body seemed to ignite. She felt herself become a leaping flame that quivered and burned, incandescent in Flynn's strong arms.

When the storm at last passed, Reb sagged against Flynn, gasping and befuddled. Her bones, her flesh had been melted away by a searing flame. She was a puff of smoke held together by skin. And if the cries of rapture hadn't been enough, Reb knew the long, quavering sigh that escaped her now had to tell Flynn everything.

Murmuring, "Oh, Reb, you're so beautiful," Flynn gathered her close, rocking her like a baby.

Beautiful? The endearment pierced Reb to the core.

Flynn reached out one long arm, turning off the light. Reb felt the covers being pulled over her, and realized that Flynn was damp with sweat, wheezing slightly from the exertion of making love to her. Fighting back a wave of overpowering drowsiness, Reb stirred, ran her hands over Flynn.

"Let me do you," Reb whispered.

"Thanks, but I don't think I'm up to anything more." As if to illustrate the truth of that, Flynn broke into several deep, harsh coughs. "I'm beat. I really just want to go to sleep. Is that okay?"

"Sure," Reb answered, nearly purring.

They embraced in the darkness, both of them weary and slightly overwhelmed by what had just happened between them.

Whoa, Reb thought, feeling stunned and oddly adrift. This sort of sex was like nothing she had ever experienced. Half-asleep, she fretted, *Is this love? Wantin' her in my sight all the time and not bein' able to keep her outside of me? Is this what it's like?* She ran her hand over Flynn's damp, solid length, verifying in the dark that her lover existed. *I don't want to love her. I don't want to love anyone, ever again.*

And then, before she could worry much more about it, she slid into sleep.

Throughout the long night, Flynn haunted her dreams.

CHAPTER 11

The next day, Wednesday, just as Chris, Reb and Flynn were finishing lunch, the doorbell rang. When Chris opened the front door, she found Allison waiting on the porch.

"Oh, Chris," Allison began, "I'm sorry. I had such a hellish day yesterday and I took it all out on you. Can you forgive me?"

Chris narrowed her eyes, viewing Allison dubiously. "The people you really need to apologize to are Reb and Flynn."

Eyeing Chris as if she were being difficult, Allison said, "All right, then." Briskly, she stepped past Chris and walked down the hall.

"You'll have to be quick," Chris warned. "We're leaving in a few minutes for an appointment. The girls are emancipating themselves so they can stay here and re-enroll in school."

As Allison strode into the kitchen, Flynn pushed back her chair and stood up, watching Allison nervously. Alf went to Chris's side. Reb merely scowled and slouched down in her seat.

Allison began to move around the circular kitchen table. "Girls, I'm sorry about last night," she said, her eyes hard.

Confusion settled on Flynn's face, and disbelief flashed in Reb's eyes.

Feeling incredibly awkward, Chris said, "Okay, thanks Allison. Kids, I've got to run upstairs and grab some documents for this meeting, so I can prove I am who I say I am. Then we'll be going."

She hesitated a moment, anxious to escort Allison to the door.

However, Allison was already moving to the phone on the kitchen wall. "May I make a quick call? It's business—and you know how outrageous the car phone rates are."

Exasperated, Chris nodded and headed down the hall with Alf at her heels.

Flynn fumbled with the motorcycle jacket hanging on the back of her chair. She pulled it free and then slipped it on.

Without explanation, Allison hung up the phone, then checked the hall to make sure Chris was gone. Decisively, she walked behind Reb and pulled the red-and-white letter jacket off the chair back.

"Hey, that's mine!" Reb yelled.

Quietly, Allison replied, "Oh, I don't think so. I know an athlete when I see one." She flicked a calculating look at Flynn as she read the back of the jacket. "Wenatchee High." Smiling, she ran a hand over the big W on the front, caressing the punctures in the wool where Reb had taken out the white thread that had once spelled "M. Flynn. Captain."

"The name's gone," Allison observed, then moved her hand to the embroidered soccer and basketball. "But there can't be too many tall redheads missing from the soccer team this season. I'm sure it will only take a phone call or two for the police to locate that someone's parents." She leveled her cold gaze on Flynn.

Stunned, Flynn stared at her. "N-no...."

Allison crossed to the wall phone. "Shall we find out?" she asked dryly, then picked up the receiver.

In one fluid motion, Reb left her chair and grabbed the team jacket from Allison. Instantly, she was heading for the back door, pulling the jacket on as she went.

"C'mon, Flynn," Reb ordered. "C'mon! We're gone!"

With a soft sound of despair, Flynn followed Reb through the back door, across the deck and then down the stairs to the drive. Moments later they were running along Sixteenth Avenue, leaving safety and comfort behind them.

Five minutes later, Chris returned to her kitchen to find Allison sitting at the table, alone. She caught the guarded expression Allison wore, then saw Alf go straight to the back door, whining anxiously. Chris's eyes snapped back to Allison's.

"Where are the girls? What did you do?"

"You'll thank me for it later," Allison stated.

"Is that before or after I wring your interfering neck?!"

They were blocks away, and had been running for roughly fifteen minutes when Flynn staggered and fell. As she lay sprawled on the uneven brick walkway, gasping for breath, she could see Reb ahead of her, running as if her life depended on it.

"Wait up!" Flynn called, but her voice was a dry croak.

With all her strength, she pushed herself up and got to her feet, watching Reb's retreating figure. *She's leaving me,* Flynn thought, trembling with a mixture of despair and panic.

The afternoon wind swept fallen leaves past her. Instinctively, Flynn began moving, following the direction Reb had taken, even as her mind reeled with indecision. *Maybe I should go back. Chris wouldn't let Dad get me. Would she?*

She peered behind her, hoping to see Chris driving along in her white pickup truck, trying to find her. But she saw no sign of Chris. Finally, she gave herself a mental shake and began walking with purpose.

She was heading for Eleventh Avenue and the warehouse where Reb's squat was.

That woman was ready to call the cops, Flynn told herself. *Nothing is worth risking that. The police will hand me over to Dad first, and ask questions later.*

Her hopes dashed, her chance of a secure life gone, Flynn knew her fate was sealed. Feeling desperate, she pushed her hands deeper into her jeans pockets and lengthened her stride. The only thing she knew now was that she had to catch up with Reb.

Last night, while she was rolling around in bed with Reb in her arms, one thing had become overwhelmingly evident to Flynn—Reb loved her. In the short time they had spent together, Flynn had come to see that Reb's true colors were in her actions, not her words. Despite the constant stream of wisecracks and sarcasm, Reb had been there for her through fights and sickness, trouble and good fortune. No one else in the world seemed to care that she was alive and struggling on the streets of Seattle—except for Reb.

Lifting her head, she looked down the tree-lined sidewalk —and saw Reb in the distance, jogging closer, returning for her.

By five o'clock Wednesday afternoon, Tom, Molly, Thea, Jane and Jennifer had answered Chris's call and gathered at the house on Sixteenth Avenue. Most of those present had also enlisted the help of close friends, and so Chris's kitchen was soon filled with roughly sixteen warmly dressed men and women.

"Thanks for coming, everyone," Chris was saying. "As most of you have heard, I spent all afternoon driving around searching for these kids, without any luck. So I'm grateful for your help."

Nearby, Jane Harada was handing out copies of the composite drawings Thea's police-artist friend had made of both Flynn and Reb. Several off-duty policemen were studying the drawings with professional interest, while a young policewoman was openly studying Jane.

Thea had a city map spread on the kitchen table. She was competently pointing out and describing the highway over-passes, the condemned buildings, and the sections of greenbelts that were popular squatter sites. As Thea finished, she assigned each pair of searchers to a specified area.

"Remember," Thea cautioned, "if you spot the kids, do not try an approach. Just note your exact location and call Chris here at the house. Everyone got the phone number? Good."

In a murmur of voices, everyone was moving. Coats were being zippered shut. Tom and his friend David began distributing the brown-bag lunches they had made.

Chris raised her voice above the crowd noise and said, "Please...Call in status reports around nine o'clock. Then meet back here at midnight, OK?"

With a wave of her hand, Chris dismissed them, and the group of sixteen searchers filed out into the cold, dark night.

Chris sat down at the table, tense and silent. Not know-ing what else to do, Jennifer moved behind her and rubbed the knotted muscles in Chris's shoulders.

Reb used her boot to grind out the cigarette butt. Sweetly melodic, the peal of distant church bells echoed be-tween the condemned warehouses that lined Eleventh Avenue. Hunching her shoulders against the damp night air, Reb counted the tolling of the hour.

"Nine o'clock, and all is not well," Reb whispered to herself.

Flynn was behind her, crouched in the shadows of the alley, no doubt shivering herself into another fever as they both waited to return to the squat. From her position at the edge of the brick wall, Reb could see Leper, Moon and Flash standing beneath the street light at the end of the block. One or more of them had been there all day, coming and going in shifts.

Only now, white wisps of fog were engulfing the street light. Reb knew that as the night wore on, the fog would drop to ground level, low enough and thick enough to obscure everyone's range of vision. Already, Reb could hear Moon whining to Flash about being tired of standing around in the cold, "waitin' for that wise-ass dyke and her girlfriend" to show. From what Moon said, it sounded as if the boys had been staking out Eleventh Avenue ever since the fight on Monday night.

Then a police car cruised by the corner, slowing down as it approached the boys. One minute they were casually slouching, griping to one another, the next they were dashing down the block, away from the squad car, and away from Reb. With a whirling display of red, white and blue lights, the cruiser gave chase.

"Flynn!" Reb hissed. "C'mere! Hurry up!"

Flynn stumbled to her side, and Reb caught her as she nearly fell. She was wheezing again, and the blazing hot face Reb touched was covered with a light sheen of sweat.

Dismayed, Reb guided Flynn across Eleventh Avenue and then down the alley toward their secret entrance. She propped Flynn against the wall, then knelt before the steel door and jimmied the lock. Quickly, she hauled Flynn inside, and once behind the safety of the locked door, took a moment to hug Flynn close.

"Sorry it took so long," she breathed.

Feeling reckless, Reb switched on the flashlight she had left by the door. She checked Flynn's face, trying to judge how severe the relapse might be. Flynn leaned against the steel door, glassy-eyed, once more burning with fever.

"I'm okay," Flynn rasped, though her voice had an other-worldly quality to it, as if she was not really in control of her faculties. "Don't worry."

Reb's heart was suddenly heavy with worry, and she stepped back from Flynn uncertainly. *Maybe I shouldn't of been so quick to run this time....*

Flynn began coughing, bending over as the fit shook her tall frame and seemed to turn her lungs inside out.

Christ, look at her, Reb thought. *She can't take this life! It's gonna kill her!*

When Flynn stopped coughing, Reb carefully shouldered the taller girl's arm and helped her up the stairs.

"How'd you stay so quiet when we was waitin' in the alley across the street?" Reb asked, casting the beam of the flashlight before them. "I heard you coughin', but it was real low...and funny soundin'."

Sliding one hand along the wall to help support her weight, Flynn didn't answer. She was breathing hard, gasping for breath as if the act of climbing the staircase was just too much for her. Seeing this, Reb stopped and let her rest a moment.

As Flynn caught her wind, she answered, "I shoved the tail end of my T-shirt into my mouth. It kinda gagged me sometimes, but it smothered all the noise I was making."

Flynn laughed softly, obviously pleased with herself, then started coughing again.

Flynn weakly clutched Reb's shoulder, her body racked by seemingly endless barks. Reb, meanwhile, turned the flashlight on the lower front of Flynn's T-shirt. The cloth hung sloppily over her jeans, not tucked in as she usually wore her shirts. The wrinkled material was soaking wet, and covered with vile-looking gobs of dark-green mucus. Reb stared at the mess, so shaken that she almost missed the fact that Flynn had finally stopped coughing.

"I gotta lie down," Flynn mumbled. "I'll be okay if I can just lie down for a while."

Reb swallowed, but the huge, painful lump in her throat remained. Willfully, she tried to maintain her composure as she helped Flynn climb the stairs to her squat on the fifth floor. Once there, Reb parked Flynn on the bed while she lit several candles. Flynn didn't even bother to take off her leather jacket; fully clothed, she crawled under the blankets.

All around the room, the cats meowed loudly, hoping that at last a feeding was at hand. The candles leapt in the slight draft from the open door, casting fearsome shadows which danced across the cutout magazine pictures of Melissa Etheridge and Hole.

Reb stepped back and gazed mournfully up at Kurt Cobain-on-the-cross. *What am I gonna do?*

For Chris, it was a long, grueling night.

As if sensing her jittery mood, Alf moved restlessly around the kitchen, his toenails clicking on the wooden floor.

Jennifer sat across from her, alternately reading and grading a pile of freshman essays. She also spent long periods of time staring into space. Chris couldn't help wondering what she was thinking about.

Nine o'clock came and went, along with a flurry of calls. Over and over the news was the same: no one had seen anyone who matched the descriptions of Flynn or Reb.

Finally, it was midnight and the volunteer search party gathered once more in Chris's kitchen. Briefly, each pair gave a discouraging account of traveling through their sector, showing people the police-artist's composite drawings. No one recognized the faces, although some recognized the names. Several searchers reported that various street youths had said that someone named Flash was also looking for two girls named Flynn and Reb. When Thea and her police friends heard this, they exchanged quick, ominous glances, which left Chris with the impression that this was the worst possible information.

The group began to disperse. Chris and Jennifer stood side by side at the front door, shaking hands and returning embraces as the men and women filed back into the night. Afterwards, Chris followed Tom and David onto the front porch. A thick fog had blanketed Capitol Hill, and as Chris waved to Tom, she lost sight of him before he had even reached his Jeep, which was parked by the curb.

They're out there in this miserable weather, Chris thought, feeling the mist settling on her face. *Flynn's never going to make it.*

Overcome, Chris covered her eyes with her hand. Sensing her distress, Alf gave a plaintive whine.

All at once, Jennifer was there, gathering Chris into her arms. "Don't give up on them," Jennifer whispered. "That Reb is one of the smartest kids I've ever met."

"I'm gonna go out and look for them," Chris stated.

"I'm going with you," Jennifer replied.

They had grabbed their jackets and were heading for the back door when the phone rang.

"Who the hell can that be?" Chris grumbled.

Tired and dispirited, she hurried to the kitchen wall phone and snatched up the receiver. "Hello?"

There was a moment's pause, then a small voice said, "Hey, lady. You gonna let that blonde bitch rat Flynn out?"

Chris gasped with surprise, then demanded, "Where are you?!"

"If you hafta put the cops on someone—you put 'em on me," Reb instructed. "I steal all the time, but Flynn, she ain't done nothin' to nobody. She just don't wanta get hit no more."

Chris grasped the phone receiver with two hands. "Reb, I already told Allison that Tom and I will dissolve the business and find another partner if she doesn't back off and leave you two alone. Now, I don't give a shit about anything you did— ever!" Hearing the intensity in her own voice, Chris struggled for self-control. "I care about *you.* That's all, Reb. I want you both to live here—with me."

She heard Reb blow out a breath, as if she'd been holding it in, more anxious than Chris had ever suspected she could be. There was another pause, then, "Flynn's real sick."

"Where are you?" Chris repeated, more gently this time.

"Meet me at the Wildrose."

"I'm on my way."

Chris hung up the phone and turned to find Jennifer standing close beside her. Speechless with relief, they embraced.

Keeping an arm around Jennifer, Chris hustled them out of the house. Alf charged ahead of them, leading the way through the fog as they crossed the deck and ran down the steps to the garage.

Moments later, tires spitting gravel, Chris's truck flew down the driveway.

Reb watched the white pickup pull up in front of the Wildrose and slow to a stop. Chris and Jennifer jumped out of either side, and then Alf bounded onto the sidewalk.

"Find 'em, boy," Chris urged.

Busily, the brown-and-white dog began sniffing the street.

They were a short distance from the streetlight, which allowed Reb to easily recognize the truck and the women, even as the fog swirled around them. However, it wasn't the fog that made Reb hesitate to show herself. She still wasn't sure if Flash and his boys had come back yet. And there was no sense in giving away her location until she was sure there were no gang-bangers lurking nearby, using the fog to hide just as skillfully as she was.

Giving a string of excited yips, Alf began running up Eleventh Avenue, straight toward the darkened doorway where Reb and Flynn crouched side by side. Reb checked the street and was unable to see anyone else moving about in the heavy mist. Decisively, she stood up and walked into the street to greet Alf.

The dog was ecstatic to see her again. His leaping attempts to lick her face broke through Reb's somber resolve. Laughing, she bent over to hug Alf and submit to a few kisses.

Then, Jennifer shocked the daylights out of Reb by rushing up and embracing her like a long-lost relative. Right behind her was Chris, whose long arms encircled both Reb and Jennifer.

"I'm so glad you called," Chris exclaimed.

"Yeah...well..." Embarrassed, Reb tried to free herself.

A series of muffled coughs came from the dark doorway Reb had just left and Reb said, "She's in bad shape," as she led the way to Flynn.

Chris draped one of Flynn's arms over her shoulders, then lifted the tall young woman until she was standing. "Let's get you home," Chris said.

Flynn moaned, and leaned against Chris.

Reb reached into her half-open jacket and plucked out the foot-long crucifix that had hung on the wall of her squat. Briefly, she rubbed her thumb over the wooden Jesus who wore Kurt Cobain's face. Then, grim with resolve, she pushed the cross into Flynn's jacket.

"For luck," she whispered, as she zipped the motorcycle jacket closed and sealed her gift safely within.

Squinting wearily, Flynn watched Reb retreat from her.

"Here we go," Chris murmured, setting off for the truck, shouldering Flynn's staggering weight.

Alf danced around Chris and Flynn, excited and happy.

Jennifer moved after them, then looked back, waiting for Reb.

"I ain't goin' with you," Reb stated flatly.

Chris and Flynn turned to face her.

Jennifer tilted her head sideways, obviously baffled.

Resolute, Reb lifted the big backpack that Flynn had brought with her to Seattle, slipping the straps over the shoulders of the Wenatchee High letter jacket she still wore. She picked up her battered wooden guitar and fingered the strand of orange nylon rope she had attached to each end for easy carrying.

"Why on earth not?" Chris asked.

Reb sidled into the street, carefully keeping a distance between her and the two older women. "Look, I know you mean well, but it just ain't gonna work. I been on my own too long," Reb asserted. "See what I mean? Goin' to school, or punchin' a time clock, always doin' what somebody else is tellin' me to do...it sounds like hell. I don't want it."

"Reb," Jennifer coaxed, "we care about you. You've had some rough breaks and you've done what you had to do to survive. But you also deserve a shot at a better life than what you have out on these streets. Don't let fear of something new and different stand in your way. You're a smart kid. You can learn to do anything you set your mind to doing."

Reb laughed. "Tryin' to build my self-esteem, lady?"

Chris stepped closer, entreating, "Flynn needs you, Reb."

Struck through the heart by that truth, Reb couldn't respond.

"Come home with us," Jennifer invited, her voice a caress in the dark mist. "At least give it a try. All of us need you. Maybe together...we can make a family."

Reb shifted her weight anxiously from one foot to the other. Her heart was beating fast and she realized she was terrified.

I can't listen to this. I already decided I was gonna turn Flynn over to 'em and then go. They can take care of her like I never could, and shit, the way she makes me feel scares the hell outta me. Taking a step backward, Reb was careful not to meet Flynn's eyes. *I gotta move on. Nothin' good ever came of lettin' myself need people. San Francisco—that's what I gotta be thinkin' about now.*

"No, thanks," Reb sighed, slipping the guitar rope over her shoulder. "It ain't for me."

And then, Flynn's hoarse voice came. "Reb, please...."

Reb knew that Flynn was half out of it. While waiting in the cold, wet doorway for Chris and Jennifer to arrive, Flynn had rested her head on the chipped paint of the threshold and fallen dead asleep. Reb had hoped to slink out of this goodbye without having to face Flynn, but that was obviously not going to be.

"Listen, you big jock," Reb joked, even as her throat ached with emotion. "Some people are like stray dogs. They need a home and someone to love 'em. And then there's other people that are like stray cats, like the ones I'm leavin' behind up there on the fifth floor. You think they're gonna hang out there and just wait for me to come back? No way. They'll take care of themselves."

Drawing herself up to her full height, Reb finished, "I found out a long time ago, I'm a stray cat. I make my own home. And I love myself. That simple."

She began retreating from them as she spoke, stepping steadily backward into the fog.

"Reb, don't do this," Jennifer pleaded.

"I hafta," she said to Chris and Jennifer, as they began to move after her.

"Don't leave me," Flynn called, her voice breaking, "I love you. I love you."

As usual, once Reb had started, it was easy to place one foot after the other. "That'll pass. You can do better than me and you know it, Flynn," she assured her. "You concentrate on gettin' yourself into college."

Flynn began crying in earnest.

Reb continued to move backwards. "Don't worry. I'll be okay."

She knew she was disappearing into the fog, for thick, white strands of it were floating between her and the women before her. With increasing determination, Reb backed up, moving faster, until she began losing sight of those ghostly figures. Alf was whining and barking, and it echoed against the vague, dark shapes of the decrepit buildings that lined the empty street. The last thing Reb clearly saw was Jennifer reaching down to take hold of Alf's collar.

Chris called her name several times, begging her to reconsider.

Afraid that she would, Reb turned away from them, clutched her guitar under one arm and began jogging in the opposite direction.

It ain't worth it, she told herself, then repeated it as she ran along, creating the verse of a song.

Much later, she climbed into the boxcar of the 2:00 a.m. southbound Burlington Northern train. By then she had half a song made up in her head. A song all about steering clear of love, because losing it was all she had ever known.

As the train rolled out of the Emerald City, she was hunched by the open door of the boxcar. Looking back, all she could see of the city was several vertical charcoal smudges emerging from a pale wash of mist; the skyscrapers were held loosely in fingers of fog, and Puget Sound was completely invisible. She was not sad to be leaving. Instead, as the train's speed increased and the chill, moist wind rushed by her face, lifting her hair, she sighed with relief. The wind meant freedom. She was no longer afraid.

Reb turned and looked ahead, searching the dark fog that cloaked both the track and the land.

She was on her way somewhere, and for now, that was enough.

EPILOGUE

Morgan looked around the table.

Chris was asking if anyone wanted more turkey. To her right, Tom and David were each loudly claiming credit for the highly complimented dressing. Molly was demanding the recipe, while beside her, Thea was grinning and spooning one last helping of mashed potatoes onto her plate. Thin and pale, but smiling broadly, Frank sat in his wheelchair. Next to him, Joel was lining up pills on the table, readying to administer the nightly dosages. On the other side of the circular table, Jane was making a low, barely audible joke to Wendy, the policewoman she'd met the night of the search party. And Allison was proudly holding the hand of her latest love interest, a raven-haired young woman named Robbi, who rowed crew at the University of Washington.

Over by the counter, Jennifer was pouring cups of coffee.

Alf, meanwhile, was circling the table, whining softly as he begged for more handouts.

The kitchen was warm and bright and remnants of the Thanksgiving meal they'd all just devoured still decorated the table in a variety of nearly empty bowls and dishes.

Contentedly, Morgan reflected, *This is my family.* It amazed her to realize that unconventional as it was, she had never felt so well-loved in her life.

Then she turned and gazed at the Polaroid photo mounted on the refrigerator. Held in place by two Space Needle magnets, the image of Reb smirked back at her. She was wearing the red-and-white Wenatchee High letter jacket and she sat on a low stone wall. Behind her, the Golden Gate Bridge and San Francisco Bay glistened in the sunshine.

Morgan knew by heart what was scrawled on the reverse side. "So you won't forget me. Rock on. I love you."

One day I'll catch up with you, Reb, Morgan mused silently. *And then we'll find out what you know about love.*

Over the noise and the laughter, Chris called out, "Okay, who wants pie?"

The whole group groaned and Tom threw his linen napkin, hitting Chris on the forehead. Chris promptly threw it back at him, making everyone laugh.

Then she caught Morgan's eye, and winked.

THE END

About the Author

Jean Stewart was born and raised in the suburbs of Philadelphia, Pennsylvania. While growing up, her primary interests were playing sports and reading books. At eleven years old, she began writing stories and journals, which developed into the habit of a lifetime. Later on, she attended West Chester University and earned Bachelor of Science and Master of Education degrees. Jean taught school and coached women's athletic teams for eleven years, then left that profession to concentrate on writing.

In 1992, her first published novel, *Return to Isis*, was nominated for a Lambda Literary Award. The third book in the Isis series, *Warriors of Isis*, was nominated for a Lambda Literary Award in 1995. She is currently working on the fourth book in the series.

If You Liked This Book...

Authors seldom get to hear what readers like about their work. If you enjoyed this novel *Emerald City Blues,* why not let the author know? We are sure she would be delighted to get your feedback. Simply write the author:

Jean Stewart
c/o Rising Tide Press
5 Kivy Street
Huntington Station, NY 11746

Our Publishing Philosophy

Rising Tide Press is a lesbian-owned and operated publishing company committed to publishing books by, for, and about lesbians and their lives. We are not only committed to readers, but also to lesbian writers who need nurturing and support, whether or not their manuscripts are accepted for publication. Through quality writing, the press aims to entertain, educate, and empower readers, whether they are women-loving-women or heterosexual. It is our intention to promote lesbian culture, community, and civil rights, nationwide, through the printed word.

In addition, RTP will seek to provide readers with images of lesbians aspiring to be more than their prescribed roles dictate. The novels selected for publication will aim to portray women from all walks of life, (regardless of class, ethnicity, religion or race), women who are strong, not just victims, women who can and do aspire to be more, and not just settle, women who will fight injustice with courage. Hopefully, our novels will provide new ideas for creating change in a heterosexist and homophobic society. Finally, we hope our books will encourage lesbians to respect and love themselves more, and at the same time, convey this love and respect of self to the society at large. It is our belief that this philosophy can best be actualized through fine writing that entertains, as well as educates the reader. Books, even lesbian books, can be fun, as well as liberating.

More Fiction to Stir the Imagination from Rising Tide Press

RETURN TO ISIS
Jean Stewart
It is the year 2093, and Whit, a bold woman warrior from an Amazon nation, rescues Amelia from a dismal world where females are either breeders or drones. During their arduous journey back to the shining all-women's world of Artemis, they are unexpectedly drawn to each other. This engaging first book in the trilogy has it all—romance, mystery, and adventure.
Lambda Literary Award Finalist
ISBN 0-9628938-6-2; 192 Pages; $9.99

ISIS RISING
Jean Stewart
In this stirring romantic fantasy, the familiar cast of lovable characters begin to rebuild the colony of Isis, burned to the ground ten years earlier by the dread Regulators. But evil forces threaten to destroy their dream. A swashbuckling futuristic adventure and an endearing love story all rolled into one.
ISBN 0-9628938-8-9; 192 Pages; $11.99

WARRIORS OF ISIS
Jean Stewart
At last, the third lusty tale of high adventure and passionate romance among the Freeland Warriors. Arinna Sojourner, the evil product of genetic engineering, vows to destroy the fledgling colony of Isis with her incredible psychic powers. Whit, Kali, and other warriors battle to save their world, in this novel bursting with life, love, heroines and villains.
Lambda Literary Award Finalist
ISBN 1-883061-03-2; 256 Pages; $11.99

DEADLY RENDEZVOUS: A Toni Underwood Mystery
Diane Davidson
A string of brutal murders in the middle of the desert plunges Lieutenant Toni Underwood and her lover Megan into a high profile investigation which uncovers a world of drugs, corruption and murder, as well as the dark side of the human mind. An explosive, fast-paced, action-packed whodunit.
ISBN 1-883061-02-4; 224 pages; $9.99

PLAYING FOR KEEPS
Stevie Rios

In this sparkling tale of love and adventure, Lindsay West, an oboist, travels to Caracas, where she meets three people who change her life forever: Rob Heron a gay man, who becomes her dearest friend; Her lover Mercedes Luego, a lovely cellist, who takes Lindsay on a life-altering adventure down the Amazon; And the mysterious jungle-dwelling woman Arminta, who touches their souls. ISBN 1-883061-07-5; $10.99

ROMANCING THE DREAM
Heidi Johanna

A charming, erotic and imaginative love story which is also the tale of how women, together, have the power to make dreams happen. Set in the Pacific Northwest, it follows the lives of a group of visionary women who decide to take over their small town and create a lesbian haven. It will delight you with its gentle humor, beautiful love scenes, and fine writing. $8.95

DREAMCATCHER
Lori Byrd

This timeless story of love and friendship illuminates a year in the life of Sunny Calhoun, a college student, who falls in love with Eve Phillips, a literary agent. A richly woven narrative which captures the wonder and pain of love between a younger and an older woman—a woman facing AIDS with spirited courage and humor..ISBN 1-883061-06-7; 192 Pages: $9.99

LOVESPELL
Karen Williams

A deliciously erotic and humorous love story in which Kate Gallagher, a shy veterinarian, and Allegra, who has magic at her fingertips, fall in love. A masterful blend of fantasy and reality, this beautifully written story will warm your heart and delight your imagination.
ISBN 0-9628938-2-X; 192 Pages; $9.95

NIGHTSHADE
Karen Williams

After witnessing a fateful hit-and-run accident, Alex Spherris finds herself the new owner of a magical bell, which some people would kill for. She is ushered into a strange fantasy world and meets Orielle, who melts her frozen heart. Don't miss this delightfully imaginative romance spun in the best tradition of storytelling. ISBN 1-883061-08-3; $11.99

NO WITNESSES
Nancy Sanra
This cliff-hanger of a mystery set in San Francisco, introduces Detective Tally McGinnis, the brains and brawn behind the Phoenix Detective Agency. But Tally is no great sleuth at protecting her own heart. And so, when her ex-lover Pamela Tresdale is arrested for the grisly murder of a wealthy Texas heiress, Tally rushes to the rescue. Despite friends' warnings, Tally is drawn once again into Pamela's web of deception and betrayal, as she attempts to clear her and find the real killer. A gripping whodunit.
ISBN 1-883061-05-9; 192 Pages; $9.99

DANGER IN HIGH PLACES:
An Alix Nicholson Mystery
Sharon Gilligan
Set against the backdrop of Washington, D.C., this riveting mystery introduces freelance photographer and amateur sleuth, Alix Nicholson. Alix stumbles on a deadly scheme surrounding AIDS funding, and with the help of a lesbian congressional aide, unravels the mystery.
ISBN 0-9628938-7-0; 176 Pages, $9.99

DANGER! CROSS CURRENTS:
AN Alix Nicholson Mystery
Sharon Gilligan
The exciting sequel to *Danger in High Places* brings freelance photographer Alix Nicholson face-to-face with an old love and a murder. When Alix's land-lady, a real estate developer, turns up dead, and her much younger lover, Leah Claire, is the prime suspect, Alix launches a frantic campaign to find the real killer. ISBN 1-883061-01-6; 192 Pages; $9.99

HEARTSTONE AND SABER
Jacqui Singleton
You can almost hear the sabers clash in this rousing tale of good and evil, of passionate love, of warrior queens and white witches. Cydell, the imperious queen of Mauldar, and Elayna, the Fair Witch of Avoreed, join forces to combat the evil that menaces the empire, and in the course of doing that, find rapturous love.
ISBN 1-883061-00-8; 224 Pages; $10.99

CORNERS OF THE HEART
Leslie Grey

A captivating novel of love and suspense in which beautiful French-born Chris Benet and English professor Katya Michaels meet and fall in love. But their budding love is shadowed by a vicious killer, whom they must outwit. Your heart will pound as the story races to its heart-stopping conclusion.
ISBN 0-9628938-3-8; 224 pages; $9.95

SHADOWS AFTER DARK
Ouida Crozier

When wings of death spread over Kyril's home world, she is sent to Earth on a mission—find a cure for the deadly disease. Once here she meets and falls in love with Kathryn, who is enthralled yet horrified to learn that her mysterious, darkly exotic lover is a vampire. This tender, beautifully written love story is the ultimate lesbian vampire novel!
ISBN 1-883061-50-4; 224 Pages; $9.95

EDGE OF PASSION
Shelley Smith

This sizzling novel about an all-consuming love affair between a younger and an older woman is set in colorful Provincetown. A gripping love story, which is both fierce and tender, it will keep you breathless until the last page.
ISBN 0-9628938-1-1; 192 Pages; $8.95

YOU LIGHT THE FIRE
Kristen Garrett

Here's a grown-up **Rubyfruit Jungle**—sexy, spicy, and sidesplittingly funny. Take a gorgeous, sexy, high school math teacher and put her together with a raunchy, commitment-shy, ex-rock singer, and you've got a hilarious, unforgettable love story. ISBN 0-9628938-5-4; $9.95

ROUGH JUSTICE
Claire Youmans

When Glenn Lowry's sunken fishing boat turns up four years after his disappearance, foul play is suspected. Classy, ambitious Deputy Prosecutor Janet Schilling immediately launches a murder investigation which produces several surprising suspects—one of them her own former lover Catherine Adams, now living a reclusive life in a lighthouse on Seal Rock Island. A fascinating page-turner. Filled with the beauty and danger of the sea and unexpected plot twists, *Rough Justice* poses an intriguing question: Is murder ever justified?   ISBN 1-883061-10-5; $10.99

How To Order

Title	Author	Price
❑ Corners of the Heart-Leslie Grey		9.95
❑ Danger! Cross Currents-Sharon Gilligan		9.99
❑ Danger in High Places-Sharon Gilligan		9.95
❑ Deadly Rendezvous-Diane Davidson		9.99
❑ Dreamcatcher-Lori Byrd		9.99
❑ Edge of Passion-Shelley Smith		9.95
❑ Emerald City Blues-Jean Stewart		11.99
❑ Heartstone and Saber-Jacqui Singleton		10.99
❑ Isis Rising-Jean Stewart		11.99
❑ Love Spell-Karen Williams		9.99
❑ Nightshade-Karen Williams		11.99
❑ No Witnesses-Nancy Sanra		9.99
❑ Playing for Keeps-Stevie Rios		10.99
❑ Return to Isis-Jean Stewart		9.99
❑ Romancing the Dream-Heidi Johanna		8.95
❑ Rough Justice-Claire Youmans		10.99
❑ Shadows After Dark-Ouida Crozier		9.99
❑ Warriors of Isis-Jean Stewart		11.99
❑ You Light the Fire-Kristen Garrett		9.95

Please send me the books I have checked. I enclose a check or money order (not cash), plus $3 for the first book and $1 for each additional book to cover shipping and handling. Or bill my ❑Visa ❑Mastercard ❑Amer. Express.
Or call our Toll Free Number 1-800-648-5333 if using a credit card.

CARD # _____ EXP.DATE_____

SIGNATURE_____

NAME (PLEASE PRINT) _____

ADDRESS _____

CITY_____ STATE_____ZIP_____
❑ New York State residents add 8.5% tax to total.

RISING TIDE PRESS
5 KIVY ST., HUNTINGTON STATION, NY 11746